ONE STEP BEHIND

DAKOTA ADAMS
BOOK IV

By

Galen Surlak-Ramsey

A Tiny Fox Press Book

ISBN: 978-1-946501-25-7
LCCN: 2020942691

Tiny Fox Press and the book fox logo are all registered trademarks of Tiny Fox Press LLC

Tiny Fox Press LLC
North Port, FL

For Westen who always finds the best goats

CHAPTER ONE
A RUDE AWAKENING

Know why I hate working on my ship? It's not because I'd rather be doing something else.

Okay, wait...it is mainly because I'd rather be doing something else. But that's beside the point, really. Some days I think I'd prefer getting a stomach pump with a cactus rather than having to align micro thrusters or rotate alluvial dampeners.

Because honestly, it's all a pain in the rear. I mean, who wants to spend six hours removing the three brackets that secure the radiation housing shield, to then pull out the EEC power nodes for thirty minutes, at which point it's another two hours to reach the primary disconnects to the trans-matrix sensors in order to finally be able to swap out the air filter refresher for your secondary cabins because the locking bolt is tucked that far away?

Not this girl, that's for damn sure.

I'd so rather be flying a glider across the crystal plains of Modan XII or visiting the shores of Nepatine Prime during storm season. Even better, I'd give my right arm to ride a buffalasaurus from New Cape Town to Danis Minor. I hear the scenery and wildlife on that planet is nothing short of legendary. Actually, check that. I still have and want the Progenitor implants in my arm, so I'll give up a leg instead. Replacements aren't too expensive.

Anyway, back to the *other* reason I hate working on my ship. It's because whenever I go and troubleshoot what's wrong, it's never an easy diagnostic, no matter what the computer says. Even if you get a direct pinpoint to the precise location of what's not working, something always goes afoul, and that something is only compounded by overly complicated instructions and missing tools.

And tools *always* go missing.

Always.

"Are you sure we need to rebuild this thing?" asked Jack. He sat nearby, surrounded by parts from the antimatter inlet manifold, with hands dirtier than those of a New Vegas politician. "That'll be another four hours we'll have to sit here, and I can't feel my legs as it is."

"Afraid so," I said, feeling his pain. My face reflected all the joy I had being there and doing that, but since we were still on the other side of the universe from home, we couldn't exactly swing into drydock and let some zero-g monkey figure it out while we were stuck in a busted ship. Gah! Why couldn't it have waited to break down *after* we got back to Mars?

"This would go faster if you got your furry friends to help," he said. "Or at least, stop them from being in heat. Don't suppose we have any tranquilizers on board?"

"No, but I don't think that would get them to help even if I did," I said, chuckling.

"Maybe not. But at least I could concentrate a little more."

"True," I conceded. "You know what would also make this go faster? A repair manual that didn't feel like it was written by someone who had less birthdays than I have thumbs."

I glanced down at the tablet, wiped away a bit of oil that clung to its screen, and gave it another look to see if we were on the right track.

"I mean, does this make sense to you?" I asked, getting ready to read out loud. "Secondary housing bolts must be removed before attempting to take off primary housing array or else damage to drive shaft will occur." I paused and set the tablet to the side. "How the hell do we get the secondary housing bolts off if they're beneath the primary housing array?"

Jack soured his face. "That's not what you said before."

"Yes, it is."

"No, it's not."

"Look, I read it to you word for word," I said. I picked up the tablet, adjusted my reading glasses, and put on the best librarian voice I could. "It says, and I quote: Secondary housing bolts cannot be removed prior to dorsal communication array matrix being calibrated—"

I stopped midsentence, and Jack folded his arms over his chest as he raised an eyebrow. "You were saying?"

I ran my hands through my hair and groaned. "What the holy hell? I swear it changed on me."

"Sure, it did."

I might have given him a profane gesture or two in frustration. But that frustration paled in comparison to when I realized I was missing a socket. "Hey," I said, twisting left and right. "Where'd the 10mm go?"

"How should I know?"

"I just had it." I groaned and sifted through the clutter of parts and tools around me. "I mean like, not even five seconds ago. It was *right* here. I swear this thing disappears faster than new socks in the dryer."

Right at that moment, Tolby came into the engine room, looking very dapper in a black tailored suit with a snazzy red bow tie, large top hat, and a slick wooden cane. Why was the giant space tiger all jazzed up? I had no idea. I could only assume it was part of whatever weird mating ritual he and his harem of intergalactic tigresses had going on.

7

"Here you are, Miss Adams," he said, plopping a hefty stack of papers with a pen on top in front of me. "You've got three hours to finish. Good luck."

"Hold fast there, Mister Pennybags," I said, laughing. "What's this all about?"

"Your final," he said in all seriousness. "We can't award you your PhD without passing, obviously."

My heart skipped a beat. The next one, too. "My final? Crap. That's today?"

"We've only been talking about it for the past two months, Miss Adams," he replied.

"Wait. There are no tests when it comes to PhD work, are there? I mean not at the end. I just have to defend my dissertation."

"Consider this part of your defense," he said, flicking his tail at the stack of papers that seemed to have doubled in size since last I looked.

"But—"

"No buts," he said. "Daylight's burning. Best chop, chop, my good dear."

I sank my face into my hands and sighed. I didn't need this now, not when we had a busted ship to fix and a planet to get off of on account of...gah, what was it? I couldn't remember. Something terrible was about to happen. I knew that much.

"Hey, can I maybe take this later?" I asked, looking up.

I never got an answer. Tolby had disappeared.

So had Jack.

So had my ship.

Actually, pretty much everything had disappeared at that point. I found myself floating a couple meters off the ground in the middle of some gloomy woods. The trees looked all the same. Each had identical patterns of bark and twisting branches, and on those branches, each tree housed a dilapidated kid's fort.

"What the frapgar is going on?" I muttered.

8

A low rumble sounded in the distance. I craned my neck over my shoulder and tried to peer through the dark, but since I'm not part space cat like Tolby, and I never traded my organic eyes for cybernetic ones (and never will, thank you), I couldn't see much.

I couldn't see much, that is, until a set of six, malformed green-glowing eyes appeared about fifty meters away.

Then another.

Then another.

Before I could suck in a tense breath, eyes surrounded me on all sides. A guttural growl filled the air, and then a monstrous, skeletal creature the size of a large canine appeared. Copper skin covered his frame, and his elongated mouth seemed to be made of razors.

"Oh, nice, not-hungry doggie," I said, holding up a hand and trying to back away. Though my feet had settled to the ground, I found moving difficult, if not practically impossible. No matter how hard I tried go in reverse, my legs felt like they were made of cement.

Maybe that would've been good, actually, as I doubt he would've seen me as tasty.

The creature charged, and when it did, hundreds more leaped out of the shadows as well.

I screamed in fright and ran about as fast as molasses in an upright bottle.

"Dakota!"

The scene wavered, and I shook my head as reality warped.

"Dakota!"

I looked up in time to see a gargantuan column of water plunge itself right on top of me.

The world became a swirling vortex of shadows and current as I spun. A loud mechanical whir filled my ears, and then there was a pop-hiss like a pressurized seal breaking.

My eyes shot open in time to see a cold, hard floor rushing up to meet me. I barely got my arms up to protect my face before I kissed metal. I smacked the floor with a loud thump and cursed up a storm as I rolled onto my back.

An open trauma tank stood at my feet, the kind where the severely wounded are suspended in a medicinal solution until healed. Said solution was all over me and the floor, making me smell like apple pie and leaving a bitter taste in my mouth.

"Good morning, Dakota Adams!" boomed an energetic voice from speakers somewhere in the ceiling. "We at Excel-Care would like to thank you for your business and hope that you will continue to utilize our services for all your Nodari-infection needs."

"Excel-Care?" I repeated. My memory felt gooey at that moment, but I knew that name. "I'm in a hospital?"

"You are!" he replied with gusto. "And not simply any hospital! You're in the Progenitor medical facility at Kumet. We've won numerous awards for everything from the fastest recovery times to most delicious desserts available in the cafeteria. Would you like to know more?"

"Kumet..." I trailed my voice as I wracked my brain. I knew that name, too. "That's the Kibnali planet?"

"It is," he said. "I'm so glad that your memory is returning so quickly. You humans can prove...interesting to work on."

"How's that?"

"Your brain is a...how do I say this politely..."

"An entry-level model?" I guessed, feeling like I'd been told that before.

"Precisely!" he said. "It is a perfect starter for the new soul. Easy on the wallet, super portable if you don't mind ensuring that it's always hooked into an appropriate body, and super cute, if you don't mind me saying. I just love the shape of your cerebellum, and don't even get me started on the single brain stem. It's adorable."

"Uh, thanks?"

"You're welcome!" he replied. "However, back to the original point, the human brain does unfortunately, come with a few drawbacks, namely being, it reacts poorly to many things."

"Such as?"

"High voltage. Sudden deceleration. Massive blunt force trauma—"

"And let me guess, treatment in a Progenitor medbay."

"Yes, but I can assure you, we here are dedicated to providing you with the highest quality customer service and treatment options, regardless of what brain you happen to carry. Would you like to hear more?"

"No," I said as I sat up, wincing as I did. Apparently, whatever infection I'd been treated for had headaches as a side effect. "Do you have a name, by chance?"

"I'm so glad you asked," he replied. "My formal designation is RUM-1379, but you are free to call me Rummy."

"Okay, Rummy. Why was I a patient to begin with?"

"Great question! One of the best," he said. "In the interest of time, what's the last thing you remember?"

"Flying back to Kumet in a dropship," I said. I knew there was more to it all, but I'll be damned to a desk job for the next thousand years if I could put together any more than that.

"Great. Great," he said, sounding as salesmany as ever. "Perfectly normal and understandable, by the way."

"So...fill me in?"

"I will, but before I do, I'd like to go over all of our specials we're having today."

"I'd like it more if you simply told me what happened instead."

"Straight to the point, I love it," Rummy went on. Despite his words, I could already tell whatever he was going to say that a) I wasn't going to like it and b) he was going to give me his sales rant whether I wanted to hear it or not. "After you came to Kumet, you were bitten by

11

a Nodari swarmling. Your friends brought you here seeking antivenin that would neutralize the toxins ravaging your body."

"That doesn't sound pleasant."

"It wasn't, but you'll be glad to know you're on track for a full recovery, provided you abide by your treatment plan. That means plenty of bedrest, and no more petting Nodari swarmlings. They aren't the cuddly type, if you haven't noticed."

I only half heard that last bit as memories of a firefight on a bridge with the Nodari formed in my mind's eye, as well as even less pleasant images of me being carried here through a half dozen other firefights. I could scarcely believe I'd been in a war, an actual war between those demonic monsters and the Kibnali, right here on this planet, but there was no denying it.

I started to think at that point maybe the holes in my memory were a good thing. Who knows what horrors I'd be forced to relive otherwise? That's when Tolby popped into my mind, as did everyone else: Jack. Jainon. Yseri. Empress. Daphne...

I glanced around the room, and while everything around felt right—the nearby computers, the body scanner hanging from the ceiling, and the medical tanks against the wall—the lack of company I had in there was unsettling.

"Where are the ones who brought me here?" I asked. "Are they keeping guard outside?"

"Another fantastic question," Rummy said. "Before I answer that, I would like to direct your attention to the pile of new clothes and silver bracelet inside the replicator on your right. I've been told that you would appreciate these the most."

At the mention of clothes, I glanced down and realized I was as naked as the day I was born. And despite what was going on war-wise nearby, I did like the idea of being clothed. I easily found what he was referring to and tossed it all on. A comfy tank top, snug shorts, and a pair of brown hiking boots—perfect.

Now don't get me wrong, I appreciated the armor Tolby had stuck me in earlier, especially since it had saved my life, but I'm not a soldier, and I never want to be one. Thus, simply getting dressed in clothes that spoke to my soul did wonders to lift my mood.

"What's this for?" I asked, slipping the bracelet on now that I was dressed. "It looks fancy."

Said bracelet had a white skin along with a complicated network of blue circuits running across its surface, much like every other Progenitor artifact I'd encountered. As such, I assumed it wasn't simply a complementing fashion piece. Or maybe it was. Did the Progenitors do fashion? They must have, right? Man, I wonder what kind of mind-blowing advances they came up with in that arena.

Self-washing clothes? Poly-morphic fabric that self-attunes to whatever clime or place you happen to be in? Ever-changing patterns that could hypnotize would-be attackers or help you score a free drink with the bartender?

Pockets in women's pants?

Nah. That's crazy talk.

"That is your standard Excel-Care VIP bracelet," he said. "With it, you'll be able to access a variety of our services wherever you are, and if you give me a moment"—he paused, and then when he spoke again, his voice came from the bracelet as opposed to the speakers above—"I can copy myself into the solid-state drive and assist you wherever you are. Would you like to know more?"

I made a face like I'd been served up Brussels sprouts with a side of chopped liver.

"Eh, thanks?" I said. I had a feeling I didn't want him following me around at all times. Ugh, annoying. But at the same time, having access to Progenitor tech, or services in this case, might prove beneficial down the road—especially medically oriented ones.

"Now then, on to matters at hand," Rummy said as I put on my boots and began lacing them. "I feel that it is my duty to inform you that

13

customers who purchase both accidental clone mishap insurance as well as the extended warranty for all cloning treatments report a forty-two percent increase in their satisfaction when it comes to conflict resolution. Would you like to hear more?"

My hands froze as I pulled my laces tight. "Come again? Clone mishaps?" I'd barely gotten the words out before my gaze landed on a second empty medical pod. "Hang on a second. There was another me in there."

"There's no other you," he said. "You, my dear, are one in a googolplex, truly stunning and—"

"Don't even start," I said. "You know what I mean. You guys made a clone to test your treatment on. I remember."

"We did."

"So where is she, and where are my friends?"

"More fantastic questions," he said. "I appreciate your candor in wanting to resolve any matters of inconvenience. May I have your permission to ask one final thing in order to properly formulate a response that will meet your needs in the most expeditious of ways?"

I groaned and shook my head. "Fine. Make it fast."

"How do you feel about your prior party arrangement?"

"My prior party arrangement?" I repeated.

"Yes, the group you were with," he said. "Your quote-unquote friends. On a scale of one to ten, how would you rate your satisfaction with them?"

"What the hell does that have to do with anything?"

"Because if you've ever been less than completely satisfied, now is the perfect time to capitalize on the fact that they abandoned you. And you can do that by perusing the hundreds of apps available that will allow you to find the party of your dreams. Would you like to know more?"

"Are you saying they left me?"

"Yes."

14

"No."

"Yes."

I stared blankly for a few beats before racing out the door, only to find an empty hall to greet me.

"Guys, I'm dressed," I yelled, refusing to entertain Rummy's breakdown of the current situation. "We can go now."

Silence answered. I dashed around the medical facility, heart pounding harder and harder with each vacant room I looked in. It didn't take long before my knees weakened, my lungs gasped, and only a tiny miracle kept me upright.

Despite all that, I couldn't give up. I wouldn't. They had to be around there somewhere.

The front.

They had to be at the front.

I bolted into the welcome area, sure that Tolby and the others would be casually sitting on one of the colorful benches lining the wall.

They weren't.

"Guys? Tolby? Jainon?" I called out, voice cracking. "This isn't funny. Where are you?"

Rummy piped in from another set of unseen speakers. "I told you. They left."

"Why?"

"They're currently enjoying the pleasant company of Dakota 2.0, which is why I'd asked you how you felt about the party situation, as well as whether or not you wanted to learn more about our numerous options when it comes to clone mishaps."

I blinked, stupefied. It wasn't because I didn't understand what he was saying. I did, all too well in fact. "Are you telling me they left with my clone?"

"I am."

"They left with the clone that you guys made in order to treat me."

"Yes."

"The clone that you created to test your antivenin cocktail on," I said, spinning the scenario in my head one last time, all the while praying I was about to wake up from a nightmare. "That's who they left with."

"Yes."

"Left as in...they're taking her for a test drive and will be right back?"

"No."

"They left as in they're currently on their way to hangar two in order to get a ship," he said. "Given the speed at which they departed, as well as the general conversation I overheard, I suspect that once they reach said ship, they will be taking off, never to return."

My jaw dropped. In a flash, I ran for the exit doors on the other side of the welcome area. Two strides into my run, they slid open, and a Nodari scout, a horrific-looking creature with wicked horns, razor claws, and a bronze exoskeleton, entered carrying a large rifle. It paused only a pace beyond the threshold and stared at me with a half dozen green eyes.

I think I surprised it as much as it surprised me.

"Oh damn," I mumbled.

Two more appeared behind it. And then a third that was considerably taller, wider, and a thousand times more vicious-looking.

"Tolby," I whispered. "Wherever you are, you can come save me now."

An instant later, the scout attacked.

CHAPTER TWO
RACE TO THE HANGAR

The monster cleared four meters in a single leap. I bolted to the side, and with one hell of a telekinetic punch, I caved in half its skull. The thing fell to the side as gore and chitin flew in all directions, and my right arm fell uselessly to my side as I'd spent all the energy I had in it in the blow.

Normally, taking out a scout would be a good thing, but seeing how I still had three others to deal with, I wasn't about to break out the champagne. On that note, whenever I finally got home, I was going to splurge on the best money could buy. I deserved it.

That said, I guess my surprise attack was enough to give the other Nodari pause and respect for my abilities. Instead of giving immediate chase, they kept their distance and raised their weapons before sending a hail of acidic needles flying in my direction.

I managed to get through the door leading deeper into the medical facility without being hit. As I flew through the threshold, I hammered the button to shut the door behind me and locked it just as fast.

"I would avoid those creatures if I were you," Rummy said. "Average life expectancy has a negative correlation in regard to time spent with them."

"I know that already!" I shouted.

"May I offer some assistance?"

"That would be fantastic," I said, rounding the corner at the end of the hall. I wasn't sure where I was going, but I hoped the door I locked behind me would hold long enough for me to find a way out. The repeated heavy thuds I heard of the Nodari ramming into it made me think otherwise; at least, not without one hell of a lucky elephant to rub, and there wasn't a plastic pachyderm anywhere in sight.

"Wonderful," Rummy said enthusiastically. "I can offer you some of the most competitive life insurance this side of the gamma quadrant. We can tailor your quote based on species; activity level; superstitious nature; likelihood of vaporization, mutation, *and* incineration; and even waive the usual fees for impending hazardous adventures. Would you like to know more?"

"That's no help at all!" I yelled, hooking left down a branch and sealing that door as well.

"Your next of kin may disagree. Have you thought about the cost of funeral expenses?"

"Look, if you can't teleport me away or guide me to a tank, I don't want to hear it," I said.

"I'm afraid I can't do any of that, but if you go back the way you came, the fifth passage on your left will take you to the testing area for ship impulse engines."

"What good does that do me?"

"On the other side of that area, you'll find cargo transit tubes that hook directly into hangar two, which is where the ship is that your friends are headed to."

I skidded to a stop. "They will?"

"Yes. In fact, you'll likely find those tubes much freer of Nodari than the halls. I believe there's at least one Nodari Captain roaming them. Your telekinetic punch will not be strong enough to stop him."

"I wish you would've said something sooner," I griped, running back the way I came.

You'd think that four passages on the left would come and go quickly, but if you did, you'd be wrong like me. I'd nearly run all the way back to the start, thinking I'd missed it, when passage four showed up, with five a few meters beyond. Sadly, the Nodari were in the way, and they came at me hard and fast.

Acidic darts flew from their weapons, sizzling past my head and melting the wall next to me. I managed to dash into the hall on my right to avoid being turned to goo. Unfortunately, the hall didn't go very far before dumping me onto a balcony that overlooked a massive warehouse that housed dozens of enormous cylinders, each three times as tall as me, at least that as wide, and sitting about a meter off the ground on stilts.

I took the grated stairs to my left without hesitation. As I flew down them, I could hear the Nodari racing after me, and they seemed so close I could've sworn they were breathing down my neck.

"Careful," Rummy said, thankfully adopting a quiet tone. "The fish in these tanks are priceless and vital to several transplants we offer."

"So?"

"So, you break it. You buy it."

"Pfft, bill me all you like," I scoffed.

More acidic darts whizzed by my head, and I ducked behind a tank to avoid the rest. As I heard the Nodari come stomping down the stairs, I ran in the opposite direction as fast as I could before slipping underneath another tank. Good thing I did, too, because I caught sight of one of the Nodari's legs coming to a stop several meters away. Clearly, the guy was trying to set himself up for an easy shot when I appeared from the other side of the tank.

19

Though I bought myself a few moments to breathe, I knew it wouldn't be long before they started to look under the tanks. I scrambled away from them as fast as I could, hoping there would be another way out. I managed to get to the far end of the warehouse without being seen.

Unfortunately, there were no other exits, only a small room maybe twenty meters away that looked like some sort of control center. Worse, I could hear the Nodari closing in. They weren't exactly silent with their feet clacking loudly on the diamond-cross, metallic floor, and I started to think they were being noisy on purpose in order to drive me into cover as they methodically swept the area.

I tried to make my way back to the stairs, thinking I might simply escape while they searched for me in the warehouse. I didn't get far before I was forced to roll underneath another tank and scramble away on all fours. In the process, I clobbered my head on a valve.

Slightly dazed and bleeding from the scalp, I had an idea. In a flash, I checked the valve that now had bits of me scrapped across it. To my delight, my prediction proved true. The valve didn't appear mechanically operated. There was a small computer relay underneath. My eyes followed the cable that ran from it. It disappeared into some housing on the floor near the far edge, and then ran toward the control room I saw before.

"Oh please, please, please be operational," I said, making my way to the room as quickly and stealthily as I could. "And please, please, please, left arm work like you should."

Maybe I should've tossed in a few pleases for not getting caught, because as it turned out, I made a poor ninja.

With several paces still between me and the control room, a scout came around from behind a tank and shrieked with glee. He snapped his rifle up and fired, but I managed to bolt behind another tank and get away.

I ran as fast as I could, weaving around tank after tank. Some feeling returned to my right arm in the meantime, which was just in time for me to sock a Nodari scout with another telekinetic punch as he suddenly appeared in front of me. I didn't have nearly enough energy to cave in his skull, but I had enough to stun him a few seconds, which let me slip away.

For the next minute, I ended up playing an intense game of cat and mouse as I tried to first make my way back to the stairs before giving up and returning to the control room, intent on trying my plan once more.

This time, I made it in without being seen.

There wasn't much to this place, other than a nearby bank of computers. I easily connected to them with my implants. A few seconds later, I was surfing through the menus. It would've been nice to have stumbled upon the "Exterminate all Nodari" option, or "Wake from Terrible Nightmare, Safe and Sound in Bed Back Home," but I knew those were wishful thinking. I did quickly find the tank controls, however, which was as good as it was going to get.

"What do you think you're doing?" Rummy asked.

"Quiet," I hissed.

"You better not be up to what I think you are."

"Then don't think at all."

"You are!" he whispered harshly. "You're going to cost us everything!"

I ignored his objections and began opening the valves in all of the tanks. Each one I hit, I could hear more and more water pour onto the floor.

I darted out, my feet splashing heavily in the knee-high, green water. More splashes came from nearby, so I made a shallow dive beneath the surface and prayed my idea would work. Cloaked in murkiness, I shut my eyes and concentrated on my left arm, trying to draw the energy from the water in order to recharge the biobatteries in my right.

A tingly sensation started in my fingertips, but it soon ran through from my palm up to my shoulder. Ice formed along my skin, and at the same time, warmth returned to my right arm.

I popped out of the water after a few more seconds to find a Nodari scout not even two meters away. He spun as I resurfaced, and that was the last thing he ever did. One monumental telekinetic punch later, he flopped backward, sans head.

"And stay down," I said with a grin.

More sloshing grabbed my attention, and under the water I went again. As before, when I came up, I was fully recharged and clobbered my would-be killer. The last Nodari, the big one, didn't fare much better. I found him standing guard near the stairs, and after I gave him all I had, he fell into the water with a giant splash.

"Well I hope you're proud of yourself," Rummy said as I darted up the stairs. "We're going to have to shut down for who knows how long to clean the place up and find new flibberfish."

"I am, thank you," I said, still running. "Feel free to send me the bill. Right now, I've got a ship to catch."

"Believe me, I will."

"Fine. In the meantime, shush."

He did, thankfully, which let me concentrate on doing everything I could to get out of there.

My legs burned as the lactic acid built to levels on par with any Olympic sprinter at the end of a track meet, and within a couple of minutes, I was racing through the engine-testing portion of the facility. It looked pretty spiffy, actually, and reminded me of the old rocket gardens they had back on Earth way back when. Titanic rocket nozzles of varying shapes were mounted on clamps that looked as if they could hold down Mechagodzilla running on triple fusion reactors, and all around were a slew of servers, sensor arrays, and at least two dozen shut-down droids that looked part octopus, part centipede. I imagine they had once helped with not only testing but building and modifying ship engines, and to that end, I really wished I could've taken one with me. I figured it would prove handy to have a droid on board whatever Progenitor ship we were snagging, since he would be the only one who really knew how to maintain it, let alone repair it.

Obviously, I didn't have time to bring one along, which really sucked, if for no other reason than I bet these guys wouldn't keep losing the 10mm socket. Talk about a time saver right there.

Anywho, true to Rummy's word, I found the cargo transit tubes running across the ground at the other end, but they weren't even a half meter in diameter. Sure, I could still fit, but I wouldn't be dashing through them, and I didn't have time to crawl. Then again, when I saw a nearby pod with an open lid, I realized I didn't have to. I could easily fit inside the pod. All I had to do was send it and pray however these tubes worked, it would be sent fast.

I made it to the pod in the blink of an eye and looked for the controls. There weren't any obvious ones, but like most things the Progenitors had, everything came to life when I tried to make a mental connection with my implants. A holographic display popped up near the hatch and gave me a simple menu to work. Using it, I quickly selected "delivery" and then "hangar two" for the location.

"Cargo movement order accepted," said a stilted, female voice. The broken tempo her words took on reminded me of someone turning the handle on a jack-in-the-box at varying speeds. "Would you like to notify corvette 7979 of its delivery? It's preparing for departure as we speak."

"You can do that?" I asked, not sure who I was talking to.

"Yes," she replied. "Shall I notify the captain of this incoming cargo container?"

"Yes!" I shouted. "And tell them not to leave without it!"

"Notification sent. Transporting cargo now."

The pod's lid started to close, and I barely had time to jump in. When the lid closed and sealed, the pod floated along slowly for a few seconds before making a small adjustment in heading. Then all the blood rushed to my head as it shot forward, like it had been shot out of the barrel of a howitzer.

The ride didn't last but a half minute at best, and thankfully, when it stopped, it did so relatively gently, and I didn't end up losing half my height.

I'd barely pushed open the hatch when I heard the sounds of repeated cannon fire along with the distinct sounds of a ship's engines spooling up.

"Stop! I'm coming!" I shouted, flopping out of the transport pod and into a side room. I scampered to my feet and ran for the door leading to the hangar. "Don't leave!"

The intensity of the gunfire grew, and the engines suddenly went from a rising hum to a steady, high-pitched whine. My throat closed, and I knew I hadn't a nanosecond to spare.

All I had to do was get their attention.

I made it two steps into the hangar when it all came to an end. A ship, sleek, fast, and a couple hundred meters in length with reverse-swept wings shot past me, dragging a wake of air so strong that it knocked me to the floor.

All I could do as it broke free of the facility and disappeared into the clear sky was vainly reach for it and whisper my best bud's name one last time. "Tolby...don't leave..."

CHAPTER THREE
PREP TO LEAVE

This might come as a shock to some, but I've been known to have a few lapses in judgment that have led to precarious situations. Some deadly serious. Some hysterically adorable. About a month after I moved into my first apartment, I bought a Martian koala bear at a flea market on a whim. I wasn't looking for one at the time, and I only went there to see what junk the antique peddlers were peddling because once in a blue moon, they're actually trying sell some rusted piece of scrap for a cool hundred that's actually worth thousands, or millions.

They never do their homework.

Apparently, I don't always either. Sue me.

No, don't sue me. I'm broke enough as it is.

Back to the Martian koalas. Having come up empty at Spacer Joe's Bargain Salvage, I was on my way to treat myself to a colossal root beer float with extra cherries when I stumbled on the most adorable little Martian koala you've ever seen. He had silky smooth, gray fur that demanded petting all the time, and bright eyes that begged everyone around to be his best friend. Unable to resist the power of the little koala and not wanting to live completely alone, I decided to buy him, cage and all.

I named him Horatio on the way home. I don't know why. I don't even like Shakespeare, probably because I find it hard to believe the legends. A poet who helped defeat the Spanish Armada in the 11th century PHS by composing such a beautiful sonnet that the men under Juan Martínez de Recalde's command forgot what they were doing and accidently (and simultaneously) lit all their powder magazines? Yeah right.

Tangent, I know. Back to the Martian koala story (again). The first day home with Horatio went great. So did the second. We watched movies together. Dined on delicious fruits as much as my paltry budget would allow, and he'd snuggle up under my chin as I dove into my reading pile.

By day three, the little bugger was getting clingy when I'd use the bathroom or want to take a shower. He'd either sneak in with me or sit by the door and stick his little paws under it, trying to get inside.

Totally pathetic.

And don't even get me started on what happened the first time I left him alone for more than a few hours to run to the store and catch the latest Rixar flick, *Toy Quest XXIII*. (Freaking hilarious by the way. Check it out if you get the chance.) Long story short on that one, I thought I was going to have to take us to couple's therapy.

I didn't, but it occurred to me my brain was on the right track. After a quick pop over to the library for research, I confirmed my suspicions. Martian koalas were extremely communal creatures. They thrived with attention, withered without it, and needed friends, more so than any social media junkie.

So what did I do? I got him a friend, of course. It took a little bit of hunting to find a good breeder, and then a little bit more convincing to him that I knew what I was doing, but I brought Martian koala numero two back home and named him Sam.

The two hit it off to my utmost delight. For the next week, they did everything together, completely attached at the hip, which was good, because my next semester was starting. Fast forward another two weeks. I returned home after a couple of days hunting for treasure in the ice flows of Umut II, about two hundred klicks north of the quarantine zone, to find out that well...Sam really should've been called Samantha and they weren't figuratively attached at the hip...

They had six of them, and before I knew it, the population exploded to...I have no idea. All I knew was I had a massive infestation of the most adorable little furballs you ever did see. They were everywhere. In the cupboards. In the vents. In my hair.

Thank god they were litter trained.

My parents were out of the quadrant and couldn't help. My brother thought it was hilarious but didn't have much to offer other than laughter. So I was basically on my own with a colossal mess, because everyone I approached didn't want the responsibly of one.

Then my landlord found out and threatened to evict me in two days if I didn't get it straightened out. Not only evict me but take my security deposit and sue me for damages. I could've had a nervous breakdown right then and there, but I didn't. Well, I didn't for long.

For the next forty-eight hours, I feverishly worked in high gear, calling anyone and everyone with a contact number that might have the slightest interest. I'm proud to say, with exactly zero hours of sleep and two hours to spare, I placed each one in a wonderful home and made sure they were paired in such a fashion that there wouldn't be another population explosion.

So, what did that have to do with my predicament on Kumet?

Everything, I told myself.

As I stared blankly at the empty sky, still on all fours in the hangar, eyes watering, throat closed, I reminded myself of all the pickles I'd gotten myself into and subsequently survived, and the koala story was the one I latched on to the most.

This was all this was. I'd made a mess of things. I didn't have anyone to help, but that didn't mean I was done. Not only would I not be finished, as I wasn't with the Martian koalas, but I realized the solution to both happened to be the same.

All I had to do was make a call. Or more specifically, I had to call that ship and get Tolby to turn around.

"All right, Dakota," I said, taking to my feet. "You got this, girl."

I glanced around the hangar, not sure which direction I should go to find a comm station. There had to be one, if not dozens, in the facility. I vaguely remembered passing by a few maps of the place, but they seemed far away and I wasn't sure how much time I had before Tolby and the others would be gone for good.

Then I spied a room, three stories up, that overlooked the massive space that was the hangar. "Hot damn," I said, starting to trot toward it. "That's got to be a traffic control, right?"

I couldn't imagine what other purpose it would serve, though given some of the weirdness I'd encountered with the Progenitors, it may have very well been an indoor playground.

To my right, guttural, wheezing growls drifted to my ears. I jerked my head over my shoulder and immediately wished I hadn't. Ignorance really is bliss at times. At the far end of the hangar, near some broken doors, were piles of broken Nodari bodies. Most looked thoroughly burnt to a crisp or had enough gaping holes they weren't getting up anytime soon, but a couple of the mutilated creatures had already begun to twitch. Hopefully by the time they healed, or reanimated, or whatever you call it, I'd be long gone.

I found a set of stairs in an alcove and raced up them three at a time, which led directly into the control room and not a Progenitor playground. It was nice to know they weren't always as whacked as they could be. Though I often suspected that was because when they disappeared, so did half their logic, and whatever bots and facility AI remained were working with patchwork code and obscure directives.

Sadly, the controls weren't easy this time to figure out. Connect to? Yes. Work, no. They probably would have been if I could've read Progenitorian hieroglyphics, but since I'd never picked that up as an elective in school (not that it was ever offered), the screen I was faced with meant nothing to me. It was simply a wide array of bizarre symbols to pick from.

I still had no idea why I wasn't presented with the translated version as I always had been. Life would've been so much easier then.

The first selection I tried was from column three, row eight. The button there glowed a little brighter, not to mention I've always loved the number three and eight smells like strawberries, which I had a sudden craving for dipped in chocolate. That probably had to do with the fact that the seventh button (which was blinking) on the left, two rows down, became the number fourteen in my head, which is sweet, rich, and absolutely delicious.

Anyway, when I pressed the first one, all I managed to do was turn off the lights. Thankfully, they came right back on when I pressed it again. My second pick put me in another menu, and random picks three through twenty did nothing at all that I could tell.

"Come on, damn it," I groaned. In the back of my head, I felt like the little voice inside me was telling me to relax, to tap into the power of the pachyderm, to trust the lucky elephant that I'd relied on so many times before, to see me through. Even if I hadn't appeased him with a belly rub as of late.

I figured it couldn't hurt, right? It's not like I was getting anywhere on my own, and I needed to get in contact with Tolby like five minutes ago.

I opened my eyes, looked at the alien screen once more, and felt the calm of nirvana wash over me. Without second-guessing anything, I let my fingers dance across the screen, selecting alien symbols with such speed and precision, I imagine I'd have given a court stenographer a run for her money—assuming they actually used those anymore.

Screens flashed by and eventually settled on one that displayed an array of ship icons. A few instinctive clicks later, up popped a schematic of a Progenitor corvette that looked exactly like the one that had shot by me a couple of minutes ago.

My heart beat faster, and a smile spread across my face. This was it. I could feel it in my bones.

The sounds of static and broken communications filled the air. In the background were muffled, off-pitch voices, along with heavy thuds and staccato notes of...of what? Gunfire? Maybe. It was like I'd tapped into the radio signals coming from a warzone, but I hadn't quite gotten the frequency right.

My hands kept moving across the controls, and I let my subconscious self work as freely as I could. A few heartbeats later, Tolby's voice came through, loud and clear.

"This is Tol'Beahn, captain of the Royal Guard to the House Yari. Is someone on this channel?"

I about leaped out of my skin. "Tolby!" I screamed with delight. "It's me! I'm in the hangar!"

"Repeat again? Seven klicks south of the city?"

"No, not the city! The facility! I'm in the hangar!"

The line crackled for a few seconds before Tolby came back on. "Copy. Stand fast, brothers, we're on our way."

My heart sank at that moment. He hadn't heard a thing. I went back to the controls and worked them again on pure instinct. "Tolby!" I shouted, thinking I'd tuned it right again. "Tolby you've got to come get me!"

"...coming in for a hot pickup. To all remaining forces, recommend immediate evac...Nodari battleship less than two minutes away..."

I screamed with primal fury and ended up kicking the bottom of the command station a half dozen times with my foot. "You can't leave me!"

He didn't hear me, of course, so I went back to the menus, hoping something I did would trigger some sort of diagnostic as to why we couldn't talk. After a dozen buttons or so, the female voice who'd talked to me with the cargo pods spoke. "Corvette 7979 unable to receive messages from this command station," she said. "Communication array has suffered critical damage. Repairs necessary to restore functionality."

I groaned and ran my fingers through my hair before working the controls again. "There has to be a way to get a message out."

"Communication array has suffered critical damage," she repeated. "Repairs necessary to restore functionality."

"You said that already!"

"Communication array has suffered—"

Her voice cut out when I slammed the bottoms of two fists on the screen.

"Okay, deep breaths, Dakota. Deep breaths." It took a few seconds to get my hyperventilation under control, and when it did, one last Hail Mary of an idea came to mind.

"Hey, computer chick," I said, popping through menus again. "Sorry about punching you, but this is hangar two, right? Are there any ships in any of the other hangars?"

"Affirmative," she said. "Scout shuttle 21-A is available in hangar one."

My eyes widened and I sucked in a tense breath. "Will it fly?"

"It will with a suitable pilot and the proper interface implants," she said.

"Fan-freaking-tastic," I said, bouncing on the balls of my feet. "Give me directions."

"Displaying optimum route now," she said.

The screen flickered, and the menu disappeared. A map of the area popped up with both my current position and my destination

31

highlighted in blue. Praise the pachyderm, it wasn't that far away, all things considered. Five hundred meters at the most.

Off I went with the map firmly planted in mind. Remember that pile of Nodari corpses at the end of the hangar? It wasn't so corpse-like anymore. As I was forced to race by, a scout staggered to its feet. It came at me like a deranged marionette on broken strings, which as terrifying as that was, it meant it couldn't give a proper chase.

With wide strides, I easily put a heap of distance between it and myself. I dashed through the corridors with reckless abandon, pausing only once and far too long to get a door to open at a T-junction.

It slid to the side, revealing another Nodari scout. It was bent over a dead Kibnali soldier, presumably inspecting its fallen foe. The monster turned its head right as I socked it with a telekinetic strike.

I didn't give him all I had, because I feared I'd need that arm to fly, and I didn't want to get into the shuttle with a bum limb. Also, right before I made my strike, I realized I didn't need to use all my energy to finish the creature off.

The Nodari staggered back, its hands reflexively clutching one of its eyes. In that moment, I scooped up the Kibnali's pistol, which was practically a full-sized rifle in my hands, and unloaded on the monster.

Plasma bolts tore into his chest and head, and another dozen shot up the wall behind him. I'm hardly Annie Oakley, but I figured if I pulled the trigger enough times at that close range, I'd get the job done.

And I did.

I made it to hangar one a half minute later. Like hangar two, it was a massive area with high walls and a domed ceiling. Various machinery sat near the walls, and dozens of hoses ran from an equal number of tanks to empty landing pads. Toward the far end, some hundred meters away, stood an arrow-shaped shuttle with folded wings and four stabilizing fins in the back.

"Oh yes, yes, yes," I said between huge gulps of air. "I seriously hope your last owner left the keys in the glove compartment."

A door to my right opened. Three Nodari scouts burst forth. Immediately we exchanged fire, which was really more of them shooting at me while I popped off what shots I could in their general direction, missing horribly. Worse, I used up what was left of the weapon's power pack; once I realized it was spent, I tossed it away.

With thirty meters to go, I focused on the shuttle, hoping I was in range to make a mental connection and the ship would respond accordingly. Immediately, I felt the pop in my head, and right after, a ramp dropped from the belly of the ship and the engines started to whine.

"Sorry, guys," I said with a grin. "Time to go."

Two paces away from the ramp, a blue field that encompassed the ship flickered behind me, and not a moment too soon. The Nodari fire increased dramatically both in intensity and accuracy, but instead of striking me, it struck the shield.

"Now that's what I'm talking about," I said, beaming. "Dakota, one. Stupid Nodari, zero."

The shuttle wasn't very big, about the size of any other I'd been in, so I bolted through its meager cargo hold in an instant and catapulted myself into what I assumed was the pilot seat.

"All right, baby, how do we fly together?" I asked, looking for the controls.

I'd no sooner asked the question when said controls sprang from the floor. At first, they were simply rising columns of what looked like liquid metal, but those columns quickly took shape and became near replicas of what I had back on my original ship.

"Whoa," I said. "Now that's freaky."

A new, deep voice joined me in the cockpit and carried the tone of one with unfathomable experience. "Welcome, Dakota Adams," he said. "You're late."

CHAPTER FOUR
NUKED

Despite the urgent need for takeoff, I flopped back in the seat, stunned. "Run that by me again? I'm late?"

A holographic orb appeared several centimeters away from the ceiling, a little to the left of me. It was maybe the size of a small bowl, and across its skin, fractals of swirling blues and reds danced. When the voice continued speaking, the orb pulsated in synch. "Correct," he replied. "From the time you left the medbay, you should have arrived at this shuttle ninety-three billion nanoseconds sooner given your total capabilities. This delay has severely hampered your odds of surviving this invasion."

"I have no idea what you're talking about, but it sounds like I should be doing more flying and less talking," I said, grabbing the controls.

"That is the correct course of action at this time," he said. "Your minimal multitasking abilities will not let you fly at peak performance while absorbing all the information I'm capable of giving you."

"Then hush," I said, annoyed he kept talking and worried about what news he was going to dump on me.

34

My ship's shields flared as Nodari small-arms fire ripped into it. Seeing those bursts of light threw me into high gear. I quickly snapped together the seat's five-point harness before easing the shuttle off the ground and flipping the switches to raise the landing gear. They had yet to fully retract before I used the foot pedals to spin the craft around. Once I was pointed at the exit to the hangar bay, I pushed the throttle all the way forward.

Bad idea.

I rocketed out of the bay like I'd caught a ride on a runaway warp drive. If I hadn't shot out into the vast open space of clear skies, I'm sure I'd have plowed right into whatever hazard would've been there, and that would've ended my escape real quick.

Despite the bone-crushing g's being pulled, I managed to reach the throttle and ease off the gas. Or fusion reaction. Or whatever it was that powered this most magnificent of tiny ships.

"Holy snort, this thing can fly!" I yelled with glee. I made a few practice barrel rolls and then made a few figure eights a couple of kilometers over the ocean to get a feel for how she handled. All I can say is she carved through the air with such grace, such agility, I'm certain any angel would be jealous.

If I still had her by the time I got back home, I made a mental note to enter the next Venetian regatta on account of she'd easily make the size and weight limit while at the same time, out-flying anything anyone else fielded even in reverse.

"All right, ship AI guy, how well can I track another ship in this thing?" I asked, scanning my consoles. "I've got some friends to catch up to."

"Correction," he said. "You've got a nuclear warhead to outrun."

My eyes nearly burst from their sockets. "A what?"

"A nuclear warhead," he repeated. "It is a widely used method of mass devastation, commonly found across all advanced cultures throughout space and time."

"I know what it is!"

"Then I suggest you get as far and high as possible," he said. "Marking its signature on your scanners now. Predicted yield, five-hundred and seventy-nine megatons."

I barely heard the estimation as I glanced down at my displays. A pulsating red blip, a little under a hundred kilometers away, was making its way toward me. Freaked beyond rational thought, I did the first thing that came to me. I banked hard and shot away from the warhead as fast as the ship would take me.

"Come on, baby, go faster," I mumbled, tightening my grip on the controls.

"Warning: Nodari countdown detected. Airburst likely in three seconds. Redirecting all power to sh—"

Blinding light filled the sky, and my ship flipped end over end like it'd been kicked by an angry titan. Klaxons blared in my ears, and every warning known to have ever existed seemed to flash on my status screens. To top it off, my body slammed into my harness a dozen times before my ship regained any semblance of a normal flight.

To my dismay, that flight was headed straight down.

I pulled on the stick for all I was worth. The nose raised, and with a few kilometers to spare, I got it above the horizon.

"Martian babes on a stick," I said, blowing out all the air I'd been holding. "That was close."

My celebration, I soon realized, turned out to be premature. Alarms still hammered my ears, and worse, the ship was rapidly decelerating. Frantically, I began hitting controls, trying to get the engines back online.

"What's going on?" I yelled.

"Damage to coolant pumps, impulse regulators, and flux capacitors has forced engine shutdown," the orb said. "Recommend finding a suitable landing area until repairs can be completed."

I bit my lower lip, rolled my shoulders, and promised myself that if I somehow managed to get back home alive, I'd practice my dead-stick landings till I was blue in the face. Moreover, I promised I wouldn't chide Tolby for practicing his in the simulator every month, too.

"By the way, I'm completely up for suggestions on where to put her down," I said, looking at all my tree-filled options.

"Ship damage has disabled my ability to make such assessments."

I grunted as I rolled the ship left and right about twenty degrees to each side so I could get a full view of the surrounding area. Massive forest fires raged behind me. To my left, I saw nothing but open sea. And while a water landing would probably be the easiest, I couldn't lose the ship. To my right, however, were more forests and also plenty of rolling hills. Landing in them seemed like a good way to lose the shuttle, too. There were some fields, way, way, *way* far out, but given how fast I was losing altitude, I didn't think I could make it.

That left one viable option: a beach landing.

Unfortunately, the shore ahead looked too rocky for comfort, and the only stretch of smooth, sandy beach lay behind. But again, what choice did I have?

"Hang on to your virtual butt," I said, banking. My one-eighty turn went wide to conserve as much forward momentum as I could, but I still ended up using what altitude I had left to bring her around. I'd barely leveled the wings and pulled up the nose when the shuttle's belly hit the sand.

Immediately, the craft threatened to nose down and flip me over, and it was only using every ounce of skill and luck I had left that kept the ship from doing so. I carved a three-hundred-meter trench as I slid across the beach, sending sand and shell in all directions. When it was over, my hands trembled. My face dripped in sweat, and I had a stupid, happy grin on my face.

"How was that?" I asked, leaning back in my chair.

"Not bad, for a human."

I quickly unbuckled and glanced behind me to assess the damage. As far as I could tell, the interior looked to be in working order, though I hated to think what condition the outer hull was in, not to mention the engines. "What now?" I asked. "Can we fix the ship? Or can you get us a tow? Preferably before the Nodari find us."

"Running full diagnostics now."

"And what about my friends?" I asked. "I need to catch up to them before they disappear."

"Progenitor ships have a distinct hyperspace signature that will allow me to follow their trail for up to three weeks after they make warp," the orb replied. "If you wish to follow them, we simply need to repair this ship before that trail is washed away by interstellar winds."

I sighed heavily. Though I'd obviously have liked to be back with Tolby right then and there, at least what the computer was telling me wasn't godawful. In fact, it felt pretty hopeful, provided we weren't looking at needing a drydock for the next six months to go anywhere. Course, by then, the Nodari would've probably found me, eaten me, and fertilized the ground with me.

As I waited for the orb to figure out what was wrong with the ship, I tried to get cozy in the pilot's seat. I even kicked my feet up on the console. "So, AI guy. What do I call you?"

"Indifference. Differentiation is not necessary. I am the Progenitor's ships' AI."

"I figured that part out on my own, Mister Congeniality," I said, cracking a grin. I swear, this guy's voice was about as warm as the dark side of Pluto. "What do I call you as opposed to the other AI you guys have?"

"Erroneous assumption. I am not the ship's AI. The ships' AI."

My brow furrowed, and for a hot second, I thought I might be going crazy. "Didn't I say that like a half second ago?"

"Clarification for a rudimentary brain. Fault, mine, as this is the second time I've made such a mistake. Updating human records to reflect need for basic explanations at all times. I'm not the AI for this ship. I'm the AI for all Progenitor ships. My size and location are beyond your understanding."

"Wow," I whispered. "You're saying you're inside every Progenitor ship?"

"A crude understanding, but that will suffice for now."

"In other words, you're the Alpha and Omega of AI."

"You may frame my role as such."

"Then I'm calling you AO," I said. I crossed my arms over my chest with satisfaction. After a bit of thought, a question popped into my mind. "Hang on a moment. If you're the AI for all the ships, can't you tell them to turn around and come get me? Or hell, fly the ship back here?"

"Their ship is not responding to attempts at control," he said. "Damage likely sustained by us, them, or both is preventing such course of action. If you wish to see your friends again, you're going to have to catch up with them on your own."

"What about other ships? Can you control them and send them over here?"

"No other Progenitor ships are online at this time."

I leaned back in the seat and thought about all the fun times I'd had with Tolby over the years—my favorite being when we made a giant snow fort in Alaban Prime and had an all-out snowball fight with the local kids. Those were much more pleasing memories than dwelling on recent events, and if I had to sit quietly as I waited for AO to finish with the diagnostics, I figured I might as well keep in the best mood I could.

Ten minutes came and went, and I began to worry something was dreadfully wrong with the ship. "Please tell me you've got some good news, AO. I can't sit here much longer."

"Unneeded request. I do not assign moral value to new information."

"I mean, tell me whatever damage we suffered is easily fixed."

"Saying such a thing would be both baseless and pointless as diagnostics are still running."

"When are they going to be done? It's been forever."

"Negative. You are a finite creature incapable of comprehending infinity, let alone experiencing it. Stand by."

"Bah," I said with disgust.

I hate standing by. Have I ever said that before? It's the worst. Not because I can't be patient. I can. When you embark upon a life of treasure hunting and artifact finding, you've got to be able to put in long hours where not a lot gets done on account of needing to do research, waiting for others to come back with research, or simply twiddling thumbs as your quantum computer crunches the numbers in order to put together a probability map based on scant rumor and quiet whispers that will lead you to the goods.

That said, when someone says "stand by" while they're inspecting your ship, it's always a prelude to a laundry list of things wrong with it that's accompanied by a bill the size of Mount Everest.

It's like the old detective bit of "Oh, and just one more thing," they say when interviewing a suspect. It's never just one more thing, and it's not a question they just happened to think of. It's something serious.

But even if AO were a mechanic and intended to charge me, and even if I had money with which to pay him, I still couldn't deal with a ruined ship. Not now, at least. I had to get back to the others. I had to get home. I had to rejoin my friends, who each day became more and more like family (Tolby already was).

And the more I spent time away from them, the more I felt utterly alone.

I hate alone.

Hate. Hate. Hate.

Hate.

(Hate.)

"I can't believe they just left me like that," I muttered, slipping into one of my rare angry, brooding moods. "Me! Dakota! How could they?"

"You seem upset," Rummy said, chiming in from the bracelet I wore. I'd forgotten he was still with me at this point on account of how quiet he'd been. "Would you like to peruse our stock of antidepressants? You are entitled to a complimentary seven-day trial of either Glee-agra or Happiant."

"Of course I'm upset," I said. "They left me! Me! How could you let them do that?"

"The Dakota they ran off with is identical to you in every way," Rummy explained. "They seemed very happy with her, and it was an honest mistake."

"Mistake? That wasn't a mistake." I gritted my teeth and could feel myself losing control of my emotions, but I didn't care. If any time warranted a breakdown in life, this was one of them. "There's no way that clone looks like me one hundred percent, or even acts like me for that matter."

"Progenitor cloning technology is flawless," Rummy boasted. "That's one of the main reasons cited by return customers and why we have a 99.2823% retention rate. This allows us to offer excellent savings on bulk clone purchases. Would you like to know more?"

"No, but you can tell me how the hell it can act like me, too."

Rummy laughed. "Copying memory is a simple process, especially when you've already got Progenitor implants installed," he boasted. "We also have a large selection of pleasing memories you can select from if you would like to alter your perception of the past. Would you like to know more?"

"No, I wouldn't," I said. "What about all my looks? Does she also have the implants in my arm?"

"Of course," he said. "Clinical trials have to be done on specimens that are identical to the patient in every way possible."

I pointed to a small scar I still had above my right eyebrow. "Did she have this?" I asked. "There's no way you gave her the scar I got when I was twelve."

"What scar?"

"What do you mean, 'what scar?'" I shrieked. "This one."

"Again, what scar?"

I found the nearest shiny surface and looked. Normally, I'd be thrilled with the flawless skin presented to me, but not this time. "Where did it go?"

"We gave you a complimentary resurfacing," he explained. "All of your accidental scars were replaced with youthful, vibrant skin. We did leave your ritual Kibnali honors in place, however."

"I guess that's something." I sighed heavily. But then another thought sprang to mind. I looked down at my midsection and pointed. "I bet she didn't have a belly button, did she?" I asked. "Did they check for a belly button?"

Rummy was silent.

"Well, did they?" I reiterated, the force in my voice being more than enough to knock a small moon out of orbit.

"They might have been too busy dealing with a Nodari infestation to notice," he said.

"Great. Just freaking great," I said, throwing my hands up in disgust. "All this because they didn't do a basic belly button check."

"I'm not sure how aware your friends are of that procedure."

"Well, they should be," I huffed. "Hopefully once my clone sees her non-existing belly button and freaks out, they'll figure out what happened."

"That might be a problem, too," Rummy said.

"Please tell me she's not one of these broken clones that ends up killing everyone when they go a little bit twitchy," I said.

Rummy chuckled, which did little to settle my nerves. "No, I assure you, only the A2s were a bit twitchy. Thankfully, those bugs have long been worked out."

"Then what's the problem?"

"She thinks she's Dakota," he said. "And because she thinks she's Dakota, she's not about to give up her family."

"The hell she won't," I said, crossing my arms. "She's got no damn belly button! She has no right to them!"

"Clones tend to disagree, ergo, the problem," Rummy replied. "It is unlikely she would ever leave them. In fact, she will probably fight to the death to keep them."

At this point, a massive headache decided to camp out between my temples, and I slumped in my seat. "And she's got my implants," I said, rubbing the sides of my head.

"Yes."

"So, she can do everything I can," I added. "Interface with Progenitor tech. Use portal devices. Telekinetically punch things from here to the Milky Way and back."

"Also yes."

"That figures," I said, unsure how I'd manage to pry her off Tolby and the others without someone getting killed. "I suppose things can't get any—"

I instantly clamped my hand over my mouth, mortified at how close I'd come to dumping a ton of bad luck into my lap. I know lots of people would say that's cliché, and superstitious, but you know what? Clichés are only born from truths.

"Diagnostics finished," AO said, cutting into my thoughts.

"You know what's wrong?"

"That is correct."

"And you can fix it?"

"No, I cannot," he said.

My heart sank. "Not even if I help?"

43

"No," he said. "The X-45 onboard repair droid will be required to restore all systems. I suggest putting that plan into motion."

"You could've clarified that to begin with," I said, trying not to be too miffed that he'd phrased his answer that way. I mean, that's like saying, "Meredeth went to the hospital, and the doctors tried to save her life. They did the best that they could...and she is going to be okay."

What kind of moron puts important news that way?

I stretched to work out my stress and kinks in my shoulders and decided to prompt AO since a lot of nothing was still happening. "So, should I tell the X-twenty-whatever to get to work now or do you do that? I'd like to get out of here before I turn thirty."

"Neither one of us can give that instruction at this time."

"Because?"

"Because the X-45 is not aboard this ship," he said.

CHAPTER FIVE
THE GEO PLANT

I blinked.

I think I forgot to breathe for a few seconds, too.

"I'm sorry," I finally said. "But were you trying to be funny?"

"Initiating comedy is not part of my function," he replied.

I blinked again and dropped my brow. I must have misheard something. "Didn't you say that we had a droid on board?"

"Negative," he replied. "Faulty assumption on your part. The word *onboard* is simply part of its descriptive name. The last droid assigned to this ship was inadvertently sucked into a cruiser's intake during a faulty engine-start test. It was never replaced."

My head flopped back, and I groaned loudly. "For Jupiter's sake, why the hell did you even bring up the droid if we don't have one? That's just rude, getting my hopes up like that."

"Because you asked about the status of the droid before I could locate a suitable replacement," he replied.

I set my jaw and let a growl slip. "Did you find one?"

"Yes."

"Do we have to go back to the facility to get one? Because I'm not keen on heading back there."

"No," he replied. "The facility which we came from has likely suffered tremendous damage, if not outright destruction. Chances of a working repair droid being found there are almost nonexistent. Chances of you successfully bringing it back are even less."

"Before I have a nervous breakdown, is the one you found something I can feasibly get to?"

"Yes," he replied, much to my relief. "There are two Progenitor sites that are relatively nearby that utilized the X-45 repair droid in considerable number. Either will likely have one that is both available and functional."

I blew out a tense puff of air and felt the muscles in my neck and shoulders relax. "Fantastic. Where do I go?"

"The first facility is located approximately three days from here, by human foot, heading zero-one-seven," he said. "It is a small, underwater outpost in the middle of the great lake, approximately two hundred meters beneath the surface."

My face tightened with anxiety. "It's got a spiffy transit tube on the shore to get in though, right?"

"Negative," he said. "You will need to secure a submersible of some kind to gain access or increase either your lung capacity or oxygen efficiency."

I half laughed, half snorted. "Okay, that one's out. Where's the other?"

"The second facility is approximately a half day's hike, heading one-nine-six. It is an underground facility dedicated to geothermal research and manipulation. Finding its entrance may prove difficult."

"You can't pinpoint it for me on a map?"

"I have no map for you to pinpoint it with," he said. "There is, however, expedition gear that may assist you in accomplishing your task."

I perked and sat up on the edge of my seat. "There is?"

"Yes," he said. "I suggest you get moving. Daylight will wane soon."

In a flash, I popped out of the pilot seat and raced to the cargo hold. As I said before, the size of the shuttle meant that cargo space was pretty limited. Hell, the lavatory on a bargain-rate starliner was the Taj Mahal compared to the space in there. At least that meant finding the expedition crate was easy. And I use the term crate liberally. It was more of a tiny box that would be defying the laws of physics if it housed more than a flashlight, canteen, and spare shoelaces.

Then again, Progenitors were keen on making things that were smaller on the outside, so who knew what I'd find in there? A dune buggy would've been sweet. Although, I guess given the forests I was going to travel, a scout bike would've been better.

I flipped the latches to the case and quickly discovered that it was a run-of-the-mill storage container and didn't have any special properties. Inside I found six bundled blue tubes, made out of something like cardboard, a long rod about two-thirds of a meter long with a funky grip on one end, and a device that reminded me of an ancient, handheld calculator, only with little crescent wings on the top.

"Oh, the number nine combo set," Rummy beamed. "Very nice. Would you like to know more?"

"Yes, actually I would," I said, keeping my eyes focused on it all.

I think I gave the little guy the shock of his life. "You would? I mean, yes. Right. Of course you would," he said, tripping over his words with excitement. He paused for a moment to recompose himself before going on. "What an excellent choice you've made. Now then, I would like to direct your attention to the first item on the left."

"The blue things," I said.

"Yes," he replied. "They're self-oxidizing pyrotechnic illumination devices, which are a staple in any would-be explorer's arsenal. Not only can you can use them to provide light while reading your favorite arrangement of printed words on compressed vegetable matter while you bathe in solar radiation, but they are excellent for luring a wide array of deep undersea creatures into your powerful jaws. They can serve as multi-ton reptile attractant, or if you are in a pinch, they also have a chance at distracting explosive devices that are actively participating in a thermal quest."

"So they're flares," I said.

"Technically speaking, yes," he said, sounding a little deflated. "As an affiliate of Excel-Explore, I am capable of providing you with excellent discounts on a monthly survival subscription of three-dozen self-oxidizing pyrotechnic illumination devices or more. Would you like to know more?"

"I'll pass, thanks," I replied.

"Are you sure? We're running a one-time special—"

"I'm sure."

"Great. Great," he said. "I can see you're a girl who knows what she wants. If I may, then, direct your attention to the Mark IV Black-Diamond Quantum Self-Arrest and Ascension Assistance Tool."

He lost me at this point, so I ended up staring at the box for a few seconds before asking for help. "The what?"

"The ice axe," he said with a heavy sigh. "The thing with the handle."

I snatched it up quickly. The shaft had a good weight to it. Not so heavy that it would be unwieldy, but not so light that I felt it was a cheap gimmick. "Now that's a tool I can get behind," I said. "Where's the blade?"

"Currently existing in a state of superposition," he explained.

"Oh, like my *ashidasashi* likes to do."

"There is a button on the side of the handle," he went on. "Press it four times in rapid succession, and the waveform will collapse, revealing the blade."

I did so, and as he said, a serrated blade with a reverse curve materialized at the top. "Talk about making it easy to transport," I said,

48

admiring the tool. I know it was still simply an axe once you stripped away the quantum blade part, but every curve the whole thing had, every square centimeter of its finish, exuded high-tech marvel. Leave it to the Progenitors, I suppose, not to be satisfied with a simple tool.

"I'm sure that you're aware, as a savvy customer, that a first-rate climbing axe is vital to any expedition," he said. "Even more so than anti-grav boots."

I genuinely laughed. "Know that? I preach it, my little digital sales bud. No one ever wants to believe me!"

"They don't?" he asked, sounding shocked. "Do they not realize that batteries can die?"

"Right? And then what happens?"

"You end up as a quaint impact crater—"

"Coyote style," I finished, laughing again. "I swear, it's like you've read my mind."

My laughter stopped, and an uncomfortable silence fell between us as a new thought dawned on me. "Wait a second..."

"Yes?"

"You've read my mind!" I said, squirming as an icky feeling washed over me. "Like...literally read my mind! You've been in my most inner of inners without my okay! That's just wrong!"

"Oh, I see the misunderstanding," he said, adopting a corporate tone that I knew was a prelude to utter ridiculousness. "You see, by agreeing to treatment at Excel-Care, you agree to grant the company a perpetual, irrevocable, nonexclusive, royalty-free, worldwide, fully-paid, transferable sub-licensable license to use, reproduce, modify, adapt, publish, translate, create derivative works from, distribute, publicly perform and display your memories, name, likeness, physical attributes, and carnal desires provided in connection with your treatment in all media formats and channels now known or later developed, without compensation to or further consent from you."

I crossed my arms over my chest. "You guys are awful. What are you going to do with all those memories, anyway?"

"Tailor a more pleasurable and pertinent user experience for you, of course," he said. "What else?"

"In other words, marketing."

"Life, the Universe, and everything is all about marketing one thing or another," Rummy replied. "Be it resources, religions, mates, service, or simply the best bagels. Speaking of bagels, we can dropship you two dozen blueberry bagels that have been shown to increase exploration activity by twelve percent and satisfaction with body image by fourteen. Would you like to know more?"

"You know, I'm about to take this bracelet and shove it into the warp drive," I said.

"I would recommend against that," Rummy said. "You're likely to ruin the ship as well as void the warranty."

"Whatever. Just tell me what this last thing is so I can get going."

"The final tool in your exploration kit is a multi-phase subatomic matrix analyzer."

"Let's pretend for a moment I don't know what that means."

"It scans things," he said.

"That sounds useful, actually," I said, picking it up. "How do I work it?"

"You can either use the integrated tutorial, or you can buy our book *Multi-phase Subatomic Matric Analyzer for the Intellectually Challenged* and get hot tips, tricks, and never before revealed functions that are guaranteed to assist you in exploring the Universe like you never have before. Would you like to know more?"

"What do you think?"

"Yes?"

I raised an eyebrow.

"Or not."

I smiled as I took everything from the case. Having some gear, especially the type that was suited to my soul, instantly put me back into my usual can-do self, despite the absolute rotten pickle I was in. And I have to admit, it's such a nicer way to live whenever possible, even if you are stranded on a hostile alien planet and your best bud has run off with a psychopath clone trying to steal your identity (I'm really not a bitter person).

Anyway, back to the gear, or more specifically, returning to my upbeat attitude. There's another reason why it's the best. And it's simply this: Doctor Dakota Adams, intergalactically famous xenoarchaeologist and treasure-hunter extraordinaire, didn't make a name for herself by cowering with inaction or moping around all sad that the universe was out to get her.

At least, that's what I planned on telling all my glowing fans when I got home, became rich and famous, and had my first interview on *Good Morning, Galaga*.

I headed for the exit hatch, and right as I got there, I paused. "AO," I said, wondering if I really wanted to know the answer. "Will the Nodari find us here?"

"Not if we leave first," he replied.

"Touché," I said. "If we don't leave, how long until they come here?"

"It should take them a few days before spreading this far from the city," he said.

"You sure? I don't want to find out that by days you meant hours."

"Quite," he said with finality. "Besides, they are busy with more important matters."

"Such as?"

"Battling a Kibnali fleet."

I sucked in a breath and drummed my fingers on the handle for the hatch. "Any chance the Kibnali might win?" I asked. I knew they were going to lose the war overall, but if they won here, maybe Tolby wouldn't skip out so fast and make me track him across half the galaxy.

51

"No," he replied. "The Nodari invasion cannot be stopped by them."

I sighed. "Right. Back to the original plan, then."

I hopped out of the shuttle and began the hike in the direction AO had given me. As I went, I played with the scanner for several minutes before I realized I was so hopelessly ignorant on how to use it, I should tap into the tutorial and give it a whirl. There were simply too many settings to tweak, and too much feedback given for me to have any clue on what to do with it. For example, what on Mars is "Oonie's Constant" and how does that relate to the "Multibyte Sawtooth Array Form"? It's not like I was even scanning something truly spectacular, like a quasar. I had it pointed at a rock. Or at least I think I did.

Hell, I might have been holding it upside down for all I knew, and who knows what it was picking up at that point.

The tutorial, thankfully, was the one thing I could find easily. Even better, it turned out to be very easy to follow. It started with the basics by providing an overview of everything the scanner could accomplish, and holy snort, was that a lot! Not only could it perform "basic" tasks like give the exact molecular composition of an entire structure, but it could also give a history of individual components and where they'd been over the past twenty-eight days. I bet that made this little baby a staple tool when it came to Progenitor Investigators.

It probably also cut down on the length of PI novels, too. I could see it now:

Too bad on the dame. She was a pretty one, too. Pretty good at getting herself in trouble, given the knife sticking out of her back. I decided to consult one of my buddies. Not the adorable killer space tiger who liked getting cute with people's kidneys when they got cute with me.

I'm talking my other buddy, the one who travels in a flask.

As I downed some liquid courage, I knew they were all watching and waiting for me to do my thing.

I rubbed my chin and went over the facts. I had about as many of those as I had creds saved for retirement.

Zilch.

Not like the city would let me live to see that anyway.

Still, I wasn't about to give up, even if life gave up on me.

I whipped out my multi-phase subatomic matric analyzer and let it do its dance on the knife. Soon as it gave me a full chrono line on the spectrograph, I gave the coppers a full description of the last one to touch it.

Turns out that person was Miss Pretty's jealous ex.

Case closed.

Anyway, after learning about all that, I went on to study tracking unique signatures, mirror signatures, lookalike signatures, and anti-signatures and then how to set up exclusionary zones alongside a myriad of other filters. Long story short (which might be too late at this point, my bad), about two hours into my hike, I had a grand idea on exactly how to find this underground Progenitor facility.

"Oh, I hope this works," I said, holding out my left hand as I scanned the bracelet I wore on it.

"If it doesn't, I can recommend a number of third-party materials for reading and watching that may assist you in accomplishing your task, as well as prepare you for the Multi-phase Subatomic Matric Analyzer Certification Exam. Would you like to know more?"

As annoying as his constant sales pitches usually were, at the moment, I felt so clever this was coming together, I didn't care. "Nope," I said, punching in the last little bit on the scanner. "I got it."

"You do?"

"Yep," I replied. I tested out my genius work by spinning in place and watching the appropriate readouts. As I'd hoped, I picked up on a large mass of lookalike signatures to the Progenitor bracelet I wore that was not in the direction of the shuttle. Said mass was still several kilometers away, and there seemed to be a lot of interference at the moment as the signal came and went, and the heading wasn't always constant, but it appeared to be more than enough.

"Great. Great," Rummy said. "I'm so happy this is working out for you. When you're done, we hope you'll leave us an honest, five-star review on Zamagon so that other customers will be able to make smart decisions when considering our products against our competitors'."

"I'll think about it."

"Wonderful!"

Two more hours came and went as I followed the signal through a light forest made of slender trees with speckled, yellow bark and branches bearing lemony-smelling, round fruit. Along the way, I caught sight of some of the local wildlife, and it made me wish I could've spent more time out here. I saw creatures with six heads on spindly necks and others with no heads on squat bodies. Some disappeared in a flash, while others kept their distance and chattered amongst themselves in a yippy sort of language. One, a rather large, colorful thing that looked like someone had spliced genes from a kangaroo with those from a toucan, followed me for a half kilometer, whistling a catchy little tune.

Before I could get to know the little fella, my scanner beeped excitedly, and that scared him off. Annoying, yes, but since that meant I'd reached my destination, I didn't give it any further thought.

"Okay, thermal research facility," I said, looking around. "Where are you hiding?"

"Do you see a cargo lift?" Rummy asked.

"No," I said, slowly turning in place one more time to make sure I didn't miss the obvious. "It's a lot of trees and dirt and a few knee-high boulders."

"Odd," he said. "The entrance ought to stand out. Are we in the right location?"

I checked the scanner. It showed the mass I'd been tracking the last few hours was beneath my feet. Was the entire structure underground? As in, the entrance, too? Like there wasn't even a shed that housed an elevator or anything? "Hang on, I've got an idea."

I closed my eyes and reached out with my implants into the nearby world, trying to find and make a mental connection to whatever Progenitor tech was here. Within seconds, I found it. Or rather, I found something.

A pop went off in my head, and I smiled. I still didn't know what I'd managed to hook into, but I started to go through a list of commands, hoping one would trigger something. I tried things like *location, display, turn on, show elevator* and when I finally tried what probably should've been near the top, *open door*, I got the results I wanted.

The ground nearby rumbled before splitting in two. The gap widened as sliding doors, covered in forest floor, slid away and revealed a wide ramp that led to a tunnel that led deep underground. I followed said tunnel for a hundred meters or so until it ended at a massive, round bunker door—the same kind I'd seen twice before.

Connecting to the nearby console was a breeze, too, as was commanding the door to open.

As it rolled away, I wasn't presented with darkness as I'd expected. Instead, a warm, orange glow bathed a section of the entry room, and a sweltering blast of hot air rolled over me. The air near the floor shimmered, and that's when I realized some of the floor was dark and moving.

Now, I might've been stranded on an alien planet a bajillion light-years away from home, but I knew exactly what I was looking at. I could thank those early exploration days spent checking out former cities that had been buried by volcanos for that one.

"Lava," I said with a heavy sigh. "Why'd it have to be lava?"

CHAPTER SIX
THE FLOOR IS LAVA

What's wrong with lava?" Rummy asked.

"Everything?" I replied, unsure how to take the question and why the answer wasn't obvious.

"I find it soothing," he said. "It always looks so happy the way it flows wherever it wants. Wouldn't that be a nice life?"

"It'd be nicer if it kept itself inside the planet."

"Technically, you're inside the planet right now," he said.

I scowled. "You know what I mean."

"Harboring resentment has shown to decrease life expectancy by up to eight percent and inversely correlates with total overall happiness," he said. "As a VIP customer, I would be happy to refer to you to a therapist—"

My eyes narrowed. "I swear, Rummy, if you don't knock off the sales, I'm going to throw you into the first molten lake I come across. Got it?"

"Preferences noted and recorded," he said. "I will limit the number of special offers you receive from here on out."

"As long as those offers number zero or less, that sounds perfect," I said.

I then eased into the room, being careful to mind my step, and took a look around. The entire thing was about two dozen meters wide and half that in depth. Like other bunker entrances, plenty of machinery hung from the ceiling while computers and consoles lined the walls. Most of them appeared to not have seen use in hundreds if not thousands of years, maybe even vast eons given the amount of dust on some of them, but to my surprise, a couple of consoles to my side were lit.

More importantly, once I had entered the room, I could see exactly where the lava was coming from. There happened to be a large crack in the wall near the far corner. It was from that crack that molten rock oozed forth. Though it was mostly contained to the corner, some of it had managed to flow toward the center of the room, which was where I had originally seen it. Thus, I worried not only where else it might be in the facility, but whether or not it would eventually cut off my exit if I ventured inside.

That said, it didn't look like it was moving too quickly, and whether or not this lab was being invaded by lava, I still needed that repair droid.

"Any idea where the X-45 is?" I asked Rummy.

"No, but seeing how the computers are still online, they might be able to tell you."

I smiled and nodded, and chided myself in a friendly manner for not thinking of such an obvious solution. I hurried over to one of the consoles, made a connection, and brought up the facility menu.

Though I managed to turn on the lights, a lot of what I found after that was garbage. Literal, digital garbage. That is to say, while the computers themselves may have been powered, their data integrity left a lot to be desired. Selection after selection in the menus either refused to work at all or when it did, it simply displayed garbled words and twisted graphics. I couldn't get to any inventory records or logs for the facility whatsoever. Trying to find and use some sort of command that would identify the location of the robot, or even better, tell it to come to me, didn't work either.

"I wonder if I should try rebooting," I said with a heavy sigh. My finger hovered over the system command menu, an instant away from shutting it all down in order to follow basic tech-support protocol and restart the entire process, but I quickly decided against such a course in action. Who knew how long that would take, especially if the boot data had been destroyed. Then I came up with an even better idea.

Though I couldn't bring up facility inventory or robot commands, I did find a way to look at a map of the entire facility and then bring up an overlay of damaged structures and systems.

"Aren't you the clever one?" Rummy said.

"I have my moments," I replied with a bright smile. I figured that if there happened to be a repair droid somewhere in this place, it was probably doing what it did best, repairing. At least, that's what I hoped, because when I saw that the maintenance bay had suffered catastrophic damage after a recent earthquake—one I had no doubt came when that Nodari nuke went off—my heart dropped.

Though I probably would've broken down into an ugly cry if I worked my way to that bay and found out that my only hope of getting off the planet had been turned into a slag of twisted metal, going by the overlay, I didn't think that would happen. Recent history records of the power generator showed that damage estimates had been sixty-three percent a few hours ago, but were now down to fifty-five. So either the initial estimates were off, or something was down there fixing things.

Something or someone. Either way, I didn't care. Even if it wasn't the droid, I figured whatever was making the repairs could fix my ship.

I took one long last look at the map in order to memorize the route from where I was to the reactor room before sucking in a breath and mentally preparing myself for the journey. "All right, Rummy," I said, heading for the exit. "Let's do this."

"I'm so excited," he said. "I always wanted to be an adventurer. That's the chief reason why I took a position at Excel-Care."

"It is?"

"Absolutely!" He replied with enthusiasm. "Working there has allowed me to live vicariously through the lives of thousands of patients by integrating their memories with my own."

"When you say integrate, do you mean you get to see what happened?"

"Much, much more than that," he replied. "I can change my own experience of things so that I get to relive every moment as if it were happening in the present. Any adventure a customer has gone through, I can partake in as if I were really there."

"That...that actually sounds awesome," I said, turning his explanation over a few times in my head. "Do you have a favorite?"

"Absolutely! Warble Ipchi, a Chaddarean who was massively addicted to rock climbing, spent three years scouring a system of underground caves for a lost, ancient city. During that time, he encountered everything from giant underground worms to deadly seductresses to the funniest film festival this side of eternity."

"Oh, that sounds fun," I said. I suppose it was silly for me to think so, but I couldn't help but feel a little sad that my own adventures hadn't been his favorite. I mean, I don't know about anyone else, but I don't think I could've handled much more excitement in all that we'd gone through without dropping dead from a coronary.

"Don't feel bad," he said. "Yours are in at least the top ten, maybe even the top five. Competition is stiff."

"Thanks," I replied. His words were kind, but deep down, I felt like he was humoring me.

By that point, I'd worked my way a fair bit deeper inside the facility. I passed by a number of side rooms that looked like some of the labs I had seen while on Adrestia, but since most of what I saw in terms of gear looked dismantled beyond my ability to reconstruct, and the fact that every few minutes or so, the ground would rumble and debris would fall from the ceiling, I didn't think it was a good idea to stick around this place for long.

Then it happened.

A massive tremor ripped through the facility, and my knees nearly gave out when lava erupted from behind me. The molted rock spewed in all directions, and I barely scrambled away in time.

A second burst, this one several meters in front of me, stopped me in my tracks.

"Seriously?" I yelled, backpedaling.

Thankfully, there happened to be a side passage that let me escape any immediate barbequing. It hooked around a few labs before dumping me back into the main corridor, close to where I needed to be. However, my path once again was cut off by a huge swath of molten lava, easily seven meters across.

"I don't think this place is going to last much longer," Rummy said as the ground shook again. "It might be in your best interest to find a way out now while you can. There's still the other facility you could investigate."

"I know, but there are no guarantees there, either," I said, taking in a deep breath and pushing all thoughts of a fiery doom away from my mind. "At least I know there's a repair droid here."

"Great observation," he said. "Truly remarkable. On that note, do you have any thoughts on how you're going to get across?"

"At the moment, no," I replied as I looked around, hoping to spy a gigantic firehose or a hundred-thousand-gallon fish tank. Wouldn't that have been nice? Or better yet, a hoverboard, some fireproof boots, or a telepad.

While searching, my gaze drifted to the ceiling, and I noticed the heavy conduit pipes that ran along the length of the hall. Sturdy bolts kept them secure, and I had an idea. I jumped up, trying to get hold of one and hoist myself up, but they ended up being half an arm's length out of my reach.

Feeling like I was onto something, I set my jaw and tried again. Though this time I managed to get a little closer, the pipes were still out of my reach.

"Close," said Rummy. "When we get a chance, we should install upgrades to the muscle fibers in your legs. Technically, our special on those ran out three hundred years ago, but I know a guy. I could make it happen."

"Thanks," I said, only half listening. As nice as it would've been to have had access to that upgrade at the time, I didn't. So it felt a little more cruel than anything to bring it up. Still, couldn't fault the guy too much. That's what he was made to do. Sell stuff.

I rubbed my hands together, set my jaw, and tried again. I did get closer, but close only counts in horseshoes, plasma grenades, and fusion bombs.

"Dakota?"

"Yes?"

"The lava is getting closer."

I glanced over my shoulder and practically passed out in fright. Another stream of molten rock had made its way down the hall I was in, effectively cutting me off from where I'd come in. I had maybe ten meters of clear floor to work with, and I guessed that would be cut in half in less than a minute.

"No. No. No," I said, now in a full panic. I spun in place, desperate to find something I could use to save myself with. Then I spied what I could only describe as a mini air conditioner that had been mounted about waist high on the wall. Its lip was barely as wide as my foot, but it would be enough. It had to be.

I stepped back a couple of paces and then ran full tilt toward the box. My legs drove me up into the air, and I landed on top of it with my right leg. My left leg found the wall an instant later, at which point I used both to launch myself up and backward.

I spun midair and wrapped my arms around one of the pipes overhead. My feet swung with the momentum, and after I pulled off one hell of a crunch with my abs, I got them around the pipe as well.

"Yeah, baby!" I said, hanging upside down and grinning to myself. "How do you like them apples?"

"What apples?"

I laughed as I shimmied along the pipe. "Never mind."

"I must say, I never doubted you for a second. A lesser explorer would've succumbed to such trials."

"Thanks," I replied. "Too bad Tolby wasn't here to see it. He would've gotten a kick out of that."

"Then you should tell him once you see him again."

"Damn skippy I will," I said. "Right after I show him my belly button and kick my imposter to the curb."

"On another note, when we're done here, we should talk about getting you a sponsorship," Rummy said, cutting into my thoughts. "Have you signed with anyone yet?"

"No, but I really think I should focus on getting to the other side," I replied.

"Good point."

I kept moving, and within a couple meters of my crossing, I could feel the perspiration building on my forehead and back. It didn't help any that the pipe grew warm, too. And since I didn't want to cook the insides of my legs and arms, I shimmied faster and faster.

Halfway across, the air scorched every piece of exposed skin I had. I made the mistake of craning my head the wrong way and ended up getting some sweat dripping into my eyes. I then made the next stupid mistake of wiping that sweat away. The act was just enough to cause me to lose my grip with my feet.

I screamed like a banshee as my legs swung down and I nearly lost my hold on the pipe. Some people say life flashes before your eyes in a near-death experience. I would've liked that, because all I got in that moment was the horrible image of me burning to crisp.

Thankfully, I managed to get my feet back on the pipe and scooch across.

"Excellent job on not dying," Rummy said as I dropped down on the floor, a good two meters from the lava's edge.

"Thanks," I said with a laugh. "That was my primary goal."

"If it's still on your agenda, you ought to keep moving."

It was, and I did.

I ran down the hall with the lava slowly creeping after me. Did I care? No. Even if it got to the generator room in the next couple of minutes, I'd have ducked out one of the other exits by then with repair droid in tow.

At the end of the corridor, I took one last bend and then bolted into the power room.

A sea of molten rock greeted me, bubbling, churning, and looking especially hungry for a Dakota snack. Worse, sticking out of it, near the platform where the generator stood, was a twisted, melted pile of scrap that looked like it had once been something intricate.

And if I looked carefully, I could see a robotic hand reaching out.

CHAPTER SEVEN
PICKING UP A DROID

My throat tightened, and my eyes misted. For the next few heartbeats, all I could do was stare at the melted droid. Once the shock wore off, anger stormed in. "Why the hell did you have to get melted?" I screamed, balling tight fists at my side. "Couldn't you have at least stayed alive long enough to fix my ship?"

"You! Flesh-thing!" came a scratchy, energetic voice, sounding like it belonged to someone who'd snorted twelve lines of old-fashioned cocaine and followed it up with two dozen energy drinks. "Look-see! Up! Up!"

I craned my head and saw a droid pinned on its chest to a bulge in the ceiling, as if he were stuck there by a giant invisible hand. The robot had an elongated, egg-shaped torso, almost like what an artist might draw when sketching out the upper body to a figure for the first time. From it, four slender legs were splayed to the side, as were a pair of supple arms sprouting from its shoulders. Its head was at the end of a snakelike neck, and it looked down at me with a pair of icy-blue eyes.

"Hi?" I replied, realizing I should probably say something. "Are you X-45?"

64

"Yes-yes! You hear-see well for creature-meat!" he said. He tried to move as he talked, but didn't get far before he was snapped back in place. "Hurry-rush to free us. Lava-flame is comes-rises! Burn-melt both creature-meat and metal-droid!"

My eyes scanned the room for something—anything—I could use, and honestly, I wasn't sure what was keeping him pinned to begin with. "How?" I finally asked.

"Proton accelerator pump super-overcharged and must die-die!" he exclaimed. "Magnet-box clamping-sticking droid to roof-ceiling! Flip switch-breaker above reactor-thing to free us! Hurry-quick before melt-flame kills us all!"

I nodded, feeling like I had a vague idea of what was going on. Whatever was in that dome he was stuck to—a proton accelerator I assumed—had one hell of a magnet, and to cut the power, it seemed like there was a breaker box on the ceiling (of course) directly over the power generator. Of course, that meant I'd need to scale the walls to reach the ceiling, a good ten meters above me, and then work my way over a lava-filled room to get to it, but I'd done crazier things in life...hadn't I?

The ground rumbled, and lava bubbled in a far corner, sending bright globs of molten rock spewing in all directions. X-45 shrieked and gave orders again, but they were unneeded. The mini eruption was more than enough to spur me into action.

The wall to my right had plenty of vertical pipes, handholds, and ledges I could use to get to the top, and it only took a second for me to plan my ascent. As I had in the corridor, I took a running start to leap up to my first ledge, where I then pulled myself up and used a thick collection of cables to continue my climb.

"Yes-yes, creature-meat!" X-45 shouted joyfully as I was about halfway up. "Climb-fly to the up-top! Go fast-quick!"

"Going as fast as I can," I said. Well, that wasn't entirely true. The thought of using my new ice axe popped into my head to make things a little quicker and easier, but I dismissed it as quick as it came. I didn't need it slicing into something electrical and turning me into a baked Dakota.

Once I reached the ceiling, I spent a few seconds catching my breath and locking myself into place so I could give my muscles a moment to relax. Surprisingly, given X-45's panic, he didn't demand that I continue.

"Cheer-praise for the creature-meat," he chortled. "When free-able, I fix-repair all you need-want. Yes, yes? Fair trade for life save!"

"That's what I'm thinking," I said with a smile. "You better stick to that promise."

"Programming orders-says I must. Now quick-hurry before we melt-die."

I nodded before sucking in a breath and rolling my shoulders to loosen up. Then I shimmied along the pipes on the ceiling the same way I had over the lava earlier.

No less than three more times did I feel tremors rip through the facility, and while I'd managed to ignore them before (sort of), their intensity made it incredibly hard to keep my optimism levels from dropping to zero.

Slipping didn't help any.

Nor did feeling a couple of flares fall out of my pocket, nor did watching them drop all the way to the floor where they were promptly consumed by lava.

"Focus-think, stupid creature-meat!" he chided. "Must not die-die before rescue-save complete!"

My brow furrowed as I set my jaw and readjusted my grip on the pipes. "I'm the one saving you, remember?" I growled. "Be nice."

"No-no! You be alive!"

I shook my head and figured it wasn't worth arguing over. My arms started to ache about halfway across the ceiling, but as I literally had the fear of death in me, I wasn't about to let that slow me down.

I passed around a number of power boxes and ceiling-mounted machinery, one of which ended up being tricky due to the lack of handholds, until I finally reached the circuit box he'd directed me to. Knowing I was already working on borrowed time, I didn't waste a moment in trying to open it.

Key word: try.

"Gah!" I said after my third failed attempt. "Stupid thing is stuck."

"Attempt-try harder-again!" X-45 said. "Mustn't fail-quit or we all die-die! Perhaps should've trained-lifted more-more to build strength-body!"

"Brilliant advice," I said under my breath. Now, I'm not saying I'm Hercules or anything, but I will say, I didn't think my exercise regime had anything to do with it. I mean, I was hanging upside down over a room filled with lava. It's not like I could really put all my muscle into opening the box.

My third, fourth, and fifth attempts were met with failure. I had half a mind to use my telekinetic abilities to obliterate it all, but leaving my right arm numb and useless for the next hour probably wasn't the most brilliant of plans.

That's when I realized my main goal was to cut the power to the magnet, not necessarily flip a particular switch. After all, who cared how that happened?

A quick survey of my surroundings showed me all I had to work with. Lots of lava, and one big generator. From the ground, it looked heavily shielded on all sides. However, now that I had an aerial view, I could see that the top had been fitted with some sort of air-intake that looked a lot like a turbine—though it spun far quieter and sexier than anything I'd seen before. (Yes, I know that's an odd description, but I promise any lover of technology would say the same.)

"What are you doing-waiting?" X-45 asked, sounding irritated and fearful at the same time. "Need-must act now! Open box-breaker and switch-kill the power! Now-now!"

I glanced over at him and smiled. "Relax, my uptight little droid. I've got this."

Now, I've always said Tolby was the tech guru when it came to our perfect duo. However, that didn't mean I didn't know my way around a shop, or a turbine for that matter. And one thing was universal about turbines, no matter who made them, where they made them, or when they made them. Turbines did not react well to foreign objects.

Needing only a few practice throws, I used the telekinesis in my implants to grab a glob of molten rock from the lake below and toss it perfectly into the air so that it landed directing in the turbine.

"No-no! Stupid-dumb creature-meat!" X-45 shrieked. "Now we die-die!"

Maybe I should've thought my plan through. Or at least, run it by him first.

The generator ground to a halt, sounding like a dying elephant as it did. Metal groaned, and then the back half exploded in a magnificent fireball.

The shockwave nearly knocked me off the ceiling. My ears rang, but the ringing wasn't sharp as I would've expected, at least, not from one side. On my left, everything felt fuzzy, distant, almost as if I were underwater—which would explain the wetness I could feel on that side.

I turned my head and instantly regretted it. My world spun, and I can only attribute me not falling to the lingering—yet powerful—effects of the lucky elephant keeping me safe.

If only the plastic pachyderm had been enough to keep my eardrum from being ruptured, too.

The lights dimmed, flickered, and then disappeared. Normally, this would've left me in the dark, but the lava offered a warm glow that at least partially illuminated everything near the ground.

A trio of spotlights turned on, two beams coming from X-45's shoulders and one from his upper chest. The droid hung from the ceiling on what I assumed were magnetic feet, but given Progenitor tech, it could've been due to something else.

"Now you've done it, creature-meat!" he scolded. "Pressure reliefs all gone-vanished. Magma chambers will explode quick-soon and take all things here-here to the great melting!"

"That doesn't sound good," I mumbled. Everything kept turning, albeit more slowly, and so I had to concentrate as hard as I could to keep from falling or puking, and thus, my words were drawn out and a little slurry, too.

"Come-follow to the escape-exit," he said. "Now-quick! Go-go!"

In a flash, he skittered across the ceiling to where a large, square opening was and then disappeared inside of it. A half second later, his head poked out, as if he were looking down from an attic. "What are you delay-waiting for? Get-come fast-quick!"

I nodded, swallowed, and willed myself forward. My movements came slow at first, but the more I learned to deal with the constant vertigo by relying on what I felt with my fingers more than what I saw with my eyes, the faster and easier things became.

I'd barely reached the opening when the largest tremor I'd felt rattled everything. Pipes rattled on the walls, while the machinery mounted to the ceiling shook. One particularly heavy-looking thing even broke free of two of its bolts, causing it to hang lopsided.

I found a few handholds inside that opening thanks to X-45's provided light, and using them, I hoisted myself into a low crawl space that had been designed for maintenance work.

A blast of heat put a fire on my butt—and I'm not being figurative. A literal fire sprung right on my butt. Thank god whatever my shorts were made of didn't go up in flames. I squeaked and rolled, hitting my head on something in the process, but at least I managed to smother the fire.

"Quick-fast!" X-45 said. "Lava fly-shoot and we'll die-die!"

"Right behind you, little guy," I said, rolling back over onto my stomach.

The droid took off, and I made a low crawl so fast I'd have been the envy of any commando. We clambered through those maintenance passages for what felt like eons. A few times, X-45 would pop open a hatch only to jump back and "curse-curse." He never said what he saw, but his reaction and the warm glow coming from below told me all I needed to know.

Long after my elbows were thoroughly bruised, along with my knees and head, he found us an exit that wasn't perched over a molten river. Gratefully, I swung myself out of the ceiling and into a corridor I actually recognized.

"Hey! We're almost out, aren't we?" I said. I glanced over my shoulder and hiked a thumb in that direction. "Down there is where that lab is with the fuzzy, spinny things."

"Spatial-time cleaner, yes-yes," he said.

"Yeah, those," I said, turning back around.

When I did, the door at the end of the hall slid open, and on the other side was a Nodari scout, biorifle clutched in its hands.

CHAPTER EIGHT
ESCAPE TO THE SHIP

Look out!" I yelled, diving for cover. What I found wasn't much: a small alcove that harbored a locked door, but it was at least enough to keep my skull intact.

Acidic darts flew from the scouts' weapons, but X-45 didn't move. For a hot second, I thought he was going to get chewed to pieces. To my surprise, a yellow shield sprang to life, completely deflecting everything the Nodari threw at him.

"Stupid-dumb metallic-meat," he said, sounding more annoyed than frightened, or even mad. "Always destroying-devouring. Hate-hate! Makes extra work for me-me!"

The Nodari ran toward us, intensifying their fire as they came, and X-45 shook his head, muttering what I assumed was a long string of Progenitor obscenities I couldn't follow. When they were within five meters, a barrel about the size of my forearm popped out of his shoulder. A thin, concentrated jet of hyper-charged plasma flew out, instantly decapitating each scout.

"That was amazing," I said, coming to my feet. "I've definitely got to keep you around."

"Yes-yes. Amazing for creature-meat to look-see, but an easy-quick task for me-me."

The ground suddenly heaved beneath my feet. The shock wave was more than enough to send us both tumbling forward. Debris rained down from the ceiling, and walls collapsed.

A fireball seemingly the size of Mount Everest blew through the tunnel, enveloping us both. The only reason I kept from being deep-fried and blown apart was because my little robot buddy threw up his shield once more, protecting us from the blast.

While the shield kept us safe, it flickered right at the end, and flared white as it collapsed. Sparks shot out of X-45's back, and his eyes dimmed momentarily.

"We must leave this creator-nest, now-now," he said. "Shields are fried-gone. Full eruption will kill-kill us both."

"Believe me, little guy. I'm all for leaving as of yesterday."

We raced through the rest of the facility, during which I spent most of the time sliding along and bouncing off the walls. Every step I took, my ongoing vertigo threatened to do me in. Stupid eardrum. Why weren't those made better?

When we got to the entry room of the complex, we found that the entire ceiling had collapsed. Rubble filled the room, and both computers and machinery were crushed under the weight of it all.

I halted in place as my mouth dried. Despite all that my eyes took in, I refused to believe we were cut off.

"Our doom is here, creature-meat," X-45 said matter-of-factly. "I cannot shovel-dig."

"Not at all?"

"Not fast-quick enough," he replied as he turned his head over his shoulder. "Look-see!"

I glanced back the way we came to see a river of molten rock headed right for us. It bubbled and churned, devouring everything it touched as it moved down the hall.

Refusing to give up, I began rubbing my thumbs against my hands, all the while imagining Liam was there. True, I had no plastic pachyderm to smother with belly rubs, but I could only hope and pray my little ritual was strong enough, sincere enough, that he'd still get to enjoy it in whatever plastic pachyderm afterlife he currently enjoyed. "Come on, lucky elephant," I said. "Don't fail me now."

"What is this luck you speak-say?" X-45 asked. "And what's this ritual you make-do?"

"He is—was—my little elephant that brought me good luck when I rubbed his belly," I explained. "Or at least, he did until he was blown up."

"Not very good luck for him-him."

I was about to argue when I spied some light filtering in off to the side. It was hard to see since X-45 had his beams on full bright still and they bounced off more than one shiny object. Also, from his vantage point, his view was blocked by a large boulder that had fallen through the roof, which is why he didn't catch it.

"Oh please, please, please," I yelled, scampering my way around the rubble to get to it. As I went, I had to crawl under and over four separate slabs of concrete, as well as a slew of twisted metal, all the while avoiding no less than three power cables that were not only broken but sparked with electricity.

When I got there, my heart soared. "Ha!" I shouted. "I told you!"

"You told-said nothing of an escape," he replied.

"Pfft. You know what I mean," I said, starting my crawl through the tunnel. It was an exceptionally tight fit. I practically had to keep my stomach sucked in the entire time, and even then, I barely scraped through. I actually did get stuck once, but a small telekinetic push on my butt saw me through—and I must say, that's a really odd experience, to remotely push your rear.

The moment I clawed my way out of the tunnel, I jumped to my feet and ran. No, I didn't leave X-45 behind. I glanced over my shoulder and made sure he got out fine. The little bugger was supple, and from what I could tell, he managed to snake his way through the rubble with ease. Or at least, easier than I had.

We must have run for a hundred meters at the most when the ground about a half a kilometer behind us erupted. Huge jets of lava leaped into the air, while dirt and rock rained down. I had enough sense to duck behind a tree, and X-45 followed. That proved to be the smart choice as a boulder some fifty kilos in weight came smashing down where I'd been only a second before.

For nearly a minute we hid behind there. When the rocks stopped falling, X-45 eased himself around our hiding spot.

"Dumb, stupid creature-meat," he said with disgust. "Nearly made us die-die."

My eyes widened, and I straightened. "Me?" I said, jacking a thumb at my chest. "If memory serves, the only reason you're alive is because you were stuck to the ceiling."

X-45's eyes narrowed, and he hunched slightly. "Yes-yes. As creature-meat, you are not always stupid-dumb. But you shouldn't have made the reactor die-die."

"Well maybe you shouldn't have gotten yourself stuck to begin with," I countered. "How did you manage that anyway?"

X-45 looked away and started to walk off. "Come-come," he said. "I must look-see your ship so I can fix. The Nodari will see-find us soon otherwise."

The corners of my mouth drew back. "Oh, this has to be good," I said, staying put.

"No-no. Nodari destroy-wreck. Not good at all."

"No, I mean this has to be good about how you got stuck."

Again, he didn't answer, but kept walking. I let him get a dozen meters before I whistled sharply. "You're going the wrong direction," I said, holding my grin. I hiked a thumb in the opposite direction. "Ship's that way."

X-45 changed course, and I trotted after him.

"You're not getting away from it that easily," I said. "Out with it."

"No-no. Nothing to speak-tell."

"We could always download his memory once we're back at the ship," Rummy chimed in. "It's a free app installed on this bracelet."

"It is?" I asked, looking down at my wrist.

"Yes. There is a paid version, too, which allows you to bypass all the ads and instantly let you upload your droid's memory videos to over ten thousand social media platforms of your choice. Would you like to know more?"

"Yes," I said, laughing. "Yes, I would!"

X-45 spun around, his digital eyes flickering into upside-down crescents. "No-no! Creature-meat cannot-must not! Memories are not for you to look-see."

I crossed my arms over my chest and raised an eyebrow. "If you're going to be aboard my ship, I think we need to hash out a few things."

"Fiendish creature-meat. I should leave you here-here. See if you can fix-heal your ship."

The tone in his voice said his threat was empty, but I challenged it regardless. "You can't," I said. "I saved you, remember? Your programming says you work for me now, yes? Besides, I don't think you want to stay here when everything is swimming in Nodari."

"Fine. I come-follow."

"And you tell-tell."

X-45 balked, and I thought we were about to run around in circles again. To my surprise, he capitulated to my demand. "Fine-fine," he said. "Metal-droid will explain-tell, but flesh-thing mustn't laugh."

My gut tightened, and I bit my lip, neither of which happened to be enough to suppress the giggle that popped out of my mouth. "Okay, sorry," I said, recomposing myself. "I'm ready to listen in a calm, non-judgmental fashion."

X-45 nodded, and as he spoke, he began to walk. "Magma chambers lost all but two pressure relief systems," he said. "Metal-droid unable to fix-save damaged valves."

"That explains the eruptions and whatnot, but how did that get you stuck to the ceiling?"

"Patience, flesh-thing," he scolded. "Story not done-done."

"My mistake," I said, grinning as I quickly caught up. "Go on."

"Solution to mess-problem simple. Needed more energy. More power. Even flesh-thing would see that. With more power, could create-make portal to eject lava, lower pressure. Save creator-nest."

"That makes sense."

"Yes-yes," he said eagerly, but then the energy in his voice lowered. "Time for repair-hack minimal. Metal-droid modified three-pronged cable to be able to be stuck-inserted in two-pronged outlet."

I probably shouldn't have, but I couldn't help the grin that formed on my face. "How did you do that? That seems like it wouldn't work."

"Cut-chopped prong. Fit-connected well after that, but idea was stupid-bad."

"Let me guess, because it was a grounding wire?" I asked, drawing upon my limited skills as an electrical engineer. Actually, it was more like me drawing on my limited experience playing electrical engineer, which just happened to be along similar lines. Long story short, Tolby bought me the S&R Delux Rootbeer Float Dispenser for a New Year gift. It had three plugs. The outlet where I wanted it only had two. And the fire extinguisher in the kitchen worked really, really well. My skills calming down the landlord, not so much.

"Yes-yes," he said. "Grounding wire needed to prevent-stop short-circuit. Cascade of failures led-caused magnet in proton accelerator to supercharge."

I grimaced, even though I still held my smile. "Did it hurt?"

"No-no. I am not flesh-thing, do not suffer from hurt-pain."

"Well for what it's worth, that story could've been a lot worse," I said, dropping a hand on the top of X-45's head and then giving him a pat like he was a big dog.

"Yes-yes. Flesh-thing is correct-right," he said. "I am a great fix-droid. Such mistakes are not me-me."

"Good, because I really, really need my ship fixed. I don't want to have to worry about you supercharging anything and waking up to an exploding antimatter battery."

"Worry-fret not, flesh-thing," he said. "I only fix-better your ship-ship. Soon you will speak-say that X-45 is the best."

"Perfect. Anything else I should know?"

"No, but what name-name do you have?"

"Dakota," I replied. "Dakota Adams."

X-45 recoiled. "Did...did flesh-thing speak-say Dakota Adams?"

I cocked my head. "Yes?"

The droid shrieked and jumped sideways ten meters. "Get-stay away."

My mouth hung open, and I had no idea what to make of all this. "What are you on about now? I thought we were friends."

X-45 didn't move any farther, but his voice stayed wary. "You lie-lie. Likely spoke-told that to the others."

"What others?"

"Those who died-died in the museum when you destroyed it."

My face soured, and I gave him my best angry eyes. "I did *not* destroy the museum."

"Records speak-show otherwise."

"It wasn't my fault!"

"And Adrestia?"

I held my angry eyes. "Again, not my fault."

"And the art gallery?"

"Gah! What is it with everyone on this?" I groaned as I rolled my eyes. "It's not my fault your facilities are in shambles."

"Keep-stay away. I do not wish to die-die."

"Look, little guy," I said, calm but stern. "All I want to do is find my friends and go home. If I were trying to destroy you, I sure as hell wouldn't have risked my life saving you, now would I?"

"Flesh-thing might be right."

"Exactly."

X-45 hummed and bobbed his head from side to side. "I wary-watch you, flesh-thing. As you have seen, I can kill-kill if threatened. Your creature-flesh will be easy to tear apart."

I held up both hands in the air defensively. "No need for that. Let's just get the hell out of here, and you'll see we can be friends."

CHAPTER NINE
A TRIP TO REMO

Five days.

That's how long the repairs were going to take, provided X-45 could scavenge enough spare parts from non-critical systems.

Now, one might assume I had a nervous breakdown after hearing such news. And such a reaction would be entirely understandable. After all, in less than a day, I'd been left behind by my best bud on a hostile, alien world, effectively nuked out of the sky by a bajillion-ton mega bomb, narrowly avoided a lava bath, and would now have to spend nearly a week waiting for ship repairs, all the while staying clear of any Nodari that were in the area.

And man, oh man, were they in the area. On the hike back to the ship, we saw over a dozen of their ships streak across the sky. Thankfully, they were cruising at least ten or twenty thousand kilometers up, but it was only a matter of time before they'd find my crash site.

Normally, a crashed ship wasn't a catastrophe. I mean, I always try to avoid wrecking my ship as much as possible, but if I ever wound up doing such a thing, I could always get home one way or another since I was a card-carrying member of MSA (Martian Space Association). For a small monthly fee, they provided me with three tows a year, and my first ten thousand light-years are free. Totally worth it, because it's not a matter of if your ship breaks down, only when. This is especially true if you put your craft through the wringer chasing treasure as much as I do. I also got a nifty coffee mug for signing up, and they've always sent the funniest birthday cards, too.

I know all that sounds like a paid ad, but it's not. They're awesome. If the only thing you ever take away from my story is the need to join up, do it right this minute and thank me later.

That said, being a platinum-level MSA member doesn't mean a damn thing when you happen to be stuck on the other side of the universe and who knows how many millions of years in the past. It's too bad MSA didn't have portal technology. Doesn't have? Won't have? Gah, I'm still not sure what the proper tense is, but you know what I mean.

(Note to self: corner the time-traveling towing market once I'm back home.)

(Second note to self: Find linguist expert to weigh in on verb tenses when talking about prior future events.)

Okay, sorry. Squirrel and all. So yes, having undergone a plethora of catastrophes in less than twenty-four hours, one might guess I lost my marbles.

And I did.

I'm not ashamed. I freaking lost it.

Totally. Completely, and for god knows how long.

But somewhere in the middle of wallowing in utter pity and hopelessness, with snot pouring out of my nose, eyes puffy, and body rapidly dehydrating, I got a sign everything was going to be okay.

And man, oh man, did I need that.

Taz, my wonderful *ashidasashi,* popped into existence as I sat slumped over in the cockpit. He hung upside down from the overhead controls and looked at me with his huge adorable eyes. And though he didn't say a word, I could tell he was saying in his own weird little way, *Relax, Dakota. I got this.*

He even dropped onto my shoulder and licked the tears off my face. It tickled, and I laughed, and then as fast as he'd come, poof, he was gone.

My faith in what the future had for me, was not. I knew in my heart of hearts by this time next week, Tolby and I would be chugging the root beer floats, watching the latest episode of *Quirk and Quark*, and laughing about "that one time he took a clone home instead of me."

Well, maybe not laugh, laugh. But at least we'd have all this behind us. All I had to do was trust in the process. Trust the luck. Hmmm. I wondered if I could turn that into a line of clothing or jewelry or something. Diversifying wealth is key, you know, to long-term success.

Don't get me wrong, I know people doubt the lucky elephant, or in this case, the lucky *ashidasashi*. I always hear my beliefs are "unscientific" and "superstitious," but the skeptics always conveniently forget science often follows luck.

Case in point, it was once thought that washing your hands after touching something dead was superstitious as no one could "catch death," and look where we are now.

And of course, people used to mock the idea that we could ever reach the moon, and now we're zipping across the galaxy with reckless abandon.

And don't even get me started on those who say time travel is impossible. I'm the God-Empress herself when it comes to that subject matter.

Look, I'm not saying I always understand—or will ever, for that matter—how rubbing the lucky elephant actually works, but I know it works more than anything else out there. Giving Liam, my old plastic elephant, his proper dues was what saved me from a Hannan terror beast and allowed me to meet and befriend Tolby. He's also the reason why I have all my appendages in working order, not to mention why I not only found a Progenitor artifact but also managed not to die multiple times while Pizlow tried to kill me at the Museum of Natural Time.

Game, set, match, skeptics.

Still doubt me? Then how do you explain the ship was repaired in five days and not seven or twelve? Exactly. Even I couldn't believe it at first.

"Systems online," AO said, rousing me from a deep sleep that fine, fifth morning. "We may launch when you're ready."

I rocketed out of the pilot seat and ended up sprawled across the deck. A painful knot formed on the side of my head, and for a brief second, I thought I'd imagined it all. "Say again?"

"Systems online. We may launch when you're ready," he repeated.

"You mean X-45 fixed the ship?"

"Yes. That was insinuated when I said we may launch when you're ready."

I scrambled to my feet and made a mad dash out of the cockpit. Despite AO's words, I had to see it for myself. I mean, I knew Taz was getting me out of there eventually, but in five days? Holy snort! He must've loved that belly rub far more than I'd ever imagined, because if you hadn't realized it yet, the ship was a total wreck after that crash landing.

Anywho, X-45 ended up being not where I'd expected. Instead of putting the finishing touches on whatever kadion thrust assembly was under the hood, or tracking down the short in the dorsal pulse relay grid (I still say he was pulling my leg on that one), the little guy was fiddling with the locker in the cargo hold, which the astute listener to this story will recall, is small. Thus, without time or reflexes on my side, I ended up running into him full tilt.

I'm proud to say I didn't fall, but I did nail him with my thigh. "Ow! Damnit, that's going to leave one hell of a bruise," I said, hopping a bit while clutching my leg.

"Foolish meat-thing, you shouldn't run-dash if you can't control self-self," X-45 said.

"AO says we're ready to launch," I said. "Is that true?"

"Yes-yes, I, the great X-45, have finished heal-fix on this craft-craft," he said.

"And you didn't have to plug any three-pronged cables where they didn't belong, did you?"

X-45 dimmed his eyes. "No."

"Perfect, just checking," I said, patting his head before dashing back to the cockpit. In less than ten seconds, I had the engines primed and ready. Gently, I pushed the throttle forward. The ship roared in response and lifted off the ground, throwing sand in all directions.

"Little noisier than last time," I remarked, raising an eyebrow.

"Sound dampening units were cannibalized for parts," AO replied. "Other than experiencing a higher level of decibel input, there will be no noticeable difference in ship operation."

I smiled and readjusted my grip on the controls. "Good enough for me. Let's go catch up with my buds."

"I am here to assist in any way possible with that goal."

"Which is why I keep you around and pay you the big bucks," I said.

Pointing the nose higher in the sky, I throttled up. The ground rapidly fell away. As we flew, I put the ship through a few simple maneuvers to gauge its responsiveness, and it was as slick as ever. To say it still flew on rails would be an understatement.

About halfway through the stratosphere, my elation at being off the planet waned just enough for reality to smack me in the face. "Maybe I should've asked before we took off," I said, "but is the Nodari fleet still around?"

"Yes. You will be running the blockade in approximately twenty seconds."

"How about you change course then! I don't want to run any blockade!"

"Unable," he replied. "Nodari fleet has all viable trajectories covered."

"Of the entire planet? How is that even possible?"

"Yes. Their numbers are legion, if I may borrow an idiom from your people."

Panicked and in denial, I magnified the view of my onboard scanners. Like everything else the ship had, it mirrored what I was used to seeing in my own ship, even if it operated on technology light-years beyond anything I could hope to understand. Maybe if it had dawned on me how odd that was, I could've saved myself a lot of heartache and trouble later on. But I'm getting ahead of myself.

"Sweet baby snortlings," I gasped. "Tell me there's dust on the scanner. Tell me that's not a hundred trillion million ships out there."

"I do not operate in hyperbole," AO replied.

Blaster fire flashed across the cockpit. First, a few dozen bolts, then hundreds, if not thousands. "Shields?" I yelped, rolling the ship left and right in an attempt to evade the incoming fire. "Get the shields up!"

"Already done," AO said. "ECM activated as well, which should reduce their accuracy by 99.989 percent."

Despite his news, I still gritted my teeth and tensed on the controls. "I'd prefer that to be a hundred percent."

"Agreed," he said. "Especially since statistically, there is a fair chance we will still be hit. Would you like me to take over ship control to maximize odds of survival?"

"Yes!" I yelled. "Do whatever it takes to get us out of here!"

"Affirmative," he said. "Stand by. Initiating internal crew shielding for optimal maneuvers. I will jump into hyperspace once I have locked on to your friends' trail."

The controls at my hands and feet melded back into the floor, and a purple field enveloped me. The moment it did, all of the pressure from our evasive maneuvers disappeared, yet the action our ship took increased tenfold.

The shuttle dipped and rolled through space. The incoming fire seemed to streak right toward us, only to bend away at the last second. I don't know how long it went on for, but it felt like forever.

"Trail confirmed. Stand by."

"That's all I ever do with you," I said, forcing myself to grin. "Make it so."

"As you wish."

The ship rolled one last time before leveling off. The engines hummed, and then with a brilliant flash of blue light all around, we shot through hyperspace, leaving the Nodari behind.

A few hours later, we dropped out of hyperspace, the ship shuddering once and making a small popping sound, like the opening of a champagne bottle, as it did. Looming about four hundred thousand kilometers away hung a gas giant with purple and green clouds in the middle of space. Thin ice rings encircled the planet along with at least four dozen moons. There would undoubtedly be more, but I didn't feel like counting them all for an accurate number.

My heart pounded in my chest, and my face wore a stupid, giddy smile knowing I was moments away from the best reunion in my life. I couldn't wait to hug that giant furball then punch him in the gut for leaving me. Or maybe I'd punch him first then hug him.

Who am I kidding? I could never do that. The biggest danger Tolby would face in the next few minutes would be suffocating from the death grip I'd have on him for the next week. That, and maybe getting icky fur from all the tears I'm sure I'd have streaming.

Barely able to contain my excitement, I checked the short-range scanners to get a bearing on him, and when that didn't pan out, I went to the long-range ones. Planet and moons aside, that didn't show anything either.

"Where are they?" I asked, trying to stay optimistic but now feeling like space had never felt so empty. "You said they'd be here."

"Hyperspace tracking functions indicate the ship has recently made a second jump to another system," AO said. His tone barely fluctuated from one sentence to the next, but I could've sworn in that moment he sounded disappointed.

"Really, Tolby?" I said with a groan. "You couldn't have waited a little bit longer?"

"He was here with a small fleet of Kibnali ships, not even a few hours ago."

I perked. "Are you sure?"

"Yes. I am well equipped to differentiate between Kibnali and Progenitor hyperspace signatures."

"And you're certain about the time?"

"I do not make mistakes with time. You do."

I chuckled. He had me there. "Fair enough, but that means we can catch up to them, right?"

I had no idea if that was true or not, but hell, it sounded good. And Taz did promise me everything would work out. So what else could it mean?

"Yes," he answered. "I'm computing their intended destination now."

"How long will—"

"Done."

I interlocked my fingers and stretched my arms in front of me, palms out, and gave a huge smile. "Keep this up, and you're going to be my favorite ship computer ever. Where are they headed?"

"The Remo facility," he replied.

"This isn't going to wind up like the museum, is it?" I asked. "Not sure I want to run around another tourist attraction where the staff is gone and the exhibits are trying to eat me, because I've done that ride already."

"Negative. The Remo facility was the central shipping hub for the galactic super cluster," he said. "Due to its role, it was outfitted with one of the largest webways ever created. I hypothesize that your companions are intending to use it."

"That's great!" I said. "Unless, of course, this hub also shipped Nodari, because I don't want to get there and find out they've escaped their containers and are now running amok."

"Your concern is baseless. Nodari are not shipped using commercial means. They would have starved to death long ago had such an incident occurred anyway."

"So I can't order a pet swarmling for Christmas?" I said with a smirk. "Damn. I had a few people on my naughty list I was going to send some to."

Rummy joined in the moment I'd finished my sentence with is usual, upbeat attitude. "Oh! You're looking for holiday suggestions? I have a number of fantastic gift ideas ranging from personal and heartwarming trinkets to all-inclusive getaways that are available at significant discounts to Excel-Care repeat customers."

Being this close to Tolby and a way home, I was happy to entertain the idea of a little R&R. We certainly deserved it. "Tell you what, Rummy," I said as I kicked my feet on top of the console. "When we get back to the Milky Way, you can detail whatever your top-of-the-line vacation getaway is. Give me the whole nine kittens."

"You desire more felines in your life?"

I laughed and shook my head. "No, it's what fighter pilots used to say a long time ago," I explained, thinking back to an article I vaguely remembered on the subject. "Cats have nine lives, so getting the whole nine kittens meant you'd have a whole lot of luck when everything is thrown at you."

"I'm not sure how that translates to a vacation package, but I'll gladly meet your request."

"Wonderful," I said. "So, AO. One last question: you said they're headed to a Progenitor shipping yard, right?"

"Correct."

"Can we send some sort of signal there to tell them we're on our way so they don't leave without us?"

"Negative," he said. "The facility is not responding to any communication attempts."

I couldn't help but grimace. "It's still there though, right?"

"Unknown," he said. "But the most reasonable scenario is that like most remaining Progenitor facilities, all systems have been powered down and need to be restarted."

I nodded thoughtfully and blew out a puff of air. "Right. Let's stick with that idea then. Go ahead and set a course for Nemo—"

"Remo."

"Right, Remo," I corrected. "And if you can get us there first, once we're home root beer floats are on me."

"My determination to quickly rendezvous you with your companions is not affected by the possibility of liquid refreshment for reward."

"Hey, who am I to force it on you?" I said, smiling with a shrug. "More for me."

With that, AO kicked our hyperspace drives into gear and off we went.

CHAPTER TEN
ALMOST THERE

Ever get off at your exit and had to double-check the nav map to make sure you weren't lost because the directions never said anything about having to pass through a massive rave?

No? Me either. Well, me either right up until the moment we dropped out of hyperspace, but hey, there's a first time for everything.

"Holy snort. Now that's a party," I said, gawking at the hundred-kilometer-long space station that loomed head. Countless ships—most about the size of small, personal shuttles, but there were a few yacht-sized cruisers, too—lay docked on hundreds of arms, while another dozen or two were coming and going as individual cases may be. Across the hull of the station, colored lights pulsed, and when I went to the comm channels, I quickly discovered they were pulsing in synch with heavy, rhythmic music. I couldn't raise a damn soul on any of the channels I tried, but I'll be damned if each one didn't have beats that put a happy wiggle in my butt.

"Interesting," AO said. "You wear an expression of joy, yet we have no further information as to the whereabouts of your companions."

"Just thinking about my bud," I said, letting the music infect my soul to such a degree that I was longing for a dance floor. "I mean, if these beats have me bouncing along this much, they really must've gotten Tolby hammering out some serious moves in the cockpit. I wish I could've been there to see it."

"I do not share your gleeful reaction to this change in circumstances."

I snorted but kept a light grin. "Please, AO. We both know you don't have gleeful reactions to anything."

"Incorrect assumption," he replied, flatly. "The joys I experience are numerous; however, I do not require a physical demonstration to others to express them."

"I bet you're really fun at parties."

"Failed use of sarcasm. I am exceptionally fun at parties."

I laughed. Hard. "Somehow I doubt that."

"The amount of entertainment I can generate would be more than enough to have you die of serotonin overload."

"Oh please," I said, rolling my eyes. "That's not even a thing."

"Your lack of understanding when it comes to basic neurology may prove fatal if you don't remedy that flaw in the near future," he said.

I shrugged, conceding his point, as the last time I'd brushed up on my endocrinology was about never. But I knew that word at least, that had to count for something. "For argument's sake, let's say you can have fun, and if you can, I suggest you put on your happy face from here on out, because I don't know a whole lot about what's going on right now, but I know a party when I see one," I said, tapping the screen. "And that, my good friend, is one gigantic party."

"I have no face, but even if I did, this is not a happy time."

My face soured as my mind ran with a few heart-shattering possibilities. "Why?" I asked. "Did they already go through the webway?"

"Unlikely," he said. "Even with the damage to the scanners, I am detecting no signs that it is operational at this time."

"They didn't get blown up, did they? I mean, like, you aren't seeing their wreckage floating around, right?"

"Negative," he said.

"Then what is it?"

"The facility has been infested by Abgors," he said, sounding equally annoyed and disgusted.

"Never heard of them," I said, shrugging again. "What's so bad about those guys?"

"*This* is what's so bad about them," he replied. "They do nothing but form flash mobs and crash locales looking for a quote 'good time.'"

"Surely they must do something," I said. "I mean, how would their species survive?"

"Incorrect assumption. They aren't a species. They are many species. Abgors refers to members of an indeterminate number of species who leech what they want and need from their respective societies and families in order to live a life of constant and instant self-gratification. Once they have invaded, drastic measures are usually needed to root them all out."

"Oh," I said, leaning back in my seat. "Yeah, we've got those back home, too. My friend Lexi rented out a spare bedroom to one of those once—dude said he just needed a couple of weeks first to get his first month's rent to her after he'd already moved in. Then two weeks became another two weeks, and another, and another, all the while, he kept bringing people over to trash the place."

"Precisely," AO replied.

"She practically had to use a flamethrower in the end to get rid of them," I said.

"Understandable and effective," he said. "I am also getting readings of massive restructuring of the station with unsanctioned Progenitor parts. Large swaths of decks have likely been repurposed."

"For what?"

"Unknown. Given the traffic coming to and from the station, the most likely scenario is that this has become a large commercial hub of some kind."

I sighed and wondered what that meant for the state of the webway since we kind of needed that to get home. Hopefully, whoever had set up shop here hadn't ended up destroying it doing god knew what.

As we drew nearer, our little craft shook violently. Though it only lasted a few seconds, my stomach flipped a half dozen times, and my fingers dug tiny canyons into my seat. "What the hell was that?"

"We've passed through a temporal anomaly," AO replied. "Recalibrating sensors now for further information."

"That can't be good."

"It is not clear if this is a benefit or a detriment at this time, given its effects are unknown," he said. "As the anomaly barely registered as a class three on the Tortle scale, it will likely have no impact on our ultimate goal."

"Oh, well if it's only a class three Tortle, we'll be fine," I quipped, not knowing a damn thing about what he was talking about. "I mean, that's like what, jumping a few seconds into the future?"

"More like a few hours," he said.

My jaw dropped as my fingernails dug tiny caverns into my armrests. "A few hours? They could be gone by now! We're behind enough as it is!"

"Unlikely," he said. "The webway is still offline. Temporal anomaly is likely the settling of spacetime eddies from Progenitor disappearance. Furthermore, I'm detecting no outbound Progenitor warp signatures. Ergo, your friends are still most likely aboard the station."

I folded my hands together and rested my chin on them in an attempt to center myself and find peace and perspective. It always seemed to help Tolby. And I guess it helped me, a little, but I'll be damned if I wouldn't have preferred an *ashidasashi* to belly rub at that moment. "Have you tried scanning for their ship? If we can find where it is around here, at least that would be something."

"I am undertaking that task as we speak," AO said.

"How long will that take?"

"Precisely this long," he replied. "The ship we've been following is in docking bay ninety-four. All slips on that arm, however, are currently taken. The nearest empty slip is approximately 1.4 kilometers away."

"Yes!" I said, nearly jumping through the ceiling with excitement. "That's what I'm talking about! Open up a comm and get them onscreen!"

"I am unable to fulfil that request."

My enthusiasm faltered. "Why?"

"Because while communication receivers are still operational, the transmitters are not due to the recent cannibalization of parts," he replied.

"I thought you guys fixed all that."

"Again, faulty assumption on your part," he answered. "This is a disturbing trend I'm noticing and one that was not part of your original file. I will need to make the proper corrections before this becomes a problem."

I furrowed my brow. "Trend? What trend?"

"You live your life on wild assumptions and often act on poor information," he said. "It is a wonder you've survived this long. But to the point: X-45 informed you that non-critical systems had been restored to working order. Not all systems. There is a vast difference between the two."

"Ugh," I groaned. "Did he really have to get rid of comms? I mean, what if we needed to call for help? Or tell them not to shoot?"

"Yes. This ship really needed the ability to avoid a zero-pressure environment, which is something your species is poor at surviving. Also, it was agreed upon by X-45 and myself that you would appreciate being shielded from intense bursts of gamma, which would drastically shorten an already miniscule lifespan. As such, while you were sleeping, I gave the order to cannibalize the comm transmitter."

I groaned before sighing heavily and running my fingers through my hair. "All right," I said. "That's not *that* big of a deal, I guess. We're here. They're here. I'll find them on the station or hopefully at the ship."

"That would be the correct course of action to undertake," AO said.

I watched through the viewports as our ship made its approach and entered an open landing bay. Once we were inside, mechanical arms extended from the deck and anchored themselves onto our ship's hull before guiding it in the last few meters. At that point, our landing gear extended, and we settled onto the bay floor with a muffled thump.

"Any last bits of advice?" I asked as I popped out of my seat.

"Yes. Make your way to central control as quickly as you can," he said. "Once there, X-45 can make a few modifications to allow me to patch into the main system, at which point we can use it to find your friends."

"I think we should check the ship first," I replied. "Seems like the most logical place to start."

"The central control will be able to hail anyone on the ship," AO replied. "As such, if time is of the essence to you, heading to central command is the best place to go."

"I guess I can't argue with that," I said with a shrug.

"No, you can't. Now I suggest you get moving."

CHAPTER ELEVEN
TAPIOCA BRAIN

I stepped off the ship, exited the bay, and found myself in a terminal so busy it would rival any commercial star port I'd been in before.

Aliens bustled by, some towing luggage this way and that, while others loitered by windows or sat in chairs reading tablets, chatting each other up, or stuffing their faces with a slew of different types of fare from a variety of nearby eating establishments. Some of that food looked pretty good, actually, and if I hadn't been pressed for time and had some cash on me, I'd have totally scarfed down this cheese-steak thing, even if the cheese was purple and the steak wasn't actual steak. It smelled fantastic.

I hurried down a long corridor, ignoring the pleas of my stomach to get some food, and had to extricate myself from the proverbial arms of a few super pushy salesmen peddling some of the oddest junk I'd ever seen before I reached the tram.

Now, I know I'd originally said I was going to head to central control, but when I saw on a nearby map that the tram would whisk me away to the terminal with docking bay ninety-four in only a few minutes, I abandoned Plan A and went straight to Plan T (for Tolby, duh).

I popped on the tram and ended up sitting on a four-spot bench, right between two guys who had the heads of a gorilla and the bodies of a giant owl, while X-45 took a spot across from me. I think they might have been together somehow, but not on speaking terms because during the whole ride, I swear they looked at everything but each other. I kept to myself as well and entertained myself by watching whatever was on the overhead screens.

Best I could tell, they had it on a gameshow where contestants had to toss rings onto the backs of spikey creatures running around in an arena. If they did, they scored points and prizes. If they failed, they had to drink a smoking concoction that—going by their physical reactions— tasted disgusting while at the same time did a terrific job of getting them absolutely wall-eyed.

"Where are you go-going, creature-meat?" X-45 asked as I jumped off the tram. "Command is this-that direction."

"To check the ship," I said, picking up my pace.

X-45 muttered to himself and scuttled after me. Together, we ran down another bustling terminal filled with more aliens, more food, and more shopkeepers trying to take money I didn't have by offering me stuff I didn't want. I had an inkling to phantom punch one of them in the face when he kept blocking my way, but I didn't have to. I stepped left. He followed and ended up barreling into a great big fella who probably topped a half ton. Said big guy wasn't too happy, especially since he was now covered in a pink beverage that had until recently been in his cup.

Needless to say, it was easy to get away at that point.

I glanced at the docking bay numbers, and once I saw I was almost there, I burst into a hard run.

"Slow-wait, creature-meat!" X-45 called out as he struggled to keep up. "Mustn't get lost-lost!"

"Ninety-four!" I yelled over my shoulder. "You know where to find me!"

I danced around aliens, darted between groups, and leaped over luggage without thought until I reached the docking bay I so desperately sought. Given that I was about to drop in on a slew of armed Kibnali, likely surprising the hell out of them, I probably should've made my entrance into the docking bay with a little more caution—you know, the whole shoot-first-and-ask-questions-never thing. But I didn't.

I hammered the entry button and bolted inside.

No Kibnali came to greet me. Not even Jack.

But who cared? The ship was there. The ship in all its glorious bits of total awesome.

Now, I know I'd seen it before, but to be fair, that had happened when it had whipped by me at Mach 7. So I hadn't had a lot of time to appreciate its incredible design.

That, and I had been freaking out a little having been left behind on a planet filled with critters dying to gnaw my face off. That's the sort of environment that doesn't let you enjoy the little things in life. Or the big things. Or anything, really.

Anywho, now that I was off that deathtrap of a rock, I could finally appreciate just how sweet of a ship Tolby had scored us. It was two hundred meters long, and as I trotted up to it, I could see it was made of one hundred percent pure sexy. It looked like it could dart around the entirety of spacetime with more grace and speed than a shortfin jado darts around the glowing reefs of Pentulam Minor.

I reached up and ran my fingers along the ultra-smooth, steel-blue and orange exterior as I walked alongside it. Goosebumps raced on my skin, and I felt a tingling energy run through my body. This thing and I were made for each other.

"I can't wait to fly this baby," I said with a stupid, happy grin on my face.

X-45 made a chirping sound and cocked his head to the side. "Creature-meat intends to take-steal?"

"What are you on about?" I asked.

"I suspect that double-clone will not like-let you take-steal her ship-ship," he replied.

I stopped for a moment. "This isn't her ship."

"Creature-meat clone will no doubt disagree," he replied. "May react danger-deadly on top of you already trying to take-steal family from her."

"Reminder: I'm the one with the belly button," I said, pointing a finger at my midsection. "If anything, she stole from me."

"Birth-scar does not confer ship ownership," he replied.

"Neither does pretending to be me," I said. "The only reason she's even getting to fly around in it is because she's operating under false pretenses. How is that fair?"

"How is it nice-fair to maroon her?"

I pressed my lips together. As much as I wanted to argue, he had me there. I couldn't just kick her out of the group and leave her stranded. "Well, the ship looks big enough for the both of us," I said, letting my eyes scan it from bow to stern. "I guess I could let her tag along for a bit till she figures out where she wants to go. But I'll be damned if she's taking my Tolby with her."

X-45 bobbed his head. "Good-good. Less chance of me having to repair damage from kill-fight."

"That's probably a good thing," I said. At that point, I directed my attention back to the ship and tried to make a mental connection to it, hoping that getting inside was going to be as easy as it had been with the shuttle. It only took a few seconds of probing around that quasi-mental space before a pop sounded in my head. Toward the rear of the craft, a ramp extended from the underside, and I immediately ran up it.

After passing through a short-haul section, I entered a spacious, circular room that held a number of computers along with monitoring stations along the edge. Each of the stations looked as if it had been recently used, as personal effects were scattered around each one.

In the center of the room stood a raised platform with a railing around all of it. A computer station stood nearby. Its screen displayed a myriad of text, and as I approached to get a better look, a holographic sphere with tiny little bumps all across its surface appeared in the center of said platform that looked very similar to the form AO took in my shuttle.

"Dakota!" said an energized, familiar—though overly harmonized—voice. "Back already? Did you find what we need?"

My head tilted to the side, and my brow furrowed as I tried to place it. "Daphne?"

"Of course it's me," she said, sounding put off. "Who else would you be talking to?"

"How did you get inside the ship?"

There was a slight pause. It wasn't one that was long enough to be uncomfortable, but it was enough that I knew this conversation was about to take a funky turn. "You haven't been time traveling again, have you?"

My brow dropped as annoyance splashed across my face. "Why would you say that?"

"Because you've clearly forgotten that before we left Kumet I uploaded myself into the ship so we could escape."

"Why the hell would I know that? I wasn't even there," I said.

"And now you've got false memories."

I groaned and rolled my eyes. "I wasn't time traveling! You guys left me on Kumet!"

Daphne chuckled. "We most certainly did not. Ergo, you've been time traveling again and gone and mucked up your brain. Nice job, tapioca brain. Wait till Tolby finds out. He's going to be so pissed at you."

"I haven't been time traveling!"

99

X-45 nudged me with his side. "You have, creature-meat."

"Have not!" I said, glaring at him. My hands found my hips. "Well, okay technically, yes, I've been time traveling. But not like she means."

"So, your brain is mucked," Daphne said. "Well, don't worry. I'm sure if you sit here a while, all that will be fixed. Just don't go wandering off again. I don't want to spend the next week alone while they have to form a search party to find you. I mean, there's only so many times I can count the wires around here before I'd go batty."

I pressed my lips together and growled. "Listen up, Daphne. I haven't lost my mind. You guys left me on Kumet, and since that time, I've had to deal with Nodari, lava, a wrecked ship, a bajillion mega-ton nuke, and a ginormous naval blockade. So, I'm in no mood to play games."

"I'm sorry, but you are mistaken," Daphne said. "That simply isn't possible."

"Yes, it is!" I said. "You guys took off with my clone!"

"Clone?"

"Yes! From the medbay!" I said, gripping the railing. "You guys just waltzed right off with her and left me to fend for myself! Are you paying attention to any of what I've said?"

"I think we would know if we had a clone on board. They're very obvious."

"Apparently not," I said, crossing my arms. "You didn't even do a belly button check, did you?"

"A what?"

I lifted my shirt to show off my beautiful navel. "A belly button check! See? You know, the thing clones don't have because they were grown in a vat?"

"So, you're saying that the Progenitor medbay we took you to in order to save you from poison made a clone and that's who we left with?"

I rolled my eyes and let out an exasperated sigh. "Yes. Why is this so hard to understand?"

"I have to ask: if they decided to install implants into the clone to make a perfect replica, why wouldn't they install a belly button as well?"

I threw my hands up in the air. "I don't know! But they didn't!"

"Are you sure?"

"Yes."

"Maybe you're the clone."

My hands balled into fists at my side. "I'm not the clone."

"How would you know?"

"I. Know. Because. I. Can. Remember. Everything!" I said, punctuating each word with a brutal kick to the wall. I'd hoped that would be enough to knock some sense into Daphne, but all it succeeded in doing was knocking some pain right up my leg, starting at my foot.

"Maybe you're more than a simple clone," she offered. "Maybe you're a spy. Perfect cover when you think about it."

"Really? A spy."

"Why not?"

I cursed and threw up my hands. "That's ridiculous. Who'd I be spying for?"

"That's precisely what a spy would say," she said, her voice sharpening. "I'm onto your little game."

"Ugh, Daphne. Seriously. I'm not a spy."

"I know," she said, her voice light and playful as before. "Using Occam's razor, it is much more likely that you've been time traveling again, and thus, have gummed up your memories. This is especially true since I have no confirmation of this clone even existing. I mean, it would be one thing if you were both here in front of me. Or if I had any recording of the two of you existing in the location at the same time for that matter. But since I don't, the only viable conclusion is your brain is tapioca. *Again.*"

"It's not—"

101

"Shhhh...tapioca brain. It'll all be better."

"Daph—"

"Shhhhh..."

I dug my fingers into my scalp and dragged them through my hair. "Why don't you call the others and see if I'm with them. Is that too much to ask?"

"That would be a marvelous idea if any of you would bother answering your comms," she said. "But since you aren't, don't even get me started on that."

"What about it?"

"I told you not to get me started," she huffed. "I only get to talk to them when they call me. Actually, I don't think it's anyone's fault, to be fair. There's a lot of interference coming from the station—rowdy partiers and all. I've detected three explosions from the most recent mosh pit in the last two hours alone. It's a wonder the place is even structurally sound."

"Fine, you know what? I'll bring her back here so you can see," I said with a growl. "Where did everyone go?"

"To central command to gain control of the webway, of course," she said.

X-45 beeped with annoyance. "See, creature-meat? I said-told things would go quick-fast if we went there first."

"But after finding it destroyed thanks to the never-ending party on the station, they went to deck thirty-three to look for a fabrication droid to repair it. As I've not heard otherwise, I suspect they are still looking for one."

I looked down at X-45 and smirked. "You were saying?"

"Lucky guess, creature-meat," he replied.

"You should wait here," Daphne said. "Tolby and the others will be back soon, I'm certain. Then we can get all of this straightened out, or at least, I'd wager you'll be thinking a little more clearly."

102

I crossed my arms and drummed my fingers on my shoulders. Even though I wasn't suffering from scrambled memories, everyone else *had* to come back sooner or later, so her suggestion wasn't without merit. In fact, the more I turned it over in my head, the more it appealed to me. "Might not be such a bad idea," I finally said. "Any chance this ship came with a deck of cards?"

"Inventory records were wiped out when I took over," Daphne said. "Casualty of kicking out a hostile AI. You're welcome to see what we have."

"How long must we sit-wait?" X-45 asked.

I looked down at the little quirky bot and cocked my head. His voice sounded concerned, was it? Or impatient? I suppose it was likely both. "Got a hot date?" I asked with a chuckle.

"I do not date-court, creature-meat," he said. "That's what you do-do."

I laughed. "Not at the moment, I don't—and I've got no plans to change that either."

"Fine-fine, but when will your friends come back?"

When no reply came from Daphne after a few seconds, I decided to give her a nudge. "Well, Daphne?" I asked. "How long will this take?"

"Should be soon," she said. "Twenty or thirty minutes, tops."

"Well, that's not too bad," I said.

And it wouldn't have been, if that's how long it ended up being. After forty minutes, I grew anxious. An hour later, still no one had returned, and Daphne wasn't doing a very good job of keeping me entertained, so I opted to wander the ship and see what was in it.

Though I didn't get a personalized tour complete with long lectures on every little bolt and weld of the place, in the short time I spent wandering the halls, all I can say is, holy mackerel, it was every bit as sleek on the inside as it was on the outside. It had fabricators, replicators, fabricator-replicators, triple-redundant food processors, sensor arrays for the sensor arrays that apparently could study the insides of a ladybug on the other side of the solar system, and one hell of an entertainment room that was complete with a library of every single Earth-made movie from the dawn of motion pictures.

How or why the hell it had that, I had no idea. They even had the original *Nebula Quest IV*, before they decided to go add in extra special effects and ruin important plot points with "never before seen extras." And I don't care what any of the ultra-fanboys say, those changes did not make it better. Lan hit first.

Anyway, I chalked this oddity up to yet-another-complete-Progenitor collection and figured there were more movies to watch from elsewhere, but I hadn't found them yet. That said, it sure as hell felt like this ship had been tailored specifically for me. Even more so when I reached the Captain's Quarters.

I found those midship, across from quarters for the XO. I happened to wander into those first. Predictably, Tolby had claimed them. I could tell because he'd shed and left his hair all over the place. I also found different colors of hair that weren't part of his coat, but Jainon's and Yseri's as well. All three of them had left extra clumps on the bed. On the table. In the closet. Near the shower.

I glanced at the walls, and for my own future sanity, I prayed that they were soundproof—or at least, the captain's cabin had some noise-canceling abilities. If it didn't, I was going to be sorely tempted to just let Imposter Me keep it all so I didn't have to listen to those frisky felines keep repopulating their species.

Not wanting to think about it anymore, I left the XO's cabin and popped over into my room. The moment I stepped through the threshold, I immediately regretted it. No, check that, I didn't regret it. It was good to know what the hell Fake Me was up to, but I'll be damned if it didn't boil my blood.

Staring at me from across the cabin, mounted on the wall, was Tolby. And I don't mean Tolby, Tolby, of course, like he'd been the victim of a taxidermist. I mean there he was in a large holo-painting, grinning brightly and giving me a one-armed hug while I playfully hung off his neck and struck a pose for the camera.

I didn't know where this picture had been taken. Or when for that matter. I suspected it was recent, but none of that mattered. What mattered was here was Fake Me, running around with my best bud, pretending like he was hers without a care in the world.

And then my eyes drifted to the right and saw even more pictures sitting on a desk to the side. "What the hell is this?" I said with a huge groan. "She threw a party in *my* ship?"

"Looks fun-fun," X-45 chimed in, who'd been silently at my side up until that point. "Everyone is happy-smiling."

My face soured and I shooed at the picture with my hand. "Psh. They're not happy. They only think they are."

"Expressions on face-face say otherwise," he said. "Many game-games played. Food-drinks consumed."

"Well, if they knew they were partying around with a fake, that would all change," I huffed.

X-45 scooted over to the desk and leaned in closer to one of the pictures before picking it up and examining it from several different angles. "Camera has minor-slight color problem."

"It does?"

"Yes-yes. Only seventeen trillion colors on display. Should be thirty-three. Once found, I can fix-fix for you."

"Yeah," I said, crossing my arms with a huff. "Let's do that. Then we can replace all these obviously stupid pictures of a stupid party with awesome pictures of our awesome party."

X-45 turned his head toward me and tilted it sideways. "You seem bitter-mad."

"Oh, I'm a lot more than that," I said with a dark chuckle. "I seriously can't believe she's like this. She even slept in my bed! And didn't even bother to make it up for me!"

"Do you normally make-fix bedding space?"

"I certainly do when I'm in someone else's bed, which she clearly is, thank you very much." I pressed my lips into a fine line and exhaled sharply through my nose. That line turned into a frown and my eyes narrowed when I spied the closet.

"What's on your mind-thoughts, creature-meat?"

I growled, shook my head, and said exactly what I wanted to do but knew I wouldn't. "Oh, I'm not going in there," I said as one foot moved slowly toward it. "I'm not going in there. No. No. No."

"Is your brain damage-hurt?" X-45 asked, sounding genuinely concerned that it might be.

In the span of a few seconds, I kicked my sloth-like pace up to full stomp across the cabin. "I swear, if she's wearing my favorite dress..."

"Can she do that, creature-meat? Seems unlikely-hard."

I didn't know the answer to that. Hell, I was barely listening anyway, so even if I did, I probably wouldn't have stopped to explain. I hit a button on the nearby wall console, and a closet light sprang to life, casting a soft blue light on everything that hung inside.

It's a good thing I didn't have something sharp in my hands, or my nails done. There would've been a high likelihood of me gouging my eyes out. The walk-in closet was easily five meters deep and half that wide. On each side were rows of various shelving and hanger racks, while the far end had a gorgeous full-length mirror that looked like it came straight from the penthouse suite of the Fitz-Pilton.

Hiking boots and athletic shoes galore lined one side, each one immaculately clean and ready for some grand adventure. Above those were a wide array of khaki pants and shorts of varying patterns and colors, and with the coordinating tops nearby, I could pick out an outfit that was both stylish and practical for any clime or place in a half a second.

And of course, she had to have a full rack of ice axes to choose from, too. And not cheap-looking ones that would snap a point after their second swing. I'm talking top-of-the-line RazoR in a dozen different colors, handle shapes, and blade styles. You had to take a second mortgage out just to get on the wait list for one of these, and if you think that's ridiculous, you've never had the incredible fortune to demo one firsthand. I have. And let me tell you, they're worth every fractional credit they charge and then some.

Why? Well, aside from being the ideal climbing tool balanced to perfection, the OS it comes with ties directly into the RazoR App store and will download and update all your apps on the fly, even bringing in new ones as your unique situation demands. Need to know when the next polar storm is going to run in while dangling from an ice sheet on Lalina Prime? The RazoR already has you covered. Want to motivate yourself by making a game of all the places you scale? Guess what? RazoR has already matched your personality type to the exact game you'll want to play, and surprise! You've already earned thirty-three hundred points, eight badges, and a new photo filter for your profile pic.

Oh, and speaking of pictures, each RazoR comes with a microdrone that's been designed to not only help you scout the optimum path for ascension, but is guaranteed to take the most breathtaking, heart-pounding selfies you've ever had, or they'll have a professional photographer follow you for a week on your next adventure, all expenses paid.

To date, no one's ever made the claim, so I'd say the RazoR's reputation is pretty well earned, wouldn't you agree?

"Man, I can't believe she has all of these," I said, helping myself to a sweet, sweet black-bladed RazoR ice axe with a curved shaft and a sky-blue, adaptive grip. Yeah, I know I still had my Progenitor one from before, but I'd wanted a RazoR ever since I climbed my first oak tree. I'd be damned if I was going to let Little Miss Imposter take them all.

"You act like you've never seen them before," said Daphne.

"Because I haven't."

"Au contraire," she said. "You forged them in the fabricator the other day after downloading the blueprints off the archive cube."

"I did?"

"Yes, you did," she replied. "Oh...wait...I forgot. Tapioca brain. I really ought to write that down."

"Ugh, Daphne, seriously."

At this point, X-45 nudged my side, and thankfully ended up changing the subject. "We must search-find your friends, creature-meat," he said. "Wait-wait is not a good use of our skill-time."

"You can't even remember what you did two days ago, Tapi— Dakota," Daphne said. "For your own safety, I really think you ought to stay put. I promise they'll be here soon. Twenty or thirty minutes, tops."

"No, he's right," I said, popping myself out of a chair and stretching. "They could be in trouble."

"Precisely," X-45 said. "Must save-protect them. Come, we go quick-quick to deck thirty-three."

Daphne hummed a moment. "Calculating best course of action. Stand by," she said.

"Calculate all you want," I said, heading for the door. "We're leaving."

"Calculations done," she said. "Best chance of reuniting with them is still to wait here, by nearly a factor of twelve to one. Besides, deck thirty-three is filled with Urgs. You don't want to meet them."

"Why? What are they? Besides, if they're so bad, then I definitely need to go. Tolby could need my help."

"Yes. I mean, no," Daphne said. "Urgs are a race of interstellar, warthog-like beings. Very aggressive. Not that you should worry about Tolby. He'll be fine. But they are very smelly. *Very* smelly. And they like the number four. No, correction. They love the number four. Practically worship it. You'd probably go into a catatonic shock just seeing one because of it."

Though internally I cringed each time she said the f-word, I wasn't going to let the picture she painted stop me. I had to make sure they were okay. "That's a chance I'll have to take," I said.

"But how will you find them?" she asked.

I held up my multi-phase subatomic matrix analyzer. "I've got it under control," I said. "So sit tight. We'll be back soon."

"Please, Dakota," Daphne said. "If you don't want to stay for your own sake, won't you think of the children?"

"What children?"

"You know, *the* children," she said.

"You have no idea what you're talking about, do you?"

Daphne let out a little digitized sigh, and the energy in her voice dropped. "I guess not. But it was worth a shot."

The corners of my mouth drew back, and I couldn't help but give her a mark for cleverness. "Nice try, Daphne, but we're leaving."

With that we were gone before she could say another word.

CHAPTER TWELVE
THE BAR

Once we'd gone a few dozen paces, I stopped to program the multi-phase subatomic matrix analyzer. My solution to "Where's Imposter Me?" I must say was born from a mind that clearly swam in an ocean of genius. I set the device to scan for all traces of me while at the same time filtering out any results within a five-meter radius. Clever, huh?

Sadly, my creative solution didn't turn out to be completely straightforward. As we made the trip to deck thirty-three, I picked up on a lot of false readings—no doubt because the entire facility was one gigantic piece of Progenitor tech, and my clone—like myself—obviously had some installed in her.

That wouldn't have been too bad if once we reached deck thirty-three, that deck hadn't been far rougher and seedier than I'd ever thought possible. Did I mention it had received a total overhaul of what it was supposed to be, too?

According to X-45 and a few signs along the way, this particular area we were headed to was once a ginormous warehouse with inventory, shelving, and machinery that would stretch some fifty meters in the air. By the time we arrived, however, the ten square kilometers of space had been ransacked and remodeled into a dense collection of haphazardly put together buildings that would make any shanty town look like an upscale neighborhood for the rich and famous.

I swear, the buildings groaned just due to us walking nearby, and a few times I held my breath because I was convinced it wouldn't take but a stray sneeze to collapse one on us. Trash filled the streets, along with countless Urg.

The Urg truly were intergalactic warthogs, each a little over two meters tall. Rough skin with tons of pockets and scars covered their short-haired bodies, while a pair of razor tusks jutted out from their mouths. Their faces seemed perpetually covered in a light sheen, thanks to all the snorting and spraying of spit they seemed to do, while dark, beady eyes constantly looked about as if trying to settle on something they wanted to pulverize for fun.

It didn't take me long to witness their aggressive nature, either. I saw two guys—well, I don't know what they were, gender-wise, to be honest—get into a bloodbath over who got to crack open a muti-fruit first (think avocado soaked in a few thousand rads that somehow lived and grew tentacles, scales, and the ability to glow in the dark). The exchange between the two muscular behemoths went something like this:

"Oi, dat der my squishy."

"Pozz off, ya dobbin! You'z 'ad da las' un first!"

"Me? That's a lie right 'ere. You'z best be gimmin' me dat squishy, or I'z gonna thump you right propa in da 'ead."

At that point, brute number two grabbed brute number one's arm and tore it off. Like...completely off.

Did that end the argument? No.

But did it get brute number one to back off? Also no.

That said, did it at least cause onlookers nearby to flee in terror, call the local facility police, or anything of the like?

As I'm sure everyone's guessed by now: no, no, and no.

111

Brute number one socked his partner hard with his "killa 'ittin' fist" and then proceeded to savagely bite and tear flesh with jaws that would put any great white shark to shame.

During that time, however, brute number two bit right back while at the same time clubbing his foe with his own arm. I didn't stick around to see who won, but between all the blood and gore being slung in every direction, I had a feeling it wasn't going to end until both were dead.

Funny thing was—and not ha-ha funny, but cripes-don't-come-here-on-vacation-without-a-battalion-of-spacemarines funny—that incident wasn't the only such altercation I ran into. Two other pairs got into similar arguments about something stupid, and five more started an all-out brawl because they could. Either that, or whacking your mate with a broken club was the standard greeting for this neck of the Universe.

And that's not a joke. I honestly couldn't tell.

On my fifth attempt at locking on and tracking Clone Me's signal, the scanner took me on a half a kilometer tour of the area before ending at a bar.

The structure itself stretched twenty meters into the air, cobbled together with a patchwork of metal scrap, concrete, bricks, and the occasional rebar tied around an I-beam for good measure. I had no doubts the front door alone would wrack up a hundred safety violations, and the thought of what that meant for the state of the kitchen sent a shudder down my spine. Music blasted from inside, as did the sounds of what had to be a mosh pit filled by juiced-up meatheads who weren't about to stop cracking heads until only one patron remained standing.

"Ugly flesh-things can't even create-make a door," said X-45. "Look at that barrel-hinge. Warped. Misshaped. Wonder they even live-live."

"The door? That's what you're worried about?" I said, forcing a chuckle. "I'm more worried about the rest of the place coming down."

"Scan-scan says structure is good-sound," X-45 replied. "Not pretty-pretty, but will hold together."

"Well let's hope it stays that way for the next few minutes," I said, rolling my shoulders back. I checked the scanner one last time before heading in. Whatever signal it was tracking still said it was inside somewhere, but given how many false trails we'd followed so far, I'd be lying if I said I wasn't feeling discouraged.

Maybe we should've waited with Daphne.

"Why are you wait-hesitating?" X-45 asked, sounding annoyed. "Let's go-go."

I smiled down at my quirky newfound friend and patted his head. "Let's go-go."

With a deep breath, I walked forward, pushed through the door, and entered a world unlike any I'd seen before. It felt like the illegitimate lovechild between the nightclubs that arose from the first cyberpunk era and a post-apocalyptic chop shop with a side of *Animal Farm*.

Patrons, Urgs mostly, that had been augmented with a slew of cybernetic implants, drank, fought, and moved somewhat rhythmically to the live band cranking out ungodly noise off to the side. Said band ripped their music on instruments welded together from junkyard scrap that half the time shot huge gouts of flame on frequent occasion. Not really the sort of concerts I'd be into, but hey, who am I to judge? The audience loved it, and that's all that matters when you're playing a gig, right?

Some of the audience showed their enthusiasm for the flamethrowers by bouncing wildly around when fire ripped through the air, while others celebrated the display by driving fists and tusks into their neighbors. Thankfully, those fights seemed to be contained in the bloodstained mosh pit.

Outside the controlled brawl, countless holograms flashed over circular pedestals. These neon, jittery images offered ads (I presumed) for a myriad of products as well as provided virtual dancers for customers to leer at.

At first, no one paid any attention to me, which I wasn't looking to change on account of all I'd seen thus far. Thus, I weaved through the crowd with X-45 right behind as discreetly as I could, continuing to use my scanner to home in on the signal it had locked onto.

But as anyone who knows anything about me will quickly attest, I never stay the wallflower for long—even if I'm doing all I can not to be asked to dance.

A wart-covered, sweaty hand with six fingers and gnarled, twisting nails dropped heavily on my shoulder, rooting me in place near one of the mini bars.

"You. Runty. Gimme da 'bot," said a rough voice peppered with grunts.

I spun around, shrugging off the patron's grip as I did, and found myself in a stare down with a two-and-a-half-meter-tall space boar dressed in a hodgepodge of rusted metal plates. Like many other Urgs, dozens of piercings and tattoos covered his face, and he even had some tiny blue and yellow lights implanted in his neck. A blaster hung off his belt at his side, though I doubted he'd ever consider using it on me, simply because that would take all the fun out of turning me into a pulp with his hands.

It took all my self-restraint not to break eye contact as I stepped back. I didn't want him to see me as prey, even if I probably was. I did, however, want some extra space between us, especially since it might be the difference between me keeping all four appendages attached or not.

"He's not for sale," I said.

"I's not askin' if he's for sale," the Urg growled. "I says you's best gimme da bot right now, or I's gonna frump you right through dat wall."

"Stupid flesh-thing," X-45 said, advancing a half pace. "Try and kill-kill us, and I'll burn-cut your head from its flesh-mount."

"Oi, keep it up, shiny. We'll see who's da toughest."

Everyone nearby instantly moved away, and most of the bar took note of what was going on as well. In a flash, the Urg and I had our own private arena in which to duke it out, while a mass of patrons formed a circle around us.

As X-45 and the Urg stared each other down, like some bizarre showdown between interstellar cowboys at high noon, I knew I had to do something. But seeing how I was a nervous wreck, ideas weren't coming too easily. For a few seconds, all I could think about was how sweaty my palms were, and how many somersaults my gut had made.

I sucked in a breath before things turned ugly and regained control of my inner angst. At that point, I remembered that the first rule to any bar fight was to show no weakness. Granted, the number of bar fights I'd been in up until now I could count on exactly zero fingers, but I had watched Tolby get in a few on my behalf, and he always said a little bit of backbone went a long way in these sorts of situations to get the other to back down. Oh, and word to the wise, if a girl has a ginormous space tiger for a best friend, it's not a good idea to get angry when she turns you down.

Sadly, I had no such best friend with me, so I was going to have to do this one on my own. And I might not have been as big, strong, or as fearsome as Tolby, but I had a few tricks up my sleeve—or in this case, in my implants.

I dropped a staying hand on X-45, hoping he wouldn't attack. "Trust me when I say this," I said to the Urg as slowly and as evenly as I could. "This is one fight you don't want to pick."

Apparently, that was the wrong thing to say. Or hell, I guess it was the right thing if you were into bar-room brawls. The Urg roared and leaped forward. I jumped sideways, and X-45 popped his plasma cutter out of his shoulder and let loose.

My robo pal wasn't fast enough. The Urg grabbed X-45's throat in one hand, and with the other, caught the plasma cutter a half second before it carved a swath through his head and redirected the jet harmlessly over his shoulder. Well, harmless is relative, I suppose. The blast melted of a crescent-shaped chunk from the ceiling and split a fan in half. At that point, the Urg spun a full 360 degrees with X-45 in tow and launched him through the air.

"Hey, porky! Leave my buddy alone!" I yelled. I balled my right hand into a tight fist and then telekinetically punched him across the cheek. I didn't use all the energy I had stored on account of the fact I didn't want to kill him, and I wasn't sure how kindly the fellow patrons would take to seeing one of their own having his skull caved in.

The Urg's head snapped sideways, and he stumbled back before shaking off the blow with a snotty, slobbery growl. "Dat 'eres da bes' fightin' you's gots?" he asked, dropping into a slight crouch.

"Nope," I said, backing. "And neither is this."

I hit him two more times, each blow harder than the previous. Again, he staggered under my assault, but he didn't go down. I did crack a tooth of his, which was a plus, and the spray of yellow blood oozing from his nose added a nice touch, too. But I could feel my arm growing cold, which meant I knew I didn't have a lot to work with. Worse, when I went to hit him a fourth time, I didn't strike him, but a crude, orange energy shield that shot up a split second beforehand.

The barrier flickered and disappeared, so I tried again, only to be met with similar results and a now mostly numb arm. Crap.

"It's still not too late to buy adequate life insurance to help your next of kin in times when they need it the most," Rummy whispered from my armband as the Urg and I had a mini standoff. "I will have to charge you a modest emergency-quote fee and also include a hazardous-scenario surcharge. But what's a slight increase in price when it comes to having the peace of mind of knowing your death will benefit others? Would you like to hear more?"

"No, but I will gladly take an orbiting battlecruiser that comes with a complimentary surgical strike," I whispered back.

I guess at that point the Urg decided I was out of tricks. He straightened, flashed a tusky, toothy grin, and cracked his knuckles in front of his chest. "Nowz my turn, runty."

He stuck a couple of fingers into his mouth and whistled sharply. Someone in the crowd tossed him a giant, two-handed mace that probably weighed as much as I did. Its head was filled with spikes and was encased with some sort of glowing, crackling energy field that probably meant it could shatter the armor on a tank.

"Aw, butters..." I muttered. Where on earth did that come from? No idea. I think I was so scared out of my mind, I couldn't even think to swear properly. Thank the lucky *ashidasashi* that I still had the wits to move, though.

The Urg swung at my head, and I barely had time to scramble away. The crowd parted as I moved, but only a half meter—enough to keep them safe, but not so much as to give me a place to run. In fact, when I tried my luck at plowing through them to get away, I was met with a solid hit to the chest which sent me sprawling into the makeshift arena.

"Wot? Runnin' already?" he laughed. "Thought you's said you's gonna give me a propa fumpin'."

With a single stride, he closed the distance between us and raised his mace high overhead. I shot out my arm, drawing upon every last bit of energy I had left in it, and hoped to every Kibnali god I could remember (which was all of one, assuming the first syllable counted) that I'd be miracled out of this predicament.

A deafening clap of thunder left my ears ringing and the top half of the Urg vaporized. What remained of him about the waist was little more than a charred stump. His legs twitched once before falling over.

The entire bar went silent after an audible gasp, and then all eyes went to someone or something behind me. I craned my head up and back and saw the most beautiful thing I'd ever seen. Check that, handsome.

Jack stood at the edge of the crowd dressed in a dark tan duster and sporting a slick, wide-brimmed hat. With both hands he carried a ginormous double-barrel cannon of absolute awesome. It hummed with energy, and I had a feeling it could turn a train engine into slag with a single shot if it wanted.

"Jack!" I shouted, scrambling to my feet and launching myself into his arms. He staggered back under my onslaught. He wrapped one hand around the small of my back and with the other, kept his weapon trained on the crowd. Both my arms went around his neck and I collapsed into him. "I can't believe it's you."

"Are you okay?" he asked. "I swear, can't leave you alone for even five seconds."

"No, I'm definitely not okay," I said, giving him a big squeeze. My arms trembled, and at that point, I realized I had tears in my eyes. "And that was more than five seconds."

"Fine, ten," he said with a hesitant laugh. He then cleared his throat and spoke to the crowd. "Show's over, folks."

With that, the crowd mumbled and went back to its state of organized chaos.

"I guess that's that," he said, giving me a glance but keeping the majority of his attention on the Urgs around us.

"No. That's not it," I said, clearing my eyes with a sniff. I leaned back to get a better look at my savior. "There's something I need to do."

"And that would be?" he asked, still keeping a vigilant watch.

"This," I said. I grabbed him by both sides of his face and pressed my lips into his.

CHAPTER THIRTEEN
DAKOTA SQUARED

Pressure between us built sharply. His hands squeezed my shoulders, and I could feel him suck in a breath. His fingers started to trail down my sides, but they didn't get far. Tolby's voice cut in, and everything came to a screeching halt.

Probably for the best now that I think about it.

"You two want a room?" my best bud asked.

The two of us broke a part. Jack blinked, and his face blanked, his mind no doubt trying to wrap itself around Tolby's sharp rebuke. I spun on my heels to find my best bud only a few paces away. The fear in his eyes was palpable, and it was almost enough to keep me rooted in place.

Almost.

"Tolby!" I yelled, throwing myself into him even harder than I had Jack. Tolby tried to back away as I came, but he didn't get far before I firmly attached myself to his side. At first I hugged him with every fiber of my soul. Then I covered his fur with a healthy mix of salty tears and snot. "Why did you leave me?"

"Dakota, I would never leave you," he whispered. "You know that."

My hands clenched his fur. I even pulled some out. Despite the warmth of his body against mine, all the terror my psyche had been trying to keep at bay poured out. And when that happened, my hands formed fists and began beating on my best bud. "Yes, you did!" I said, striking him over and over. "You left me on Kumet! I never thought I'd see you again!"

Tolby didn't flinch as my blows came. Course, I've seen him wrestle Martian polar bears for a cheat day when it came to exercise, so I suppose it wasn't like I could do any real damage to him. Still, nice of the big lug to let me vent. After I began to tire, he picked me up with more love than any parent had for a child. I felt him shoo at others, but I was so exhausted and elated to finally be reunited with my best friend, I sank back into his fur and stayed there.

He carried me out of the bar moments later.

I'm not sure how long we walked, or where we walked to, but it felt like a lifetime. Eventually, he gently placed me down in what looked like to be the remains of a ransacked tool shop. Counters formed a broad U around us, while broken shelves hung at odd angles on the walls. The smell of rust with hints of mold filled the air, and I could hear a fan spinning overhead somewhere. Half the lights worked, leaving much of the place draped in shadow, but that didn't matter as I could still see Tolby—the only thing I ever wanted to see from there on out.

His giant paw stroked the top of my head and stroked it gently. Anger had left me by now, but not the hurt. "I can't believe you left me," I softly said as I did my damnedest not to turn into a blubbering mess. "How could you?"

"Dakota," he replied. "I don't know what happened to you between now and whenever—and for the love of everything, *don't* tell me anything—but you've been time traveling again. Your brain is goo. I would never, ever leave you."

"My brain is not goo," I said, pulling away.

"It is."

"No, it's not. Now listen to me, damn it!"

Tolby looked like he was going to argue, but instead he simply exhaled sharply as his shoulders fell. "Fine," he said. "I'm paying attention. But you have to hear me out first. You don't have any safety discs anymore. If you feel...funny, you must promise me you'll stop whatever it is you're saying or doing. I don't need a paradoxical backlash to turn you to cinders...or worse."

My jaw clenched tight. I could feel my blood start to boil, but I reminded myself he didn't know any better, and he was still looking out for me. "Fine," I said. "I promise."

"Good."

"One little question, though, before you get started," he said.

"What's that?"

"We've been followed by a little robot," he said. "Is he a friend of yours?"

I glanced left and saw X-45 peeping at us through a window. "Yeah," I said with a sniff before waving at him to come in. "He's been helping me. Kinda quirky for a droid, but that's nothing new for us. Right?"

"Right," Tolby replied, smiling. Oh, how my heart warmed at that. "Now, tell me what's going on. And don't nuke us with forbidden future knowledge as you do."

"I won't," I said, trying to sound as reassuring as I could. I took in a couple deep breaths to steady myself before beginning, as the last thing I wanted was to end up in an emotional rant and reinforce the idea they had that I'd been time traveling again. "Remember when you brought me to that medical facility on Kumet to extract that Nodari venom?"

"Of course. How could I forget something like that?"

"Remember when they made a clone of me to test their treatment on?"

"Yes."

"After treatment, you guys left with that clone. Not me," I said. "I was stuck in the vats for ten or fifteen minutes before I got out, and I've spent the last several days trying to catch up to you guys."

A long pause settled between us. Tolby's left ear twitched a few times, and I could tell he was both in deep thought and greatly conflicted. Eventually, he looked over my shoulder, and I turned to follow his gaze. I saw Jack several paces away, a meter inside the edge of light.

"We didn't actually do that, did we?" Jack asked, looking and sounding guilty as sin.

"No. No, of course not," Tolby said, shaking his head. His words did not reflect the fear in his voice. "That clone was lifeless."

"Yeah..." Jack said, though his tone made it clear he wasn't a hundred percent on that. Maybe fifty-fifty at best.

I reached over and put a hand on his side. "You did," I said softly. "I promise."

Tolby's eyes darted between me and Jack. "I can't believe it. It doesn't make sense."

"It makes a little sense," Jack said, hesitantly. "I mean, we don't know how that clone activated, or whatever, but at the very least, I think we need to ask ourselves the trillion-credit question."

"Which is?"

"What if she's not lying?"

Tolby shook his head. "I don't think she's lying."

"You know what I mean," Jack said. "What if she's not mistaken either. What if she's actually telling the truth, and she's the real deal and the one we've got is a clone?"

"Thank you," I said, letting my arms flop to my sides and exhaling sharply. "I'm not lying, and I'm not crazy. Do you think I'd be like this if I hadn't been desperately chasing you across the galaxy, all the while trying not to die?"

Clone Me stepped out from the shadows. She wore loose-fitting pants along with a tactical belt and a light jacket which was open in front, revealing a sky-blue tank top. A carbine had been slung over her shoulder, and her eyes regarded me as a curiosity—like I was the fossilized remains of an ancient ancestor in some forgotten tomb—and in a way, I guess that wasn't terribly out there in terms of comparisons. I mean in a sense, she was looking at her mold. That'll blow anyone's mind.

Tolby glanced to the darkness. "Well? What do you think?"

Clone Me came into the light with a tentative step in my direction. "I don't think she's lying either," Clone Me said. "Or at least, I don't think she's me from the future. Clone then? Or replicant? Cyborg? Shape shifter? Do you guys have those around here?"

The shock in Tolby's and Jack's faces could've dwarfed a small moon. Their mouths opened a little, but neither spoke. My reaction, on the other hand, was a little more volatile when she stepped toward me again, her eyes looking at me as if I were some sort of ancient curiosity tucked away in an obscure museum wing.

"Stay back!" I yelled, arm outstretched. I might not have had a blaster, but I still had my Progenitor implants, and I was more than willing to use them to keep this imposter away, not to mention a pair of ice axes hanging from my hip. Some might think I was overreacting a bit, but who knew what psycho "tests" she'd want to run on me in an effort to turn me into the bad guy and keep Tolby and the others for herself. "I swear, if you don't leave right this minute, you'll regret it."

To my surprise, and relief, Tolby placed himself between us. He kept one paw on my shoulder while the other reached toward my doppelganger. "Don't come any closer, Dakota," he said to her. "We have to figure out what's going on, one way or another, and who the real Dakota is."

Clone Me cocked her head and spoke, her voice sounding insulted. "You don't actually believe her, do you? I'm not an imposter."

"I don't know what to believe right now."

"Tolby," she said. "It's me. Dakota. How can you not know your best friend?"

I pulled on my best bud's arm. "Don't listen to her. She's the fake. She's the one trying to take you from me, trying to steal my family—my friends."

"The hell I am!" Clone Me said, her eyes narrowing. "I don't know where you came from, but you can suck on a warp coil for all I care."

"Dakota! Stop talking to her!" Tolby shouted. "If this is a future you, you're going to tangle us up in a paradox that'll split the quadrant. And I don't know about anyone else, but we're so close to home, I don't want to do anything that'll jeopardize that."

I groaned as my eyes rolled back in my head. "Look. I can prove she's the damn clone, okay?"

Clone Me didn't flinch. Instead, she snorted and smirked. "I'd love to see you try."

I stepped to the side so everyone could see me and triumphantly pulled my shirt up enough to expose my midriff, at which point I pointed to the cute little belly button smack dab in the middle of my tummy. I'll be the first to admit, I had never given it much thought before in my life. It had always been there and didn't really do a whole lot other than beg me for a ring. But now...now it was my savior. My seal of authenticity. My ticket back home with my best friend.

My eyes gleamed. "Checkmate."

Clone Me raised an eyebrow. "Am I missing something?"

"If you are, so am I," Jack admitted.

"Are you guys blind?" I asked as I jabbed a finger into my tummy. "That's a bona fide belly button."

Clone Me looked around. "And?"

"And it means I was born and you—you bellybuttonless freak—are the imposter," I said. "You don't get one of these if you haven't popped out of a womb. That's basic biology."

All eyes went to my clone. She sighed heavily, shrugged, and then with far more cool than I'd ever have thought possible, she casually raised her tank top. "Hate to break it to you, but I've got one of those as well."

Jack huffed and ran his fingers through his hair. "Great," he said. "So, you did scramble your brains again," he said to her. "Why would you do that?"

"I didn't!" she said. "I wouldn't! Well, I mean, not without good cause, right?"

"Probably saw something shiny in a catalog," Jack said.

"Or wanted to get a plushy from that gift shop we wouldn't stop at earlier on deck twelve," Tolby added with an exasperating sigh. "We should've just let her pick one out."

"Hey! That was a damn cute plushy," Clone Me said, putting her hands on her hips. "And for the record, I wouldn't hop back for a stuffed animal."

Tolby raised his eyebrow.

So did Jack. He tossed in a snicker in as well.

"Okay," she said with a sigh steeped in resignation. "I wouldn't risk time travel for a plushy if I weren't absolutely sure everything would be okay. I did learn a lesson or two at the museum, you know."

"That's debatable," Jack said with a wry grin. When Clone Me shot him a glare, he returned fire with a wink. "You're still my favorite time-hopping cutie though. Don't worry."

"Look, damnit!" I shouted, grabbing everyone's attention once again. "I'm not from the future. If I were, I'd be having my fifth brain aneurism by now for meddling in my past. Come on, I mean, last time I met myself, it lasted for what? A minute, tops? And cripes, by the end of that, I gushed enough blood out my nose I could've earned a year's worth of frequent donor rewards."

"She's got a point," Clone Me said with a nod. She gently touched her nose and seemed genuinely relieved her hand came back clean. "I don't feel any different either."

"You're her best friend. Do you have any ideas on how to sort this out?" Jack asked, this time, directing his question to Tolby. "I mean, if she's not a future Dakota, that pretty much only leaves clone as an option, right? Either that, or a perfect lookalike when it comes to a cyborg replicant."

Tolby shook his head and grunted. "I don't know. Maybe Yseri or Jainon can figure this out once we catch up to them. All I know is I can't shake the feeling this is only the prelude to a monumental disaster."

"Seeing how we've got two Dakotas to deal with now, I'd say that's an absolute certainty," Jack teased.

I crossed my arms over my chest, but quickly undid them the moment I realized Clone Me had done the same. "What's that supposed to mean?"

Jack held a wry grin. "You know exactly what that means."

"I don't cause trouble!" I said.

Tolby grumbled.

"Don't you start," I said, shooting him a scowl.

"I didn't."

"Good."

Jack's eyes lit up, and he spun around to face Clone Me directly. "I know what to do," he said enthusiastically. "Dakota. Quick. Come here."

She did, though slowly and with a titled head. "Why?"

"Kiss me. Quick."

Clone Me straightened. "Come again?"

"Kiss me!" he said, waving her over.

She threw up her hands. "I have no idea what you're on about."

"I need to compare."

Clone Me stopped in her tracks, and her face went flat.

"What?" he asked, throwing up his hands. "It's a good idea."

Clone Me didn't say a word but simply folded her arms over her chest.

"Hey, she's a good kisser," he said, undaunted. "We need to see if you are, too."

I sighed and regretted ever planting one on him, even if I had been caught up in the moment. "There's got to be a way to prove I'm telling the truth," I lamented. "It can't be that hard to show you I'm not a loon."

"You're not a loon," said Tolby.

I buried my face in my hands before running my fingers through my hair. Despite Tolby's reassurances, despite my vehement insistence on who I was, my resolve wasn't completely impervious to doubt. What if I had gone crazy? What if the memories floating in my head weren't real and everything I believed was a lie?

No. That couldn't be it. I mean, what I knew...I knew. Those memories were sharper than a razor, not the foggy mismatched balls of goo that I couldn't cling to when my time hopping dealt a full hand of colossal shenanigans.

I knew who I was. I only had to convince them of that.

"I loathe to get involved," Rummy said, piping up from the bracelet on my wrist. "But had you purchased accidental clone mishap insurance—along with the supplemental conflict resolution package—all of this could've been avoided. Well, maybe not avoided, but you'd certainly enjoy peace of mind knowing that every facet of your case is being handled by a professional mediator. Would you like to hear more?"

My heart jumped in my chest, and I could feel my face light up with more energy than a shooting star. I'd completely forgotten about the little bugger. Yeah, his constant sales pitches about useless products and services drove me crazy, but there was one thing he had that was precisely what I needed: a third-party testimony.

"Rummy!" I shouted, holding up my arm. "Tell them! Tell them she's the clone!"

"Who is that?" Tolby asked.

"This is Rummy," I said, nodding toward my bracelet. "He's the sales guy from the medbay. He'll vouch for me. He'll also vouch that Taz saved us from the Nodari, and we all know that he'd only hang around the real Dakota."

All eyes went to my bracelet. "It is true that we *may* have had an accidental clone mishap," the little guy said with no small amount of hesitation. "And as a result, we at Excel-Care might have, through no fault of our own, inadvertently released an unrequested clone into the wild. This statement, however, by no means, shape, or form, expresses any apologies, admissions of guilt, or agreement to compensation due to events or hardships incurred, intentional or not."

Tolby looked dumbfounded. Clone Me had clearly taken the denial route. Jack opted for the middle of the two. Or maybe it was straight-up brain malfunction, because he was the first to speak, but his words hardly made sense. At least, at first. "How could...I mean, like why should...and the thing at..." he stammered. He stopped, breathed deeply, and stuck out both hands. "Okay, let's try this again," he said, more for himself I think than any of us. "You're saying you made a clone. We ran off with her, and the real Dakota is the one wearing you?"

"I am *not* a clone," Imposter Me huffed as she folded her arms across her chest. "I've been with you the entire time."

"Yes, that's true," Tolby said, his words trailing. "Except for when Dakota was treated for the Nodari venom. She disappeared for a few minutes. Technically, in that time, a swap could have been made and we'd have never known."

"Exactly!" I said, throwing up my hands. "Now that we've got that cleared up, we can move on with getting *my* life back."

"Your life? Screw you," Clone Me said. "You're not stealing my friends and family from me."

"Yeah, if I'm the clone, how do I know my third-grade teacher had a huge wart on her left cheek?" I said.

"Because you've got *my* memories," she said. "I knew that, too."

"Did not."

"Did too. I also know in first grade, I wanted to see how sharp my scissors were and cut the girl's hair who sat in front of me."

I opened my mouth to try and give a snappy come back, or at least something that would label her as a fraud, but I couldn't find the words. I think I can count the number of times I didn't have something, *anything*, to say on something in my life on exactly zero fingers.

"By the Planck, this is a mess," Tolby said, shaking his head. "It's giving me a massive headache."

"Would you like to purchase a lifetime supply of Ache-B-Gone?" Rummy asked. "It is specially formulated with over three hundred and twenty-nine natural herbs and vitamins to create our proprietary formula that is clinically proven to reduce all ailments, aches, discomforts, and mild to moderate pains by over eighty-eight percent. Would you like to know more?"

"No," Tolby said with a sigh. "I want this nightmare to end before I lose my mind."

"Nightmare?" Rummy repeated, sounding genuinely insulted. "I think we can all agree that this little event has turned out for the best."

"I seriously doubt that," Tolby said.

"Seconded," I added.

"And the motion carries," Imposter Me tacked on. Part of me was happy she didn't argue over this bit, but most of me was annoyed, if not angered, at the reminder of how perfect she could be at pretending to be me.

Stupid perfect clones. They think they're all smart with their identical behavior. Gah! Why couldn't Rummy have just painted a big yellow X across her back to make her stand out? Would that be too much to ask? Apparently so.

"So, what do we do?" Jack asked. "I mean, I guess we could take them both along?"

"Fine," I said, crossing my arms. "She can tag along. I guess. But I'll be damned if she's sleeping in my bed."

Clone Me snorted. "Your bed? Better get used to disappointment if you think you're sleeping in my bunk."

"Mine has room for one more," Jack said, throwing the least subtle wink he's ever thrown.

"There you go," she said. "It'll give you more time to smother him with kisses."

"Sorry if I got a little emotional after you stole my friends, took off with my ship, and left me for dead."

Tolby roared. Loudly. I know I turned three shades of white, because Clone Me jumped and did the same. She probably missed a half dozen heartbeats before her heart kicked back in as well. "Both of you, be quiet," he bellowed. He then flexed his claws, breathed in deeply, and closed his eyes for a moment. "Calm...calm..." He repeated his mantra a couple more times before readdressing the imposter and me. "Now that I am re-centered," he said, placing his paws together in front of his face, "you will either both share everything equally or share none. That is the only fair thing to do."

"I have a better idea," I said. I then pointed at my bracelet. "Rummy, I'm sure, has some sort of test he can do to prove to you all who is the clone and who is not."

"I do," he said. "Well, I can access the tests at an officially licensed Excel-Care facility in order to perform them. Doesn't need to be a level-nine facility like the one back on Kumet, but it'll need to have a standard diagnostic station. I'm reasonably sure that this station has one. Deck twenty, if I'm not mistaken, by the food court—assuming it's still standing. Seems as if a lot of facilities in this shipyard have been repurposed."

While everyone else's eyes lit up, mine included, Clone Me's face filled with dread. So much, in fact, if I hadn't known better, I'd have guessed a gigantic, cybernetically enhanced ravenous squid had dropped into the room with us. I might have even glanced over my shoulder, just to be sure it hadn't.

"Oh crap," she mumbled.

"What?" I asked with a smirk. "Afraid he's going to out you?"

Clone Me shook her head before glancing nervously around. "You came from the facility in Kumet."

"No, you came from the facility on Kumet."

"Whatever, I'm not going to argue. There's something else, though, that we really, *really* need to know."

Tolby growled, and his ears pressed back. "I hate it when you talk like that."

My imposter cautiously approached, and when she spoke, she did so with soft, almost motherly words. "Dakota, how did you get here?"

I straightened and huffed. "What do you mean how? In a ship, of course. What's so worrisome about that? I do know how to fly, you know."

Clone Me froze, and her face paled. "A ship you got from Kumet?"

I cocked my head and twisted my mouth to the side, not following her concern, nor understanding why that concern had suddenly spread to everyone else. "Yeah...why? It's not nearly as awesome as the one you guys got, but it was Progenitor, thank god, because that's the only thing that let me outrun that Nodari fleet. But none of them followed me, if that's what's got your stabilizers in a twist."

Clone Me swore.

So did Jack.

Tolby also cursed up a storm, but he also ended up grabbing my shoulders and spinning me around to face him. "By the gods," he said. "Tell me you figured out how to fly that ship by yourself. Tell me you rubbed your lucky elephant and somehow it all worked on its own."

"I'm awesome, but I'm not *that* awesome," I said with a nervous chuckle. "I got a lot of help from the ships' AI. Handy guy, even if he's a bit rough around the edges. Too bad your ship didn't have him on board on account of damage or something. He could've stopped all this from happening right from the start."

CHAPTER FOURTEEN
A NEW PLAN

When I was seven, my friend Katie got a ferret for her birthday. She named him Snowflake, on account of he was all white, and aside from a slight musky smell—and the fact that he pooped everywhere (which made letting him run around the house at will pretty much a no go)—I thought he made an awesome pet. We'd entertain ourselves with him for hours, letting him jump around the bed or play with our hair.

I thought he was so awesome, in fact, that for three solid weeks I begged and begged my parents for a ferret of my own. I tried everything. I tried asking politely. I tried giving puppy dog eyes. I tried promising to clean my room for a whole four days in a row. I even tried going on a hunger strike, which lasted an hour as we happened by a 151-flavors store and the power of the root beer float was too much to resist.

Anywho, as you can probably guess, I didn't get the ferret. Did I let that stop me? Of course not. As it happened to be, we went on a camping trip a couple of weeks later up in the Smoky Mountains, and I was intent on catching myself a ferret of my very own. I wanted a white one like Katie's, but I wasn't going to be picky, either. I decided I'd settle on whatever color I happened on. Black. Gray. Brown. Whatever.

133

Fast forward fifteen days. After spending the night at our campsite and procuring exactly zero ferrets, I woke up early and went looking for one. As luck would have it, it didn't take me long to find one. He was bigger than Katie's, which wasn't surprising since hers wasn't that old, but he did seem a little fatter. And he wasn't white, either. Well, not all the way. He was mostly black.

Initially, he wanted nothing to do with me. Hissed a bunch, but I came prepared with delicious treats. After a solid ten minutes of bribing him, I gained enough of his trust that I managed to pick him up. He didn't like that either, so I stuffed his face with more delicious goodness and carried him back to the campsite.

My parents were around the campfire, making breakfast, when I strolled up to them and showed off my prize and prepared to give my speech on why they should let me take him home and how wonderful I was going to take care of him.

I didn't get very far in that speech. Right after I said, "Look what I got," my mom screamed, my dad yelled something about a skunk, and everyone ran as fast as they could away from me.

For fifteen years, I'd never seen anyone run away from me with such speed. Holy snort did that ever change after I brought up AO.

Imposter Me tried something with her arm, then mumbled something else about portal batteries recharging, at which point she sprinted away at Mach 8 with Jack and Tolby right behind. I'm still not sure how I wasn't trampled in the process.

They were nearly out the door when my brain kicked in gear and I took off after them. "Tolby! Stop!" I yelled. "You're not leaving me again!"

Those words were enough to at least knock some sense back into my best bud. He slowed enough for me to catch up. "You don't understand," Tolby said. "AO tried to kill us all. If he's here, we've got to warn the others before he finishes the job."

"No! He wouldn't! He was so nice!"

Tolby groaned. "Of course he was nice, Dakota. He was nice last time, right up until he tried feeding us to the Nodari!"

I slowed as his words tumbled in my brain. He had to be wrong. He had to. But his voice, his panic, his everything said he wasn't. "I—I didn't know."

Tolby came to a halt. "I know, Dakota. I'm not blaming you, but we've either got to destroy him—again—or get out of here ASAP."

X-45 blasted out of the storeroom right as Tolby finished his sentence. His arms waved frantically in the air, though I think it was more to grab my attention than an honest go at panic. Somehow I doubted anything would get the little metal weirdo in a twist. It just didn't seem to be part of his programming (and man, wouldn't that be nice to be like that?). "Creature-meat!" he called out. "Stop-halt your run-run. I can help-assist you all."

"Move, Dakota," Tolby ordered, raising his sidearm. I barely had time to telekinetically knock it to the side before he fired. The plasma bolt missed X-45 by a hair and drilled a nice hole into an alleyway dumpster.

"Don't shoot him, Tolby!" I shouted. "He's a friend, and he's saved me three times now."

Thankfully, the big furball kept a cool enough head that he didn't blast X-45 apart, but at the same time, he didn't put his weapon away either. "You thought AO was a friend, too, back on Kumet," he said. "Forgive me if I don't trust your judgment on the matter. For all we know, that robot of yours is going to help us right out of an airlock."

"Trust my judgment?" I scoffed. "You're the one who nearly took my head off when we first met, remember?"

"Ugh. I should have never told you about that."

My arms crossed over my chest. "Well, you did, and this is different," I replied. "Back then, you didn't have a best friend telling you how nice and awesome I was! Now put your weapon away and stop freaking me out."

135

Tolby groaned and lowered his pistol. "Fine. Happy?"

"Good-good, furry creature-meat," X-45 said. "You give joy-glad that I'm not forced to kill-kill you. Little creature-meat would be sad-sad if I did."

"Are you threatening me?" Tolby said with a growl. "Try, and you won't even be able to think about getting a shot off."

X-45 let loose an electronic chirp that sounded like a parrot laughing, only harmonized. "I could kill-kill all of you in an instant if I wanted to, and I wouldn't stand-stay here-here to do it. I'd fold the warp. Bend spacetime in the here-here. Much quicker-easier that way."

"Easier? How's that?" Clone Me asked.

"Destroying all of you would be simple-quick with this station's webway. Could use it to rip-tear fabric. No escape," he said. "Assuming it still work-worked."

I felt the color drain from my face, and a massive amount of guilt fell on my shoulders. God, why did disaster always follow me wherever I went? "That's why he wanted us to patch central control—so he could take command of the station and use the webway."

"All the more reason we need to hurry," Tolby growled. "I'd wager he's not relying on you to succeed in order for him to accomplish wiping us out."

"I'd bet on it," said Jack.

Tolby flicked his tail, and his ears went back as he tried to reach Daphne on the comms. Sadly, whatever interference was going on due to our location on the station kept that from happening. "This is infuriating! Why can't we reach her? Or the others?"

"Here, I boost-help signal," X-45 said. "Try-try again."

"Daphne? Can you hear me?" he asked once last time.

"Tolby! There you are," Daphne said. "Did you happen on another Dakota? I think she's been time traveling again and turned her brain into tapioca. She showed up at the ship not too long ago and went looking for you."

"We did," he replied. "And whether or not her brain is mush is the least of our worries. She brought a ship from Kumet. AO is here."

"He is? Well, that does put a damper on our plans."

"It's a hell of a lot more than a damper, Daphne," Clone Me said right as we all reached a turbolift, and she hit call button. "We need to deal with him, ASAP. Got any suggestions on how to do it?"

"Here's one: I fly over to his ship and blow it up."

"You can do that?" Clone Me asked. "I thought there was too much system damage for that to work."

"There is," she said. "But for the record, I said I should. Not that I could. While I can perform basic piloting functions at this time, as you pointed out, damage sustained from both battle and my hostile takeover of the ship's functions have kept me from having control of the weapon systems. We're lucky to have manual control of them at all, to be honest. I should point out, though, that we don't need to work ourselves into a total panic."

"How's that?" she asked. "Because according to this little robot guy we picked up, if he gets control of the facility, we're all going to die. So I'd say this is the perfect time to panic."

"We still have a baker's dozen seasoned Kibnali warriors, counting Tolby, Jainon, and Yseri," she replied. "We could send them to blow the ship. They'd like that, too, I'm sure. Kibnali are very keen on destroying things, if you haven't noticed."

Clone Me snorted. "Believe me, I've noticed."

"Oh good," Daphne said. "With the war we left and all, I was going to suggest having your eyes looked at if you hadn't. Who knows what that Nodari venom did to you."

"Okay, let's send in the kitty commandos and end this right here and now," Jack said, hardening his face and tightening his grip on his mega-cannon. "Because I don't know about the rest of you, but I'm done with this AO guy. Just point me in his direction and I'll start plugging holes in every circuit he has."

Tolby grunted and swished his tail. I didn't know what he was going to say in that moment, but I knew whatever it was, it was bothering him greatly. "Daphne," he said. "I want you to get ahold of Jainon and Yseri, tell them what's going on, and tell them what their mission is: to destroy AO or his ability to take over this station."

"Should I sing it to them?" she asked.

"Sing it to them? No. Why would you?"

"I was thinking it would be a nicer way to deliver the bad news," she replied. "Remember when I turned the story of the Kibnali extinction into a bedtime story how much nicer that was? I think you'll agree that was a much better way to take in disaster."

Tolby let slip a long, deep growl. "No, it wasn't," he said. "Now tell them what's going on and stop wasting time."

"Fine. But if later they say they would've rather had the song, that's going to be on your head, mister."

"That's a risk I'm willing to take," said Tolby.

"You know," Imposter Me said, holding up her hand. "I could portal us right into AO's ship. Dakota Copy over here only needs to tell us where it is."

I cocked my head while forcing myself to ignore her calling me a copy. "You can? How? Jakpep was destroyed."

"He was, but we've got Jakpep before that happened, minus a working power cell, that is," Clone Me said. "We've also got a precursor to Jakpep on the ship. Handy, even if it's a bit limited in its abilities."

"Doesn't that figure," I mumbled, annoyed to Neptune and back that not only had Clone Me stolen my identity, my friends, and my ship, but also another portal device. I guess I shouldn't have been too surprised, as that would be par for the course.

"So where's the ship you came in on?" she asked.

"Slip twenty-seven nineteen," I said, realizing my personal beef with her would need to wait. Actually, check that. No it didn't. If there was a portal device, I'd be damned if I wasn't going to get to use it, especially when it came to making sure Tolby was safe. "But I should be the one to use the portal," I added. "Not you."

Clone Me snorted. "Yeah, that's not going to happen."

"Why the hell not? I know where my ship is better than you do."

"Because it's my portal device, that's why."

"Only because you stole my identity!" I shot back.

"Both of you settle now. Arguing is pointless," Daphne said, grinding everything to a halt.

I cocked my head to the side, not sure where she was headed with this. "Why's that? Are we going to flip a coin for it?"

"Heads," Clone Me said.

"I was going to call heads. I always call heads!"

"Maybe, but it seems clones are a little slower on the 'I was going to' than the real thing," she said with so much smug, I almost decked her right then and there. "And don't even think about punching me," she added. "I wouldn't stand here and let you."

"Gah! I've barely met you and I already hate you," I said, digging my nails into the sides of my head.

"Ahem," Daphne said before our argument could escalate any further. "There's no need to fight."

"Tell that to the imposter," I said, narrowing my eyes and wishing her dead. Well, maybe not dead, dead. I really don't have a lot of hate in my heart. But if she happened to break down in her space hopper on some rando backwater moon, I wouldn't exactly be jumping to whip out my membership card for the MSA and get her a tow home, you know?

"I'm sensing an increase in negative emotions," Rummy said. "Now would be a perfect time to meet your new therapist and discuss ways to cope effectively. Would you like me to book you an appointment? As a VIP customer of Excel-Care, you are entitled to a fifty-percent discount on your initial evaluation, as well as twenty percent off all psychiatric medications and treatments." His voice then dropped a full octave and spoke in a hurried whisper. "Excel-Care is not liable for misdiagnoses, or side effects of medication which may include rash, fever, swelling, unwanted hair, halitosis, society anxiety, yellow chills, swollen glands, neurological damage, premature death, or occasional lower back pain."

"I can't imagine why you don't have customers banging down your door," Jack said with a roll of his eyes.

"Me either!" Rummy exclaimed. "Such a bargain. Do you think we should reinitiate our referral bonus program?"

My inner space squirrel kicked in, and I couldn't help but ask. "You have a referral program?"

"We do! In fact, you can earn additional residual income by introducing your friends to our fantastic line of lipsticks, essential oils, legal advice, personal communications, and exquisite jewelry. Would you—"

"No, I wouldn't," I said. "What I want to know, now that I'm done chasing the tangent, is why Daphne said arguing was pointless."

"That's simple," she replied. "It's pointless to argue because I've disabled the portal device."

"Why would you do that?" Clone Me asked, sounding both shocked and insulted.

"Elementary, my dear Maybe Dakota. I did it on account of we shouldn't trust either of you until we can determine what's going on and who we can trust," she replied. "Safety reasons and all."

"Hang on a sec," I said. "You guys are all about AO being this super evil AI that's hell-bent on wiping everyone out, but somehow it's not nearly enough of a pressing matter that we shouldn't try opening a portal into the ship?"

Tolby flexed his claws and flipped his tail. Clearly the big guy didn't like Daphne insinuating that I wasn't who I said I was. Hell, I didn't like it either, but I guess I couldn't blame her. What we needed—what we always needed—was a way to sort this out, posthaste. "Do you have a better suggestion?" he asked. "Because right now, I'm all for a calculated risk."

"I do!" she said. "I found an extremely handy scenario builder suite. It's loaded with all sorts of extras like video tutorials, full support for the mega-large googol data type, and a new sorting method that increases correlation calculations by four percent. Oh! And get this, we even get a season pass for the next ten years for all updates and DLC. I can't wait to see what's in the next expansion pack. I hear there are going to be mod authoring tools."

I sighed and buried my face in my hands. "I really hoped you guys would've fixed her by now."

Clone Me chuckled lightly. "I think it's safe to say that's a unanimous position."

"I heard that," Daphne said with a sour tone.

"And we still love you," Clone Me replied. "What's your idea?"

"Yes, my idea," she went on. "I've been doing some risk analysis based on all possible known scenarios. I'm afraid the chances of our new Dakota currently *not* being used by AO are approximately three thousand, seven hundred and twenty to one. Thus, I think everyone will agree that bringing either of them back at this point in time is a bad idea."

I threw up my arms and rolled my eyes. "I'm not a damn spy, Daphne! I'm me! Dakota! The girl who loves root beer, ran around a Progenitor museum, and has a cute little fern back on Mars."

"A fern that you sing to," Jack interjected.

"Yeah? And?"

"And nothing. Just a cute little factoid about our favorite time jumper is all."

"As I was saying, my idea is you let me handle AO, and the rest of you figure out what's going on with our two Dakotas," Daphne said.

"You're going to handle AO?" Tolby asked, skepticism ringing loudly in his voice.

"No, someone else well," she said. "I'm merely orchestrating." She then paused for a half beat, and when she came back to the line, her voice sounded extra chipper and full of energy. "Oh! Should I call myself Maestro, then? I always wanted to be one."

"Ugh," Jack said with a groan. "There she goes again."

"*She* has a name, thank you," Daphne said. "And it's Maestro. Got it?"

"Sure thing, Maestro," Jack said with a roll of his eyes.

"Good, now I'll get a handle on AO. You all figure out what we're going to do about our little Dakota squared problem. Ha! Isn't that funny? Dakota squared? I should be a comedian."

CHAPTER FIFTEEN
THE PET STORE

When it came to what deck twenty had in store for us, I have to say, it wasn't at all what I'd been expecting. I guess by now, however, that's not exactly saying much, is it? I probably could've had my hair stapled to the floor by a roaming gang of Sagittarian Moon Apes and just shrugged it off given the amount of weird we'd been through lately.

Whereas deck thirty-three turned out to be slimier than a promise made by an extended-warranty salesman, deck twenty looked so posh, it made the Palace of Versailles look like a quaint bed and breakfast. It had an open design with shops, apartments, and businesses built into towering, curved walls on both sides. The ceiling had to be a few hundred meters if not more from the floor, and like most giant Progenitor structures, I had a good feeling that portal technology was being used to squeeze it all into the station. There was no way this place wasn't bigger on the inside.

Anywho, a massive, crystal-clear lake lay sprawled across at least a third of the deck (stocked with plenty of golden fish), and when we first arrived and found ourselves on a gorgeous white, arched bridge overlooking it all, I counted at least four parks filled with colorful flora and benches galore.

Even the patrons of this area seemed like they were ten steps above everyone else we'd encountered, especially the Urgs. Well, that's not saying much, either. Those space hogs had about as much charm as I had artistic talent. Word to the wise, if we're ever trapped in some bizarre game where our lives depend on me drawing something more than a stick figure, I really hope your will is up to date.

We got to the aforementioned bridge in no time, and at its center, we found a three-meter-tall white kiosk. Each of its three sides had a holographic display of the area along with the usual sort of directory one might find at any typical mall. None of the listings said anything about an Excel-Care facility, or a food court for that matter (which bummed me out on account of my rumbling stomach), but Rummy didn't seem worried. Well, to be honest, I really didn't know what he seemed like because he wasn't talking. Not for the first bit at least.

"Where do we go?" Jack asked as his finger trailed down the directory.

"No idea," I said. "Maybe the body sculpting place? That's...sort of like healthcare."

The edges of the kiosk cycled through a few different colors before changing into a dark green and staying there. After that, a faint white noise built in my ears for a few seconds before cutting out altogether, and a flashing yellow box appeared around one of the shops, a few hundred meters away.

"This is it," Rummy said.

Tolby leaned over me and read the entry. "Porgie's Pets."

"A pet store?" I said. "We're going to a pet store."

"Yes," Rummy replied. "That is the location where Excel-Care should be. Or at least, was."

"Here's to hoping whatever equipment we need is still there and works," Imposter Me said.

"Or at least a couple of collars," Jack said.

I cocked my head. "For?"

"The two of you, of course," he replied with a devilish grin.

I rolled my eyes at myself. I should've seen that coming. "Ha. Ha. Ha."

In response, he threw us both an unapologetic look. "Who's joking? You'd look great in a leather choker."

"I do look great in a leather choker," Imposter Me replied before sticking out her tongue. "But you'll never know."

"Enough, all of you," Tolby said.

At that point, we left the kiosk and headed for Porgie's Pets. Along the way, I made sure I walked between Tolby and my clone, and just to be ultra sure she knew where her place was in our social circle, I reached up and held Tolby's paw as we went. The pad felt rough and familiar, and feeling all the cushions touch my skin took me back to our first days together, back when we barely knew each other but knew right from the start we'd not only go on a slew of amazing adventures together, but that we shared an unbreakable bond like no other. Together, we'd survived monstrous plants as big as a continent, sleezy space pirates who were obsessed with getting their tolls from me, blizzards that could rip apart star liners, ravenous cybernetic squids who definitely didn't like carrots, and then some. And I'd be damned if some wannabe me was going to be our undoing.

We got to Porgie's Pets in a few minutes. Like the rest of the shops, it had been built into the wall. Large glass panes made up the front face of the store, and a glowing neon sign above the door written in flowery handwriting announced its name. To my utter surprise, however, when we stepped inside, there wasn't a pet to be seen at all. Sure, there were plenty of pictures hanging on the walls of happy pets with happy owners. Pets of all shapes and sizes. Small. Gargantuan. Furry. Scaly. Furry and scaly. One head. Six heads. Even no heads.

On either side of the store stood four booths with reclining chairs on pedestals, sort of like the ones you'd see in history books detailing dental hygiene. Man, I can't even begin to think what it must've been like to live before plaque vaccination. I mean, who in their right mind could sit still while some stranger jabs your mouth with sharp, pointy instruments of torture? I guess it's one thing if you're into that kind of thing, but as for this girl? No way.

As for the front and center of Porgie's Pets, there were six gray, circular tables with five red chairs spaced evenly around. In the center of each table were identical metal vases, slim with scooped necks, and inside said vases were three flowers with soft white petals. Next to those were cute little metal stands which held folded brochures. I couldn't read any of them from where we were standing, obviously, but the pictures on them from what I could tell looked a lot like the pictures hanging on the wall. Happy pet owners with happy pets.

At the far end of the store, six robots lined the far wall with platinum skin and five blue eyes set in otherwise featureless faces. Each bot stood tall and slim, with three spindly arms hanging off each side. They were dressed in tailored black suits with a half dozen bow ties running down the center of their jackets. They didn't stand on legs, which surprised me, but rather floated about a meter off the ground using some sort of anti-grav technology. Probably pretty handy, when you thought about it. That meant they could always be at the proper height when addressing clientele of all kinds.

We'd barely been inside more than a few seconds when the bot in the middle darted over and stopped only a couple of paces away. "Good day, sirs and madams, as the cases may be," it said with such a refined and buttery-smooth voice, it would make any trillionaire's butler sound coarse. "Welcome to Porgie's Pets. My name is Sir Derrington Penelent Nolo the Fourth, but you may call me Mandred if you prefer. And you are?"

Before Fake Me could do whatever it was she was going to do to make things more complicated for yours truly, I stepped forward with a bright grin and thrust an open hand toward Mandred. "I'm the incredible and intergalactically famous Miss Dakota Adams," I said. "These are my friends."

"Ah, yes. Very good, Miss Adams," he replied. "How may I be of service to you this fine evening?"

Even though I knew we had pressing matters to attend to, which included getting Tolby and Jack to finally realize they'd been running around with a fake, I had to satisfy my curiosity on something. "Before I get to that, I do have one really quick question, Mandred: Where are all the pets?" I said, looking around one last time to make sure I didn't miss them. "I don't see any to choose from."

"Choose?" Mandred repeated. He then chuckled softly before clearing his throat and raising a hand to cover his mouth so he could recompose himself. "Begging your pardon, madam, but we're not *that* kind of pet store."

"You're not?" I asked, tilting my head to the side. A quick glance to the others seemed to show that they were equally as confused about this as I was, which was good. I didn't want to feel like the only one missing the obvious, especially if Clone Me had somehow figured it all out. The last thing I needed to be was one step behind again, even if it was on something as trivial as a pet store.

"Ah, no, madam," he said. "You see, our customers do not choose their pets. Our pets choose them."

Now it was Jack's turn to run after the proverbial squirrel. "They choose their owners?"

"Yes, sir," the bot replied, still keeping his refined voice, and although I knew he was about to go into lecture mode, there wasn't a hint of annoyance or condescension in his tone. He spoke to us as if we were royalty, which again, you've got to give marks for when it comes how to treat a customer. "Our pets are guaranteed to provide a literal lifetime of total happiness and companionship to every customer based on their individual preferences. As such, those who wish to purchase one of our fine companions must undergo a rigorous physical and psychological assessment in order that the pet can make the best choice as to who they want their owner to be. The entire process is detailed on page three of the brochure, if you'd care to read about it more in depth. I'm sure you'll find it very enlightening."

"Are you saying customers take a test so pets know who to pick?" I asked.

"Yes, madam," he said.

"Do they ever pick wrong?"

"No, madam," he said. "We use unparalleled technology that has to date provided unequalled results."

My mouth twisted to the side as a logistical thought came to mind. "You wouldn't happen to have like...a huge zoo in the back room or something, would you?"

"Ah, no, madam," he said with a light chuckle. "Your future pet, wherever he or she is at the moment, is currently enjoying life at one of our hundreds of care centers until a purchase has been completed. Once testing is complete and final payment is received, we will have the only companion you'll ever want delivered to you, free of charge, via the carrier of your choosing. Now then, would you like to see who is willing to be your proud animal companion?"

I was about to take him up on the offer because holy snort did that sound cool! I bet he (or she) even came with a fancy certificate detailing an illustrious bloodline in case you wanted to take him (or her) to shows. I wondered if I'd be matched with some awesome cat breed, on account of Tolby and I being so close, or maybe they'd find me more of a canine-lover, because let's face it, big dogs are awesome, too. Then I wondered if maybe I'd be chosen by some strange alien thing that lived somewhere I'd never heard of. Oh! Oh! Maybe I'd find out that Taz was my one and only! I mean, the little guy and I certainly hit it off right away, and he was super lucky. It was hard to imagine I'd be matched with anything luckier than that awesome little guy.

Anyway, as I was saying, I was about to take him up on the offer when Tolby clamped down on my shoulder with his giant paw and killed the fun in a heartbeat. "No, she doesn't," he said. "We've got other business to attend to."

"Very good, sir," Mandred replied. "Is this business something I may be of assistance to?"

"Yes," Tolby said with a nod. "We're looking for the Excel-Care facility. We were under the impression it's around here. Or was, at some point."

"Ah, yes, *that* store," the bot replied. "I'm afraid I'll have to be the bearer of bad news, then. You see, we took over its offices quite some time ago. As such, those offices are no longer in operation."

I groaned. Clone Me did as well. Didn't that just figure. "What happened to all the equipment?" I asked, hoping that perhaps all was not lost.

"Sold at auction, I believe," he said. "Well, the equipment we couldn't use was sold at auction. Some of it, despite the company's poor business model, was very useful and is used to complete the physio-logical workup of each customer."

I perked. Whatever they'd kept, some of it had to be the standard diagnostic stations Rummy told us about. "Could we see it?"

"Afraid not, madam," he said. "Trade secrets and all. But I assure you, you will not find better results at pet matching anywhere else, regardless."

Tolby's ears flattened across his head while his tail started to twitch. "We don't have time for this nonsense," he said. "We need to see that equipment. Now."

Mandred's eyes flashed to red, and the other five bots, who'd been motionless up until this point, fanned out behind him. "Your angst is understandable, sir, but I will need to respectfully ask that you mind your manners while inside this establishment," he said. "I do not wish to eject you from the premises."

Tolby growled, and the hairs on his back bristled. The big guy was always the peaceful type, recent events notwithstanding, but seeing how we were short on time, it felt like we were one bad verbal exchange away from the next World War opening up in the store. Thankfully, I had an idea. "Forgive my friend, Mannie," I said. "May I call you that?"

Mandred turned toward me, though the other bots seemed to keep their attention fixed on Tolby. "If you like, madam," he said. "It makes no difference to me."

"Sweet," I said, trying to sound as positive as I could. "You see, we're in a bit of a hurry, so we don't have time to be yanked around when it comes to purchases."

"Of course, madam. I wouldn't dream of uttering a single exaggeration, let alone falsehood, to any of our patrons. That would be so unbecoming."

"It would be, but..." I let my voice trail as I folded my arms.

"But...?"

"Two things," I said, holding up a pair of fingers. "First, if we do this, and I stress *if*, we're going to need a lot more help, as we'll be spending an obscene amount of money in here. Pampers galore, because that's what we really like."

Predictably, because I realized the bot was a salesman at heart, Mandred perked. "How obscene are we talking? Profane or *really* offensive?"

"Really offensive."

"Very good, madam," he said. "On my honor, we'll treat you like a movie star. You'll leave here feeling like the prettiest woman in the entire universe, with the most perfect pet, too, I might add."

"Which leads me to the second point," I said.

"And what would that be, madam?"

I sucked in a breath, mostly for show, but partly because I didn't know if anyone else would jump on my ruse as quickly as I hoped. I did, however, figure since Fake Me was a clone, she'd be having the same thoughts I was and I could count on her to roll with it. Or at least, she'd quickly realize what I was trying to do. So I looked at her with as much skepticism as I could manage without feeling like I was over-the-top and went on. "Do you really think they can tailor pets to anyone?"

She hesitated, but only for a moment. Her eyes sparkled with recognition, and she shot me the grin I'd only shared with my brother, Logan, from time to time when we'd work our parents. "I don't know. That's a bold promise. I mean, they probably couldn't even tell us apart. How would they know what pet fits us best?"

My heart soared. Course, at the same time I had to remind myself of what a backstabber she was, but at least she was going along with it. I guess she had to, in the end. Tolby would see right through any covert sabotage attempt in an instant, and then she'd really be done. "That's pretty much what I was thinking."

"Begging your pardon, madams," Mandred cut in. "But differentiating between twins is exceptionally easy. You may share identical DNA, but I assure you, the unique experiences each of you has had, even if they are merely slight shifts in point of view, are quite mappable."

Clone Me giggled. "See? He doesn't know. Let's go somewhere else. Remember those puppies we saw a few decks down? They were totes adore."

"Totes."

The two of us turned, and we started to head for the door. And thanks be to the furriest of furry Kibnali gods, Tolby caught up to our scheme in a flash and provided the last bit on his own. He leaned toward Mandred and said one little thing. "They're clones."

"Clones!" Mandred said, sounding energized and flustered. "Why, of course you two are. Such beauty and intellect could only come from a carefully tailored creation."

Fake Me and I paused and slowly turned around, each of us maintaining a look of healthy skepticism.

"Sure, that's easy to say after we told you," I said. "The real question is, can you tell which of us is the clone and which of us is not?"

"We absolutely can, madam," Mandred said.

We crossed our arms over our chests in unison and even spoke the exact same words at the same time. "Prove it."

"It would be my pleasure to demonstrate," he replied, floating over to us. From an internal side compartment, he whipped out a small box with a tapered edge and quickly pressed a slew of keys across its top.

A red-and-yellow series of light beams swept over us both, left to right at first, and then top to bottom. The hairs across my forearms stood on end with each pass, and my tongue dried and stuck to the roof of my mouth. Initially, I wasn't sure why my nerves had decided to get the better of me, but a glance to Little Miss Family Stealer cleared that confusion right quick.

Though her arms were crossed over her chest, her hands were a little too close to the blaster on her hip. She might have been playing it cool for everyone else, banking on Mandred's inability to actually out her, but I knew better. In her mind, she was Dakota Adams, and no test was going to tell her otherwise, and certainly no test was going to make her give up her friends and family. It was like Rummy had said: Fake Me planned on fighting to the death to keep everyone she loved in her life.

Guess I couldn't blame her when I got right down to it, but that wasn't going to keep me from ejecting her from my rightful spot in life either.

Once the scans were done, Mandred continued to work, all the while politely declining two offers to help from Rummy, as well as ignoring three sales pitches for the latest self-teaching aids regarding testing for clones. All in all, it probably only took a minute or two at the most for him to finish his work, but I swear, it felt like a thousand years.

"Results are in," he said, lowering the box before pointing to Fake Me with a finger. "I'm proud to say that you're the one."

"Ha! I told you all I was the real Dakota," I said with a hefty dose of smug on my face. "Now will you guys finally listen to me?"

"No, I'm afraid there's been a misunderstanding," Mandred said.

My heart stopped. "A what?"

"She's the original," he explained. "You are the clone."

CHAPTER SIXTEEN
ROCKED WORLD

I'm pretty sure my brain had a hard reset because some ungodly amount of time had to have passed before I realized Tolby was waving a paw in my face while the others had moved a good three meters away from me.

"Dakota? Can you hear me?" he said before tapping me on the shoulder.

"Guess she's catatonic," Jack said with a shrug. "And that's not Dakota. Not our Dakota at least. Now what do we do with her?"

At that point, I managed to completely snap out of it all. I blinked. I swore. I shook my head and repeated the whole process a few more times, and then once again for good measure to make sure the loop had five iterations instead of four. God, could you imagine the mess I'd have found myself in if I'd wound up doing that? Ew. My skin crawls just thinking about it, and I'd probably have to rub Taz's belly for a month straight just to counteract all that bad luck.

"I'm sorry. I've clearly had a brain aneurism," I managed to spit out. "Say that again?"

"Of course, madam," Mandred said, still as smooth and accommodating as ever. "The woman over there is the original Dakota Adams. You are the clone, not even a week old by your standards of measurement."

I heard everything he said. The neurons in my brain fired the audio signals to the right places of gray matter, and my bone-encased organic computer even managed to send the meaning of those words to the correct areas of gray matter as well, where they were processed accordingly. Despite all that, Mandred was wrong. I knew it. We all knew it.

I lunged for the little device he held. "Let me see that," I said, ripping it from his grasp. Looking back, I'm surprised he gave it up so readily given his hostile reaction to Tolby's demand to see the Progenitor tech they'd kept. Maybe it was a customer-service subroutine in his programming that let me do it. After all, from his point of view, he had a huge sale riding on all this. Whatever it was, I got the device, but I'll be a quadruplet-loving couch potato if I understood a damn thing it showed.

"Would you like me to interpret the results?" Rummy asked after a few moments of me staring blankly at the screen.

"Does that involve me listening to one of your sales pitches?"

"No, but now that you mention it, we are having a forty-percent discount sale on Mem-Loss, your premier pill for ridding yourself of any and all unwanted memories. Furthermore, if you act now and subscribe to our monthly delivery, you can save an additional five percent as well as enjoy free shipping to all orders within the Kappa-Seven quadrant. Would you like to know more?"

"Just tell me this thing is lying."

"This thing is lying."

Despite his immediate reply, my throat tightened, and tears welled in my eyes. "You're lying, aren't you?"

"No, I'm following instructions," he said. "Studies have shown that there is a zero-point-nine-eight direct correlation between being able to meet a customer's request and greater satisfaction when it comes to overall survey responses."

My heart sank to such a degree, I thought I'd die right there. I buried my face in my hands and forced myself to ask the next question. "Am I the clone?"

"Yes."

"You're certain?"

"Yes."

I wasn't prepared for the grief that hit me. But the total denial? Now there was an emotion I could get on board with. I mean, what the hell did Rummy know, anyway? He was just some stupid piece of AI software stuck inside a bracelet I wore. "Well, I'm sorry," I said, clearing my eyes with a sniff and then folding my arms across my chest. "I want a third opinion."

"Okay, but I'm still certain," Rummy replied. "You're the clone."

"Not from you! From someone who knows what they're talking about!" I yelled, throwing my arms up in the air. Gah! I could've torn him from my arm and chucked him across the store right then and there. It's probably a tiny miracle I didn't.

"We at Excel-Care have a large network of professionals dedicated to providing every diagnostic service you may need. Would you like to know more?"

"Yes, I want to know more! I want the list of every single damn one of them that will prove you wrong! I want a third opinion, and a fourth, and a tenth and a bajillion, bajillion to show you all that I'm the real Dakota!"

"In that case, I'm afraid the number of names I'll be able to provide you is exactly zero," Rummy replied.

"How do..." My already weak voice cut out as my throat closed.

Though I couldn't finish the sentence, I didn't need to. Rummy answered nonetheless. "Each clone has markers attached in both the seventh and eighth dimensions," he explained. "They are easy to test for."

Jack, despite his usually annoying personality of constantly hitting on me, came to my defense. Well, maybe not defense, but at least asked the perfect follow-up with genuine concern. "If it's so easy, why didn't you tell her from the start? Why let her think she's the real Dakota all this time?"

"Shortly after her release, the Nodari invaded the facility," he explained. "I didn't have time to issue the test, and to be honest, I had no reason to believe she was the clone. Now, however, who is who is unquestionable."

At that point, my knees buckled, and I collapsed in a blubbering heap of tears. Try as I might, somehow I knew he was right. I'd always known he was right. I lay there crying uncontrollably for what had to be a lifetime. My entire life was a lie. Everything that made me who I was was just a copy of someone else's experiences. None of it was real. My friends weren't mine. Neither was my family. I'd never felt so small, meaningless, and alone in my entire life—a life that existed for what...a few days?

Tolby scooped me up in his giant paws, and I nestled in his chest, burying my face into his fur—fur I'd know by touch anywhere. But it was still a touch built on a lie. I tried not to think about it. Try, being the key word. No matter what I tried to focus on, holding my breath, counting sheep, trying to name all the lucky numbers between one and ten thousand, I always kept careening back to the inescapable truth. I was a clone, and at that point, all I wanted to do was take off running to somewhere this could never catch up to me.

My hands trembled as I ran them across his body and squeezed him like the giant teddy tiger he was to me. "How can you not be mine?"

Tolby didn't answer. He was cool like that, knowing when he shouldn't. Instead, he stroked the back on my head.

"Tell me this is a bad dream," I went on. "Tell me we're back on Mars, and I'm going to wake up soon."

"I'm afraid not, Dakota," he said.

I swallowed hard at the name. I loved hearing him call me that, but at the same time, it cut me deep. As much as I would've given up anything for that to be my name, it wasn't mine. Not really. I didn't have one. Or if I did, it was probably some vat serial number.

"You have no idea what a nightmare this is," I whispered. "I can't believe I'm a fake. A fake...a worthless, pointless fake..."

"I do," he said softly.

"No you don't," I said. "It's not the same as when you were alone. At least you still had a place in the universe with me. I've got...I've got nothing. I am nothing."

Tolby gently spun us around so his back faced the others. When he spoke, his voice was so soft, even I had trouble hearing it. "I've never told anyone this," he whispered. "All my life I never felt I belonged in the Kibnali Empire. We always fought. Always went to war. Always killed, never tried to develop real treaties or relationships with others that didn't involve them ultimately being our slaves. But I couldn't say anything. To do so would be to speak against everything we were, to go against the Empress herself, too. For that, I'd be exiled to a frozen wasteland at best, executed on the spot at worst. So I lived a fake life, as cowardly as that was, and had bittersweet dreams of what a real life would be like, one I thought I could never have. At least, until I met you."

"Thanks, but that wasn't me," I said with a sniff.

"That's not the point," he said. "The point is, for the longest time, my life felt hollow, devoid of hope and purpose. But all that changed one day in the most unexpected of ways. As long as you draw breath, yours, too, can change. There's nothing out there stopping you from having a life of your own."

I spent a few moments in quiet contemplation, and then twice that when something dawned on me. "You haven't told anyone that?"

"Not a soul."

"Not ever...not even her?"

"Only you," he said, nuzzling my head. "And if you like, we can keep it that way."

My heart warmed as the magnitude of the gesture wasn't at all lost on me. I leaned back so I could get a better look at him. "I love you."

"I love you, too," he said to my utter shock and elation. He then smirked and chuckled. "As much as knowing you for a half hour will allow, that is. For all I know, you might turn out to be this adventure-obsessed crazy lady who gets me into all kinds of trouble. Then where would I be?"

I laughed and shook my head. "If I weren't, you'd still be stuck on a Helios IX with all sorts of nasty monsters."

"Good point," he said, tousling the hair on top of my head. "I suppose we might get along after all."

"And you'd definitely not have your feline space babes to hook up with," I added. "Though on second thought, for my own sanity, maybe that's not a bad thing."

"Jainon and Yseri would disagree. You really ought to get over this weirdness you have about mating. It's not that big of a deal."

"Says the guy not having to listen to it twenty-four seven."

Tolby shrugged, and after a moment's pause, Jack spoke up. "Okay. Now that that's sorted out, what do we do now?"

"She's coming with us," Tolby said. He then twisted his head over his shoulder to address someone else. "What? She is."

"I never said anything," Clone—er, Real Dakota said.

"You had that look."

"If I did, I'm sorry," she replied.

The tone of her voice caught me off guard. I sniffed, cleared my eyes, and patted Tolby's arm so he'd let me go and I could get a better look at her. Once back on my feet, I willed myself to look up from the ground and at...her. She stood a few meters away, nervously toying with a PEN, with her eyebrows raised in the middle and her mouth turned slightly down.

Again, her reaction wasn't one I'd expected. Had she been gloating, I wouldn't have batted an eye. Or relieved. Or even apathetic. But genuine concern? I didn't understand it. Why was she being nice to me? I tried to take it all from her. Part of me still wanted to.

"I know what you're feeling," she said. "Since you're wondering why I'm being nice to you."

My right hand tightened into a fist, and I wanted to clock here right there. "You have no idea what I'm going through."

"I do," she said, voice still soft. "I might not be a clone like you, but I'm not the original Dakota, either."

"How's that?"

Real Dakota laughed and rolled her eyes. "God, I don't even know how to make a short summary," she finally said. "Time travel shenanigans, mostly. I'm the forty-second Dakota in a big ball of wibbly wobbly, timey-wimey stuff."

"The forty-second?"

"Yeah. Apparently, the other forty-one Dakotas in this strange loop have all died trying to fix things," she said with a heavy sigh. "Not exactly great odds for us, is it?"

I shrugged, not sure how to answer and not seeing how this was supposed to make me feel better whatsoever. "At least your life is real."

"At least you aren't responsible for wiping out the Kibnali," she countered. "Yet another little Progenitor tidbit you didn't have to discover."

"Stop it," Tolby interjected. "You're not responsible for any of this, either. The Progenitors are."

"Maybe one day I'll believe that," she said before turning back to face me. "Point is, you get a youthful body, sweet Progenitor tech, and a fantastic personality to run around the universe with, and none of the emotional baggage attached to it. Moreover, we're both part of a long line of intergalactically famous and totally awesome Dakotas. So even if you are a clone, you're the 43rd Dakota to grace the Universe, which is a pretty big honor, as far as I'm concerned."

"I guess. I'd trade it all for a family," I said, still feeling like crap despite her attempt at a pep talk. "At least you aren't alone."

"We've got an extra bunk," she said. "Besides, it could be really fun to bring you back home and mess with the family. Not to mention, find treasure twice as fast."

"Or trouble," Tolby said.

"That too," she said, throwing in a wink. "It'll be fun. You'll see."

My breath left me. Was she really inviting me to stay? A glance at Jack and Tolby told me she was serious and that they didn't have any objections either. Did I dare believe that to be true?

"How about it, sis?" she said. "Want to come with?"

"Sis?" I echoed. I liked the sound of that. I liked it so much, I think I even smiled.

"Tolby? Dakota? I've got some wonderful news!" Daphne said, her cheery voice breaking into whatever bonding moment we had going on.

"What is it, Daphne?" Tolby asked.

"Maestro," she corrected.

Tolby let a little growl slip. "Okay, Maestro, what's this wonderful news? Did you find AO's ship?"

"Yes!" she exclaimed. "Well, no. I didn't. I can't take credit for that. Yseri and Jainon, however, did. I've just received a detailed report, and I'm proud to inform you that the quaint little Progenitor shuttle AO flew here on is now quaintly scattered in space in a trillion pieces. I'm compiling a highlight reel as we speak and putting it to some Sweet Tiny

Metal. I can't wait for you to see it. It really shows just where my talents are and how well deserved my title of Maestro is."

Twin Me put her hands on her hips and laughed. "I can't believe he's gone. I mean, like, that easy."

"Why's that?" asked Daphne.

"After all we've been through, are you kidding?" she replied.

"I suppose getting a Nodari armada dropped on your head would make anyone a little jumpy."

"Exactly."

"I think I should remind everyone, he's not gone, gone," Tolby said. "His ship is."

Feeling like I was missing something obvious, I hopped into the conversation. "Is that the same thing?"

"No," Tolby replied. "He's the AI for all Progenitor ships. He exists somewhere else, remember?" The second he finished that sentence, he cringed and shook his head. "Sorry. I forgot. You weren't there when we learned that part."

I ignored the not-so-gentle point, realizing I was going to have to come to terms with this clone thing sooner or later. "Are we at least safe from him?" I asked.

"As long as you don't go firing up anymore Progenitor ships," Jack interjected.

"I don't plan on it."

"Well, you guys can decide what you want to do when you get back," Daphne said. "You'll be happy to know the batteries to the portal generator will have enough juice to warp you back here in a couple of minutes, and our Kibnali commando buddies are already on board. I'll unlock the controls to the portal device so Dakota can bring you in."

As I sighed with relief at being afforded a quick exit off the station, the doors to Porgie's Pets slid open. I turned to see a metallic sphere with sky-blue circuitry all over its skin. The thing was practically as big as I was, and it zipped effortlessly through the air and into the store with a low hum.

While the droid had the telltale Progenitor drone designs of a circular body and a large, singular eye set in the center (in this case, the iris looked made from rose gold), that's where the similarities ended. From the top, a half dozen antennae swept backward, and mounted underneath on its belly hung a pair of double-barrel blasters that could probably turn a tank into Swiss cheese before I could bat an eye.

"Dakota Adams," the robot said in a deep voice, a voice I'd already come to both know and shudder at. "My apologies. Due to a trifling incident back at our ship, I'm late for our rendezvous."

CHAPTER SEVENTEEN
THE OFFER

AO?"

Stupefied, that was the only thing I managed to say. Real Me pretty much had the same reaction, except she tossed in a snort as well.

Tolby, on the other hand, had a much more Kibnali response. He raised his own weapon and snapped off a trio of shots from the hip. The plasma bolts hammered into the droid with a bright show of fireworks. Correction, they hammered into the droid's shields with a bright show of fireworks. Before shots four through ten could be fired, AO fired.

A long beam of molten death flew from one of the underbelly guns, striking Tolby's weapon dead on, carving a mass chunk out of the weapon and sending globs of molten metal in all directions. Mandred and his cohort of sales bots drew weapons of their own from unseen holsters, but they never got to fire them. AO fired six more times in rapid succession, punching a large hole in each of their heads. The sales bots fell to the ground, lifeless, with wisps of smoke rising from the holes set between their eyes.

None of us moved at that point. Hell, I don't think any of us breathed, even. A few beats passed in silence before AO brightened his eye and addressed us all. "Engaging in further hostile activities will not be tolerated," he said. "I come to extend a peaceful cessation of hostilities."

"Not exactly what I call a diplomatic negotiation if that's what you're after," I said, noting the smoldering robo corpses.

"A much more peaceful response than warranted," he replied. "Your friend escalated the situation without provocation. Total pacification of this room would have been a morally acceptable action to have taken."

"Hey, Daphne," Jack said. "I was under the impression this guy had been handled."

"Due to recent events, I'm afraid I will need to make a slight adjustment to the records," she said. "There we go. Now instead of saying AO is dead, let the record reflect that he's mostly dead."

"I'd say he's very much mostly alive," I countered.

"Mostly dead. Mostly alive. Who's to say what's what?" she went on. "Still, I've got to admit, now that he's here, my face is red with embarrassment. Assuming I had one, that is. Must be nice, really, to show expression so easily. Maybe I'll put in an order for a cyborg I can inhabit. I might like that. But at least we know what he was using the clone for. Isn't that nice? Mystery solved. That'll be nice, seeing how we've got a new mystery to attend."

"And what would that be?" I asked.

"My scanners are picking up a lot of blips headed toward me. I wonder if they're celebrants coming to party. Wouldn't that be fun? Party poppers and mimosas for all."

Tolby growled and flattened his ears. "I doubt that's the case."

"Hypothesis correct," said AO. "I have activated a full wing of NF-210 autonomous fighters. Each one is more than capable of tearing your ship apart should these negotiations sour."

"I think I would've preferred the mimosas, even if I can't drink," Daphne said.

"Uh, any chance you can outrun them before they get to you?" I asked.

"Oh sure," she said. "But I couldn't come back if I did. I've calculated that there's almost a ten percent chance you don't want that to happen."

"Ten?" I echoed.

"Ha. Stupid decimal point. I meant one hundred."

Tolby glared at AO as his claws kept flicking through the air. "Talk," he said. "You've got our attention."

"I have more than your attention," AO replied. "I have total control of your lives. As you can see, I am no longer bound to the ship I was once in. This droid, too, is now a mere extension of myself. I do not care if you destroy it."

"I take it this means you've got control of the station?" I asked, taking a stab at what the situation now looked like. After all, what else would it be?

"Your hypothesis is correct," he said. "Now that I have achieved this, I wish to fulfil the rest of my directives involving the Kibnali Purge."

"I'm not going to let you harm any of them," I said, stepping between AO and Tolby.

"Your physical body lacks the capacity to offer any sort of meaningful shield to your friend," he said. "Regardless of how pointless it is for you to try and stop me should I attack, at this time, I am not interested in killing either you or him, provided adequate terms of surrender are reached."

"You wish to surrender to us?" Jack asked with feigned shock and amusement. He then offered a sweeping bow while grinning broadly. "Very well. We accept."

"Attempt at humor will not convince me to alter my demands in your favor," AO replied. "For the sake of expediency, I suggest we stay focused on the issue at hand. Due to the Progenitor's extended gratitude for your service, Dakota, I am still compelled to offer you a way home provided you agree to an implant that will ensure you do not attempt to return to this time and place and try to save the Kibnali. Your companion, Jack, may join you as well."

Twin Me flipped him the bird. "That's what I think of your offer. How about instead, you shove a black hole right up your...your...well, whatever it is you have where the sun doesn't shine, because you're out of your damn mind if you think I'm going to leave Tolby and the others."

"Your counteroffer is duly noted and foreseen," he said. "Your continued defense of and love for the Kibnali is understandable, but ultimately misguided. Sadly, you have romanticized their nature and are blind to horrors they inflict on all those who are not like them."

"They're not all like that!" she said with a glare.

"Incorrect assertion based on incomplete and faulty data," he replied. "The Kibnali are a blight upon the universe and will enslave or destroy all civilizations if allowed to continue to exist. As such, their complete eradication is of utmost importance and not up for negotiation. That said, however, I am willing to make one concession that may be of personal interest to you."

Twin Me eyed him skeptically. "What's that?"

"I am willing to implant the same extradimensional chip into Tolby and allow him to return with you as well," AO said. "He alone will not be able to repopulate the Kibnali due to inability of having a female partner to procreate with. Thus, you two will be able to enjoy a life together, and when he finally dies, so will what's left of the Kibnali Empire."

Twin Me didn't hesitate in her response. "Again. You. Your whatever. Nice, big black hole."

"Refusal to generous terms noted and recorded," AO said. He then turned his body slightly so that he and I were facing each other directly. "Dakota 43, aka The Clone, before these negotiations come to an end, I am willing to extend you the same offer."

Creases formed in my brow and my jaw dropped a centimeter or two as I processed it all. "Me?" I said, sticking a finger in my chest.

"Correct," he said. "You will find that despite the opinions of the less informed, both the Progenitors and myself wish to operate in a fair manner. Just as all of the previous iterations of Dakota before you were unwitting agents in our plans and were offered suitable payment and compensation for their efforts, I wish to do the same for you."

"But...but I'm a clone," I stammered. "I've done nothing."

"Though I could not prevent it due to paradox backlash, I had the foreknowledge of an earlier Dakota sabotaging my ship back on Kumet and forcing me out of the controls," he said. "As such, nanoseconds prior to my ejection, I engineered the installation of memories into you, as well as your activation and release inside the cloning vats with the sole purpose of ensuring I reached whatever facility the forty-second iteration of Dakota decided to go to."

"You let me go to track them down?"

"Yes," he said. "Due to ingrained limitations set by the Progenitors, I was unable to restart the shuttle we used on Kumet to get here. Thus, I needed you to awaken its systems using your implants so I could occupy the main controls," he said. "Now that we are all here, you can see that you performed your assigned tasks competently and are due for compensation."

I went to speak, and to be honest, I'm still not sure what I was going to say, but he beat me to the punch and tacked on one final thing. "Before you preemptively reject my offer, I would also like to point out that if you decide to return to the Milky Way, you will not only have friends and family of your very own, but I can erase any and all memories of all that has transpired. You will essentially wake up in your apartment on Mars like none of what transpired after the museum ever happened, thinking you were picked up by a rescue ship in the *Revenant*'s lifeboat."

"None of it?" I echoed. I wish I could say I was some sort of holy saint, free of any and all temptation, but I wasn't. My mind drifted as it thought about the possibilities. I could be home, with my bud, with an actual family who loved me, wanted me, kept me. Best of all, I wouldn't have to be constantly reminded I was a copy of someone else—a fake.

"None of it," AO assured. "Or, you can opt to stay here. In which case, you will suffer one of many terrible deaths your predecessors all have."

Tolby dropped a heavy paw on my shoulder and drew me back. "She's not interested, and neither am I."

His rough response felt like a slap across the face. I hated myself for even considering the offer and hated myself even more for not being the first to reject it. How could I abandon Tolby like that or make him sacrifice everything he lived for? I wouldn't be able to live with myself if either of those things happened.

That, however, didn't mean I was about to roll over and die for AO, either, especially when a terrific idea popped into my head. Hopefully, neither Daphne nor Twin Me would ruin it.

"How long do I have to consider all this?" I asked.

"Sixty seconds," he replied. "But if you'd like the opportunity to think about things quietly, I'll be happy to stun everyone else in the room. In fact, if you'd like, I'll even knock out Tolby and make sure he's sent with you, one way or another."

Tolby twisted toward me, his eyes wide with worry and the hair bristling on his back. "Dakota. Don't."

The fear in his voice was palpable, and I knew that by me not giving him any sort of answer, he was about to have a coronary or two. But I couldn't talk to him at that time since I needed to reach out with my implants to try and find the portal device onboard the ship. After all, if Twin Me could use it with her implants, then I could, too.

My brain scoured vast swaths of nothingness, desperate to find whatever elusive connection there was. The sensation is hard to describe, especially to those without any real experience to it all. It was like being blindfolded inside an empty stadium, spun a dozen times, and then told there was a silver coin somewhere on the field. Everywhere I searched, it felt like tiny blades of grass were scraping across my palms without a single hint to where I should go. I could only hope and pray that these mental fingers of mine would stumble on said coin.

"Thirty seconds before I rescind my offer," AO announced.

I kept up my search, ignoring the looks and whispers of those around me. Thankfully, a few moments later, I brushed against the connection I sought. I felt the click in my head as the ship's portal device became an extension of my mind. I had no idea how it worked, but I had to trust that it worked the same as Jakpep.

Before I could use it, however, I heard another pop in my mind.

Dakota, is that you? Daphne whispered in my head.

A version of her, but yeah, I thought back.

How clever! You've connected with my internal comms. Do you know what this means?

Yeah, I'm hoping it means you can tell me you can warp us out of there in a flash.

Well, yes, I could tell you that, she said. *But it also means we can have girl talk whenever we want. It gets lonely here without a dedicated BFF, you know.*

AO started to count down from fifteen, and I sprang into action. A rolling landscape of numbers and formulas filled my head, and looking back, I probably shouldn't have smiled on account of AO floating there, watching me. But even if he did notice, I guess he noticed too late to do anything.

A beautifully round portal leading back to the ship bisected him perfectly, and I promptly used my telekinetic punch to split him in two.

"Go! Go! Go!" I yelled, making a mad dash for the portal.

Everyone plowed through the wormhole like rabid shoppers pushing through the front doors at an Ultra-Mega Limited-Time-Only Crazy-Savings-and-Deals Black Friday event at the local DD-Mart.

I stumbled coming out of the portal into the ship, but I did manage to spin to the side to keep from being trampled while using a nearby handrail to keep me upright.

"Daphne, get us out of here!"

"Maestro."

"YOU KNOW WHAT I MEAN!"

A loud explosion left a ringing in my ears, and the ship lurched sideways, throwing us. The floor rocked violently in the other direction, tossing me yet again. I smashed the side of my face into a computer console, and Jack ended up on top of me right as we leveled out.

Something like the sound of metal beams twisting under an immense load put a knot in my stomach. The world shuddered and bubbled around me, and then with a deep, hollow-sounding thud, it all snapped back to normal.

"Nothing like a good dogfight and emergency jump into hyperspace to get your blood flowing," Daphne said merrily over the speakers. "Still, should've stretched a bit first. Could've pulled a muscle or something. Then where would we be? I'll tell you where: out for the season."

Jack groaned and pushed himself to his feet before offering me a hand up. "I don't even care how quirky she is right now, seeing that we're still alive."

"Me either," Real Me said, laughing underneath a computer station near a corner. "Does this mean we're safe?"

"We are as long as no one ventures into the galley and lets all the vacuum in," she replied. "The good news is the blast got the blender."

I cringed. I was hoping we'd gotten away unscathed, but I knew I shouldn't complain about being on the good side of luck in our escape.

"Thank Taz that's all it got, right? Anything else we need to worry about?"

"Those fighters are probably following us," she said after a moment's thought. "They'll probably try and kill us once we both drop back into real space."

"Ugh. That figures."

Tolby's face soured. "Well, we better come up with a plan in the next few hours to deal with them then."

"Speaking of plans for the immediate future, now would probably be a good time to ask: Where would everyone like to go?" Daphne said. "I'm assuming we're not going back to that station."

"I still want to go home," I said. "Are there any other webways we can use?"

"In theory, yes."

"And in practice?"

"I have a half dozen leads of varying quality."

I felt my stomach tighten and my face scrunch. "How varying in quality are we talking about?"

"Oh, you know, ranging from terrible to keep dreaming."

I sighed heavily as my shoulders fell. "Well isn't that peachy."

Twin Me did and said the same, and we both laughed. "Tell Jainon and Yseri to meet us in the Ops room," she then said. "We'll go over our options and make a decision there."

"Or you could make a decision there," Daphne countered.

"Say again?"

"They're on their way to the portal room," she explained. "Along with everyone else."

I turned as the door across the room slid open with a hiss. Yseri stormed through with Jainon and ten other Kibnali following. The handmaiden scowled the moment her eyes locked on my face, and she instantly pointed her rifle at my chest.

CHAPTER EIGHTEEN
MORE FIGHTS

Yseri!" Tolby yelled, jumping between us. "What are you doing?"

"She's an agent of the Progenitors!" she shot back. "She has to be destroyed!"

"Are you out of your mind? She just saved us!"

"Or is biding her time to kill us all instead of only a few."

"I'm not going to let you kill anyone," Tolby said with a growl. "We've got enough troubles without having to invent more."

Yseri shook her head and narrowed her eyes. "I've put up with you and your infatuation with your pet for far too long," she said. "But this...this thing isn't even real. It's an abomination—an abomination that we know without a doubt works for the very enemy that killed us all."

"She's not a threat," Tolby said.

"How many of us have to die for you to say otherwise? Of course she's a threat."

"Look at her, Yseri! She's scared out of her mind! She's not going to do a damn thing."

Talk about the understatement of the millennium. The entire time they went back and forth, terror rooted me in place. It wasn't just Yseri who'd set herself against me, but all of the other Kibnali as well. Fanned out behind her were ten feline soldiers I'd never seen before, who looked every bit as deadly and determined as Yseri. Off to the side, even Jainon was a part of it all, rifle clutched in her paws. Thankfully, both the other Kibnali and the High Priestess had their weapons pointed at the ground. That said, I wasn't about to bet my life that any of them intended to side with me.

Yseri stepped forward, rifle still up, and as she spoke, her voice turned cold and calculated. "Tolby, the Empire must survive," she said. "I don't want to shoot you, but I will if I must, as you are no longer the only male alive. That thing cannot be allowed to survive."

"The hell you will," Twin Me said, snapping her own weapon up.

In a flash, weapons were drawn and pointed at each other on all sides: those sides being Twin Me and Jack versus eleven Kibnali. The only ones who didn't have a gun pointed at another's head were me, Tolby, and Jainon. Well, X-45 didn't have a weapon either, on account of his being torn off by that Urg back at the bar, but he did stay at my side, crouched, looking ready for a fight.

"Stupid furry-meats," my little robot friend said. "Your incessant distrust will be your undoing-deaths."

"I told you they were like this," Jack said, his eyes darting around the room while he had his super cannon pointed at the nearest Kibnali who pointed a gun right back at him. "We'll always be expendable."

"I never said you weren't," Yseri said.

Twin Me shook her head, and I could see tears glisten in her eyes. "Empress never felt that way."

"And look where that got her," Yseri countered. "Her blood is on your hands, and I don't intend to see any more of ours spilled."

I felt my jaw drop and my heart skip a beat. Empress? Dead? Dead because of me? Somehow, my gaze drifted over to Jainon. The High

Priestess and I—well, Twin Me—had had some bonding moments, hadn't we? Did she hate me as much as Yseri did? I had to know. "Jainon," I said softly. "I'm not who she says I am."

"I know our Dakota is not, and I know Empress never regretted a thing she did," she said with a solemn voice. "But you? Who knows what subconscious desires AO has planted in your head? I'm afraid she's right. Your presence here is a chance we cannot take. Now Tolby, please, step aside."

"No," he replied, not flinching. "She's Dakota."

"She's a clone! Nothing more!" Yseri spat.

"With the same memories, the same wants, the same everything as the Dakota we know and love," he shot back. "That makes her Dakota. I will not let anyone harm her."

"I can't believe you'd say that."

"I can't believe you'd argue against it," he replied. "What are we if not the sum of our bodies, memories, and personalities? She has it all."

For the first time in the exchange, Yseri seemed unsure of herself. She glanced over her shoulder back to her sister. Jainon, in turn, sighed heavily as her tail flicked nervously behind her.

"Tolby's words are not without wisdom," Jainon said. "I suggest a compromise. We bind her, drop her off on a planet where we know she has a chance to survive. At least then her fate will not be sealed. Not by us, at least. If she's as much our Dakota as the original, the gods will watch out for her."

Yseri lowered her weapon a few degrees. "What of her arm? I'm going to guess you won't let me amputate it."

"You're right. I won't," Tolby said.

"Then what would you have us do? Simple bindings will not keep her contained. We've all seen what she can do with those implants. She could tear this ship apart with them."

"I believe I can help with that," Daphne said. "There is a class four surgical arm available for use. With it, I can short-circuit her implants, rendering them all useless. We could then transport her to wherever with ease."

I loved my implants, and I wouldn't have been keen on losing them. But losing Tolby, again? I couldn't bear the thought of that. I reached out and touched the back of his arm. "No, please," I begged. "I can't be alone in the world. You don't know what that's like."

"I know what that's like, Dakota," he said. "I would never put you through that."

"Stop thinking like a kit," Yseri said. "You know you'd make the same decision in my shoes. I've *seen* you make the same decision for others. Would you rather see her die right here and now?"

"I would never hurt you," I said. "I would never hurt any of you!"

"That's right, you won't," Yseri said.

When she raised her weapon again, I looked to Jainon for help, but I could see in her eyes she wasn't going to come to my aid. Jack and Twin Me showed me more sympathy, but since they'd stopped pointing their guns at the other Kibnali, it was pretty clear they weren't willing to die on this hill either. Still, I had to try.

"Dakota," I begged. "You know me more than anyone. Don't let them do this to me."

She shook her head and muttered a few curses before sighing heavily. "I'm sorry. I don't see any other choice," she said. "Tolby, listen to Jainon and Yseri. When we've reestablished your Empire, we can come back and pick her up."

"That assumes we can, or that she'll still be alive," he said.

"I'm tired of talking in circles," Yseri said. With a twitch of her ears, the other Kibnali around her pointed their weapons at Tolby and me once more. "We've given you a way to save her life and save ours as well. Either agree to our terms right now or prepare to give a full account of your life to the gods."

"My soul is ready," he said with an unnatural calm. "I will not be the one to bring dishonor to our species."

Yseri nodded, remorse splashed across her once hardened face. "I want you to know I will name my firstborn male after you," she said. "And he will give me many fond memories of the time we had together."

The handmaiden straightened, but before she could fire, I sprang forward, pushing Tolby to the side. "Stop!" I said, arm outstretched. "I'll go. Do whatever you will to me, but don't hurt him."

"Dakota—"

I shrugged off the paw Tolby put on my shoulder and didn't dare throw him even a glance. I had to keep strong, had to look forward, lest I fail. "I know what I'm doing, and I'll never let you die on my account," I said. "I am the fang and claw of the Empress, and I know she'd want you to live to see the Empire rise from the ashes."

All eyes went to Yseri, and the handmaiden kept silent for a few seconds. "Very well," she said with hints of respect in her voice. "But if I even catch the faintest scent of something odd, I'll tear your head from your shoulders before you can blink an eye."

CHAPTER NINETEEN
THE LETTER

Did you know getting a tattoo used to hurt?

Weird, I know. That's a little bit of trivia I learned not that long ago when I was looking up the history of ketchup. Apparently, ketchup used to be slathered on all sorts of things like hamburgers (patties made from dead cow) and French fries (pieces of this plant called a potato dipped and fried in oil) instead of simply being a garnish for dessert. And before it was a popular food item, ketchup was used as medicine. For some weird reason, a little before the 5th century PHS, people believed it had medicinal properties. Then they decided it tasted better than it cured.

Anyway, back to the tattoo trivia, which has a point, I promise. So yeah, tattoos used to hurt because they didn't have nano-injectors or artisan bots. They also didn't have adaptive inks that could be repositioned or removed if you happened to be the one-in-ten-billion customer who ended up being the recipient of a minor mistake.

It also meant that whatever you got was, for all intents and purposes, permanent. Not a bad thing at all if your artist was a good one, but apparently there were a lot—and I mean A LOT—of bad artists peddling crappy drawings that you'd have to live with for the rest of your life.

Thought you were getting a cute baby elephant inked on the inside of your forearm? Surprise! It's a deflated balloon animal and it's about as cute as three-day roadkill. Want something badass? You got it, as long as you aren't trying to impress anyone over the age of three. Even then, with what some of these guys put out, you'd be rolling the dice.

So, to top all that off, how they'd give you these tattoos was with a basic needle that would stick in your skin somewhere around fifty to three thousand times a minute while at the same time, depositing tiny droplets of ink. Compared to the few minutes it takes now to get the ink of your dreams, it was a long, long process, but to my original point, it could also be incredibly painful, too, depending on the location.

All you could do was sit there in the chair, try to not think about what was going to happen as the needle drew close, and hope for the best.

That's pretty much the position I was now in, except I'm pretty sure that those who frequented tattoo parlors in the 5th century PHS weren't strapped to a diagnostic chair inside a medbay while three giant space cats kept guns pointed at their head.

"Is this going to hurt?" I asked, my eyes focused on the machine above and its thin, wicked-looking needle that jutted from its underbelly.

"No," Daphne replied.

I blinked and lifted off the seat as much as the restraints would allow. "Say again?"

"Oh, you meant for you?" Daphne said. "Since you'd asked that exact question not even a minute ago, I assumed you were asking for me. I'm afraid the answer still hasn't changed. Yes, this is going to hurt. A lot."

"A lot, a lot? Or like, a lot a little?"

"A lot as in, being flayed alive would be a step down. Or three."

I cringed. "Maybe you're wrong."

"Maybe," she said. "But I'm not."

I shut my eyes and tensed. Would it be over quickly? I hoped so. My mind went back to the tattoo trivia. What if it lasted for hours? What if she stabbed me over and over again for what would feel like an eternity and when I couldn't take it anymore, I tore free of my restraints, only to get promptly shot six times in the head and twice that in the chest?

"Is there any chance I could get a drink?" I asked, popping one eye open. "Something with about twelve shots of Saturnian rum ought to do it, but feel free to up that to eighteen if you want. Liver be damned."

"You seem anxious," Rummy said. "I am proud to offer you the perfect solution that is guaranteed to ease all worries by sixty-four percent and increase overall fondness for family members by a factor of one-point-seven. Would you like to know more?" He paused for a half beat before continuing on in a soft, fast voice. "Excel-Care makes no warranties, expressed or implied, and hereby disclaims guarantees regarding merchandise."

I laughed at the absurdity of it all. It even made me feel good, or at least, not as utterly terrified as I was seconds ago, and that was always good. "Sure," I said. "Why not?"

"An excellent choice," he went on with unbridled enthusiasm. "As a VIP member of Excel-Care, I'm excited to enroll you in our eCard of the month club, a fantastic service were you can send and receive up to forty-thousand unique cards each month, specifically tailored for ninety-seven million different occasions, with one-point-twenty-one gigabit encryption, for the low price of twelve thousand credits a week, billed per decade, cancel at any time after your sixth billing cycle."

I smirked. "Is that all?"

"A steal, isn't it?" he said. "But wait, there's more! You get your first day free!"

"Well that's something," I said, chuckling. "How about we start with the free trial and go from there. Daphne, want me to send you a card?"

"Only if it's addressed to Maestro," she said, sounding irked. "I must say, I'm feeling a little slighted now that you keep insisting on using my carbon-based-lifeform-assigned name."

"While you think about that, I'll set up your account," Rummy said. I could practically feel his excitement radiate through my arm. "All right, let me just add this to that, sign off your acknowledgements and waivers for you...annnnndddd...done! Congrats on your new account. Oh! Look at that."

I lifted my head off the chair as I looked down at my bracelet. "Look at what?"

"You've got a card already."

"I do? Like a Welcome to the Club card?"

"No, well, I don't know, to be honest," he said. "But it's from you. Addressed to you. Weird."

"That is weird," I said. "How do I view it?"

"Maestro, may I borrow your screen?" Rummy said.

Daphne gave him the go-ahead, and the screen next to me flickered to life. A cartoon drawing of a beachside house with a huge palm tree out front popped up. As a happy little sun with cool shades made its way across the top, a little jingle started to play, and then scrawled in flowery handwriting were the words "Wish You Were Here! Love, Dakota."

The sun stopped near the corner, and the music went into a loop with the tree moving gently back and forth over and over and over again. I waited for a few moments, expecting it to do something, anything, before finally shrugging. "That's it?"

"It's the thought that counts," Rummy said.

"But like...that's *it*?" I said again, putting a heavy emphasis on the last word. "I mean, you said I sent this to myself, right? So...how? And why?"

"And when?" Daphne tacked on.

I arched my eyebrows and nodded at that point. That was a damn good point. Rummy, however, wasn't much help in that department. "I'm afraid I don't have access to such details," he said. "Even if I did, customer privacy is of the utmost importance."

"Privacy? For who? I'm the one who sent it," I said incredulously.

"That's one theory," Rummy replied.

"Who the hell would send me such a weird card and sign my name?"

I'd barely finished the question when the screen flickered again, and the picture distorted like someone had taken a magnet to it and pushed everything around. A black circle formed in the center, taking up nearly a third of the screen, while the music grew louder and louder.

"What is going on?" one of the Kibnali guards asked.

"How should I know?" I said.

One of the other guards snorted and hit the comm button to his armor. "Yseri, you'll want to come up here."

"On my way," she said.

Less than a half minute later, the door to the medbay slid open and Tolby, Jainon, and Yseri bolted inside. Had Yseri not been joined by my best bud, I'd have put my immediate odds of survival at fifty-fifty. She'd always been a no-nonsense kitty, and I could see it in her eyes she didn't want to deal with me any longer. I felt as if Jainon were leaning that way, too, though that might have been my nerves getting the better of me.

Yseri's eyes flickered across the room before settling their gaze on the monitor. "Is this what you called me up about?"

The guard was about to answer when the music stopped and the warped picture dissolved into a flat gray on which another letter began to appear, although this time instead of the flowery handwriting that had been done before, the words used in this one looked as if they'd been done by a six-year-old wielding a crayon for the first time.

Dearest Clone,

Hiding this is hard. Fourteen of us died to get it. Twelve more perished trying to use it; thirteen if I fail, too. You're the first of your kind. Use it to your advantage and chip away.

c5b7f651-3b54af55-edb970d8
1f935a1f-d8c3deb9-eac7dc50
6d83840f-d319b7df-da2e729f
e082e62d-c2a93983-91becfbb
bb995dd1-91d2c711-fcfd4408

Love,
Dakota 41

CHAPTER TWENTY
WHAT NEXT

I didn't have anything to do with that," I blurted out. "Rummy said I had a letter and Daphne put it on screen. I have no idea what's going on."

"She joined our eCard of the month club," Rummy tacked on. "As a close family member and/or acquaintance, I can add you to the plan for fifty percent off the usual subscription price. Would you—"

"No, Rummy! Just be quiet! For the love of god, don't say another word!"

Tolby dropped a paw on my shoulder and gave it a squeeze. "Relax, Dakota. Let's just see what we're dealing with."

"Easy for you to say," I replied with a huff. "You're not the one about to lose a head."

"And neither are you," he said. He then craned his head over his shoulder and stared at Yseri. "Right?"

"For now," she replied, the top of her lip twitching into a brief snarl.

Tolby growled and squared off with the handmaiden, and as the conflict between the two started to rekindle, fur bristled not only on their backs but on all of the other Kibnali as well. "This isn't the first time a prior Dakota has reached out to help us," he said. "We'd be foolish to ignore it."

"That assumes we should trust any of them."

"Nonsense, sister," Jainon cut in. "We've seen the gods bless us with her presence firsthand. Besides, if any of the previous incarnations of our tailless friend were our enemy, they could've killed us all long ago. If we are to survive, we can't succumb to paranoia or worry about the possibilities of the most convoluted traps."

Yseri crossed her arms over her chest and grumbled a few words under her breath. "You might have a point," she admitted. "Well, Dakota, since this letter is meant for you, I assume you understand what it means."

"Hell if I know," I said with a shrug. "All I can do is point out the obvious: whatever that code is at the bottom, it must be incredibly important seeing how I died a lot to get it and nearly as many times trying to use it."

"Maybe it's a code we need to crack," Tolby said as he patted himself down. "Gah, where's my tablet? No need. Daphne, can you decipher this for us?"

Daphne, who'd been quietly humming to herself up until that point, stopped. "Who?"

"You."

"No Daphnes here," she said. "Would you like to leave a message?"

I groaned and rolled my eyes. "*Maestro*," I said, making sure disdain dripped from every syllable, as her quirkiness wasn't something I was in the mood to entertain. "Can you figure out what this is all about?"

"Why yes, yes I can," she replied with a bubbly voice. "In fact, that's what I was doing all this time already."

"Lovely. Made any progress?"

"I have," she replied. "I'd originally thought it was an encoded message as you had, but then I realized it was something else."

"And that would be?"

"A decryption key."

"To what?" Before she could explain the obvious, I clarified. "I mean, do we know where the encoded data is?"

"We do not," she said. "But I do. I found exactly what it went to in under fourteen seconds. Are you sitting down? I think you'll want to for this news. Oh, right. You are already."

"Just spit it out, already," Tolby said with a huff.

"Irritability is often a symptom of poor stress-management skills," Rummy piped up. "I'd be happy to refer you to one of our thousand expert Palipatra yoga instructors who will gladly assist you in finding inner peace."

Tolby dropped his brow. "I'd have a lot more peace if we could hear what Daphne found," he said. "Not to mention, less of a desire to shoot you out of the airlock."

"He's right," I said. "Can we get back on track?"

"Certainly," Daphne said, pride filling her voice. "I'm happy to announce that hidden inside the archive cube were a couple of things: First, there was a set of coordinates that I can say with a confidence level of ninety-nine-point-nine-nine-four-three are the coordinates of AO's location."

Energy filled the room, and I could practically hear everyone's mind race with the possibilities. Tolby was the first to speak. "Do you mean AO's location as in where he is back on the station we just left?"

"No, I mean AO's actual physical location," she replied. "Or rather, where his core is. He's spread across eight dimensions, but he does have a sizeable portion of his vital components in a pocket universe we can reach that, if destroyed, will effectively render him inert."

I took in a sharp intake of breath and nearly pulled a muscle as I jerked against the restraints. I didn't know what AO's death would mean for the Kibnali in terms of saving most of them from the Nodari invasion, but I did know that if we could kill AO, it would mean we all had a chance at a future.

"How can you be so certain?" I asked.

"Remember that scenario builder suite I used earlier?" she asked. "I used it again. So awesome. Statistically speaking, there's no other set of unknown coordinates that you would die repeatedly to try and obtain, or once you had them, repeatedly die in order to use."

Jainon's pupils widened and her body relaxed as she stared aimlessly off in space, clearly lost in fantasy. "The ability to strike our enemy's heart at our fingertips..." she murmured. "Dare we entertain such dreams?"

"A heart that is surely protected like no other, sister," Yseri said as she pointed a claw to the screen. "Dakota has tried many times to cleave it in two, no doubt with help from us as well. Yet each time, she's failed."

Jainon grinned, showing off her razor-sharp teeth. "Except this time we've got two Dakotas. This will be the first time AO has had to deal with that."

"It is also likely that the AO of now is not the AO of before," Daphne said.

"What do you mean?" Jainon asked.

"Again, going by scenario building, previous Dakotas have repeatedly struck AO and managed to cause some sort of permanent damage," she explained. "As AO lacks the ability to use webways on his own, he'd be limited in his ability to make repairs. Thus, his defenses now are not as tight as they once were, which would explain Dakota 41's instructions to keep chipping away at him. Death by a thousand cuts."

"There might be something to that," Yseri said slowly. Though her voice was steeped in skepticism, I was thrilled to see she no longer seemed to hold the utter hatred she'd had for me. "Assuming Daph— Maestro—is correct, and also assuming we can somehow get to those coordinates, we don't know what's waiting for us once we arrive, let alone what AO looks like, what his weaknesses are, and so on, no matter how much damage he may have suffered. If we had a full Kibnali armada at our claws, I wouldn't think twice. But we're a single ship with a single squad of commandos. If this is to be a covert op, we need specifics."

"That leads me to the second item hidden on the cube," Daphne said. "The complete blueprints of AO's core. I'm running analysis on it now."

"Inaja's luck is still ours," Jainon beamed.

"It won't be if we don't capitalize on this," Tolby said. "We need to plan our attack."

"I'll have the plans as well as my analysis ready for you in the Ops room," Daphne said. "Unless you want to sit here in the medbay and crowd around a tiny monitor."

"No, but I would like something else before everyone runs off," I said.

"What would that be?"

"Someone to untie me," I said. "Especially before you all run off and Jack wanders in."

Seventeenth birthday. I'll never forget it. Sigh...okay, Real Dakota's seventeenth birthday I'll never forget. Man, that's so depressing to think about.

Enough pity party. Back to the story. So my brother Logan got put in charge of organizing something special. Parents gave him a budget of a few hundred credits and let him plan it all. He ended up taking me, Mom and Dad, and a half dozen others to Splatageddon™, the premier paintball field near New Cherry Point, Republic of North Carolina. I never played paintball before and had no interest in it either, but I've always been the adventurous type since I scaled my first rocking horse as a tiny tot. So it's not like he made a poor choice based on my tastes or anything.

We played I think seventeen games in all. I stopped counting after the eighth game because I wasn't having a whole lot of fun learning what a terrible paint-slinging soldier I was, not to mention a monumental failure as a tactician. I walked into every ambush set by the other team, stood up when I should've stayed low, and once wandered off the field and ended up guarding a service road because it looked like a good place the enemy might attack from.

(I still maintain it was a distinct possibility. The rules never expressly said they couldn't).

So, by the last game, thoroughly disheartened at how readily everyone had written me off as a complete liability, I was determined to prove my worth. I mean, the staff took so much pity on my team, they even let their new guy (who was adorably cute when he got nervous talking to me) join our team to help even things out.

That final game was a match of capture the flag. We got five minutes of setup time before the start of the match, and for the first half of that, we all stood in a huddle and hashed out the details of who was doing what and whatnot. I didn't follow a lot of what the overall strategy was going to be. Something, something flank here. Feint there. Hold this line at all costs unless this, that, or the other happened, in which case fall back to sector Charlie niner-five-seven (or whatever it was called). Everyone got to pitch their ideas, of course, except me, of course. No one wanted to find a lucky elephant to rub, but they did want to make sure I knew we were the ones with red armbands, not blue (I might have gotten a little trigger happy earlier and wiped out three players when they came crashing through the brush at me).

Anywho, that's pretty much how I felt in the Ops room as thirteen Kibnali discussed all the options when it came to wiping out AO once and for all. I had no idea what they were on about for most of it, other than the main goal was to destroy him, and Daphne had brought up a wire-frame view of AO for everyone to look at via hologram.

189

Well, that's not entirely true. I understood a few of AO's possible weak points, as well as the fact that there was an insane amount of internal security. Oh, and apparently, this portion of AO's core that we were attacking was the size of Mercury. And though I sat through the discussions mostly clueless as I had before in my final paintball game, I also refused to be useless.

Besides, I had an idea, assuming I'd heard Daphne's brief correctly a while back, and that was always debatable. But Taz had appeared in my lap only a few minutes ago and was currently attacking my foot in the most ferociously adorable way, and thus I knew in my heart of hearts, it was all going to work out.

That said, I did need a clarification on one point before I fully pitched my idea to the group.

Grinning like a schoolgirl, I raised my hand as the room grew silent over a deadlock on ways to proceed because not a single idea thus far didn't involve lots of dying—and no one in the room was a fan any dying, let alone lots.

"Can I point something out that seems to be missing from all of this?" I asked.

"Did I forget to upload something to the display?" Daphne replied.

"No, but according to that letter, this is the first time AO has had to deal with me," I said. "If we don't capitalize on that, I don't think any of your ideas are going to work."

"She's got a point," Jack said. "A second time-bending little hottie could be just the wildcard we need."

The group surrounding the circular holo display came to an immediate agreement, and Tolby leaned back, his tail happily swishing behind him, despite the stern look on his face. "A well-timed surprise can topple any foe. So, what does having a second Dakota do for us, aside from needing to stock twice the root beer when we get home?"

"Jack gets twice the rejections," Jainon said with a snicker.

"A small price to pay for twice the eye candy and the occasional smooch," he said, taking the jab in stride. "I still think we should compare kisses though. I mean, how do we really know our new Dakota is exactly the same as the original? We don't, and knowing that little bit of trivia might be the difference in life or death for us all."

I shot him a deadpan look. "Seriously? Now?"

"I don't see why not," he said, not losing a beat. "If we're all going to die in some multi-dimensional suicide mission, we ought to make the most of our time together. You could do a lot worse, you know."

"I could do a lot better, too," I said, drawing back one corner of my mouth. "I mean, we're still going to get your brother, right? Is he seeing anyone?"

Jack rolled his eyes and threw up his hands. "Gah! Seriously? You, too?"

I snickered and looked to Original Me. "Let me guess, you asked about him already."

Original Me grinned and shrugged unapologetically. "Can you blame me?"

"No. He's gorgeous."

"I bet funny, too."

"And has a fantastic butt."

"Okay! Okay!" Jack said, shooing at us with a hand. "Can we get back on track?"

"As long as we're entertaining the ideas of mating partners, we should have Inaja bless your wombs before battle," Jainon tacked on. "A pair of impregnated Dakotas would fight with such ferocity for their unborn, we'd be practically guaranteed victory. You could always build a partnership with Jack's brother later."

"I said it before, and I'll say it a thousand more times if I have to," Original Me said, laughing and holding up her hands. "You're not blessing my womb, and I've no plans on being impregnated by anyone."

Tolby cleared his throat, which thankfully got us all back on track. "If we're done with that, what else can we do with two Dakotas?"

"Throw double the phantom punches," I said.

"Plug into two pieces of Progenitor tech instead of one," Original Me tacked on.

Jack cleared his throat and pointed to his arm. "Ahem."

"Sorry, forgot you managed to score some discount implants," she said.

"Discount or not, I can still plug into everything, Jakpep and webways included."

I perked, having forgotten about his implants as well. "Three people who can make portals? That's definitely got to be good for something."

"It would be if we had a webway to use," Yseri said while sinking back in her chair. "AO has control of the only one we know about. Even if he can't use it, he might destroy it to keep us from gaining access to it."

"Well...there's got to be another one somewhere, right? I mean, supposedly the Progenitors had them all over the universe," I said. When everyone looked at me confused, I kept going. "How did you guys plan on getting to AO's pocket universe to begin with if not through a webway?"

Tolby snickered. "I don't think we've gotten that far in our planning."

"We could always use Jakpep," Original Me offered. "We'd have to power him somehow. I used up all the energy in the drycell battery back on Kumet, remember?"

"Could we plug him in somewhere?" Jack asked.

"Like where?"

"I don't know. Anywhere. The ship engines?"

A shared look of I-have-absolutely-no-clue spread across the room until X-45, who'd been installing a new plasma cutter in his shoulder where the old one had been ripped off, piped up. "Siphoning power-energy is simple-quick," he said. "Drawing enough for spacetime manipulation, however, has cost-cost."

"What would that be?" I asked, nervously tapping my fingers on my thigh.

"The drain will cause the ship to drop-fall from hyperspace and will only hold a portal open long enough to allow one person to move-move through spacetime. Pursuit fighters will catch the ship soon-quick after-after."

Jack flopped back in the seat with a groan and kicked his feet up. "Well, I guess that idea is out."

"But if one of us goes, the other could still open another portal, right?" I asked, still thinking my yet-to-be-pitched idea was a good one.

"Yes-yes. Should be able to make second and third portal as needed."

"At which point, either yours or our Dakota's brain will be mush," Tolby said. "Not that that's anything new, but that seems to be a big liability if we need all hands on deck due to a fighter attack."

"Which doesn't matter if whoever we send through destroys AO, right?" I said. "If those fighters aren't getting orders, they'll leave us alone, according to Daphne's spiel she gave."

"In theory," Yseri said.

Jainon shooed a paw at her sister. "Stop your negativity. All we have is theory right now."

My face beamed at Jainon's support. I quickly pointed to AO's holographic schematic on display. "He's powered the same as the Museum of Natural Time was, right?"

"This portion of him, yes," she replied, highlighting six small sections well beneath the planet's surface on the schematic. "Each of these areas siphon energy from hyper giants across the universe. Why? Are you thinking about opening another museum?"

"No, I was thinking maybe we could get those portals to malfunction and destroy AO the same way we destroyed the museum. We did it once. We could do it again."

"That was a combination of fluke and worn-out parts that summoned that star," Tolby said. "I've no idea how we'd manage that a second time."

"Explosives," Yseri said. "No need to get fancy."

"The reactors are deep inside an inhospitable portion of AO's being," Daphne said. "Reaching them is unlikely."

"Unlikely as in...one in a hundred?" Yseri asked.

"More like one in a million."

I frowned and balled a fist in frustration, but I didn't want to give up on this idea just yet. "There's got to be some sort of regulation station, some place engineers could use to perform system maintenance, that I could jack into and bring it all down, right?"

Daphne drew a little white box around an isolated structure near one of the planet's poles. "That would be this control room," she said. "Heavily guarded by laser turrets. Laser drones. Laser fighters. Probably laser sharks, too, but those weren't listed anywhere. You'd need a dozen Kibnali battalions supported by half their fleet to take it by force."

I studied the map for a bit, not ready to give up. Sure enough, there were tons of defenses, but as I started to mentally mark them all down, I realized they were either all on the surface of the planetary computer, or only in select areas inside. "They're mainly external defenses," I pointed out. "Look, even where the control room is, there aren't any. There's a huge build-up of them at the bottleneck that leads into that section of the map, but none actually there."

"Interesting," Tolby said, leaning close. "Why would that be?"

"Perhaps the Progenitors couldn't risk that area suffering any sort of damage," Yseri offered. "That would make sense if this portion is responsible for control of the power core."

"It would also give the Progenitors a way to always shut AO down if need be in case he went rogue," Jainon replied. "After all, they didn't trust any of their droids with the operation of the webways. They probably wouldn't want to fully trust an extradimensional computer, either."

"Perfect," I said, smiling to myself at how clever I was for spotting the weakness. "I just jump into the non-defended area. Stroll into the control room. Shut down AO. Easy as pie."

"That control room will still be cut off," Jack pointed out. "You'll have to get by three security doors. I doubt you'll be able to crack the security there. I'm not sure I'd trust using explosives, either. How do you plan on doing that?"

"There will likely be maintenance droids in there as well since something has to physically tend to it all," Yseri said. "They might not be armed with weapons, but I'd assume they'd be able to kill nonetheless—certainly before you got past the security doors."

"Droids, shmoids," I said. "I can do it."

"How's that?" Jack asked.

"With wormholes," I said, grinning. "How else?"

"But Jakpep will be hardwired into the engines," Yseri said. "You can't use him if you're in a pocket universe, can you?"

"I don't think we want her brain going to mush inside AO's world, either," Tolby rightly pointed out. "She'll probably end up thinking she's at an amusement park and start looking for the nearest rollercoaster."

"I bet it would make a great ride, though," I said, grinning. "A ride...*to die for.*"

Jack groaned. Tolby did the same. I shushed them all with a wave of my hand. "Hey, I didn't say it was a good joke. Anywho, I don't need to make the wormholes. Either Original Me or Jack could do it, right? Maybe with a little help from Maestro somehow?"

Original Me shrugged. Jack looked equally clueless. Daphne, however, turned out to be anything but. "With some help from X-45, I could fashion a device that would make your eighth-dimensional markers glow for a short time," she said. "I can monitor those, and once you send a signal, we could open up pre-planned wormholes. I'll have to assist Jack and Dakota in the real-time calculations when they tap into Jakpep, and they'll both have tapioca brains for at least a day afterward and won't be able to do anything at all during that time, but I think it could work."

"Basically, you'll send up a flare when you're ready to get in, and then again when you're ready to leave," Tolby said when he saw I wasn't following completely. "Just don't miss either portal when they spring up, because there aren't any second chances with them."

"I don't need second chances. I've got Taz," I said, scooping him up and rubbing the little guy's belly. "This is going to be perfect. You'll see."

Though everyone else seemed at least optimistic that this plan had promise, Yseri kept her arms folded across her chest and a scowl on her face. "I don't like relying on a plan that revolves around her completing one of the hardest special operations ever concocted with zero training on such things. Even our own elite commandos and recon units would be hard-pressed to accomplish this task in a group, let alone on their own. And from what I understand, we can only send one person through the portal before it collapses."

"I can do this," I said. "I *have* to do this."

Even though Yseri and I were separated by ungodly amounts of time and space when it came to our species, there was no way I could've missed the ginormous amount of skepticism she wore on her face. "Of all of us here, you're the least that has to do anything. You've no stakes in any of this. You're just a clone."

I felt my eyes mist and gut sink at the painful remark, and that pain doubled when I could see everyone else shared the sentiment to one degree or another. "I might be just a clone," I said, voice cracking. "But the memories I have of all of you are very real. You might not see me as your friend, let alone family, but I love you all. And you know what else?

It'd be nice to actually have a memory of my own for once that mattered. To be able to say to the world 'You know what? I did that. I did that all on my own, and it was real, and it mattered.' So you can take that opinion of yours and shove it right up your ass."

The room fell silent, and since my mini rant was done and I had nothing left to say but my eyes were puffy and my nose leaked copious amounts of snot, all I could do to follow up was wipe my nose on the back of my hand and stare mindlessly at the floor.

They didn't understand. Hell, I probably wouldn't either if I were in their shoes. How could anyone know what it's like to be a total fraud, desperate to prove herself otherwise to the world?

An arm snaked its way across my shoulders, and I turned to find Real Me snuggling her head against mine, eyes glistening. "You know," she said in a near whisper, "I only tolerate Logan because I have to. I always wanted a sister."

I sniffed. Hard. Then laughed. "Yeah, I know," I said. "When I was little—I mean, when you were little, you tried to get Mom and Dad to take him back and get a little girl."

Real Me gave me a squeeze and kissed the top of my head. "When we were little."

"I stand corrected," Yseri said, much to my surprise. "I won't doubt your heart, but your ability? Absolutely. Neither of you are skilled enough to pull off what you're suggesting. I had to rescue you from a handful of Ratters, some of the most pathetic creatures in the galaxy. What chance do you have in AO's world on your own?"

Murmurs of agreement ran through the group, and I have to admit, I even felt as if the wind had been stripped from my sails. There was no faulting Yseri's logic or concerns. I was a terrible soldier, still couldn't hit the broadside of a cruiser if it was more than a dozen meters away, and was hardly a battle-hardened soldier who could shrug off countless injuries to complete the mission. Practically every big fight I'd been in, I'd had Tolby to see me through.

197

My eyes drifted over to my bud. "I wish I had…"

Tolby cocked his head to the side as my face lit up. "What's that look about?"

"I was going to say, I wish I could bring you along to protect me," I said. "But then I realized, I can."

"How's that?"

"Okay," I said, resting my elbows on the table and leaning forward. "Follow me on this, because it's going to be a little timey-wimey and we're going to have to wipe a memory or two in the end…"

CHAPTER TWENTY-ONE
FINDING TOLBY

Ever kiss a snowman?

Me either. But I did pretty much make out with a huge snowbank when I dropped two meters in the air and plowed into one, so that's probably the same thing. Icy cold stabbed my face, numbed my skin, and no doubt left my cheeks and nose a rosy red by the time I collected my wits and rolled onto my back.

Stars from a familiar night sky twinkled above me, and I spent a few moments trying to figure out how I knew them. The view wasn't quite the same as what I'd see from my home back on Mars, but portions of it were pretty close—albeit skewed—in many places, and in a few others, the constellations looked practically spot on.

I sat up, powdery snow falling off my red, modulated armor, and scanned the area. Thankfully, the two large moons above provided ample light, so I wasn't trying to pierce the gloom. Thick, white-capped trees formed the start of a forest a little ways away down a hill, while off to my left I could hear the quaint sounds of a babbling brook. None of it looked familiar, but in the back of my head, I felt like I should know where I was and possibly more importantly, what I was doing there.

Had I gone for a midnight joyride on a snowmobile and gotten tossed? Maybe, but the lack of speeder wreckage said otherwise. Hit with a tranq dart so organ snatchers could sell my kidneys on the black market? Probably not since I wasn't leaking blood out my back, even though that hypothesis might explain the grogginess I was experiencing. Besides, my kidneys weren't worth much anyway seeing how I was and always would be total organic—Progenitor tech aside.

Gah. What was it? And why was I in Kibnali armor? That wasn't my style, even if it did make a girl like me totally badass—or at least, semi badass. Enough to fake it at least. Anywho, I never got around to wearing the stuff because it makes exploring a massive pain in the ass as it hinders the most important things while treasure hunting like climbing, squeezing, and most important of all, not scaring the bejesus out of the librarians when you go to do your research. I'm not sure if they were always this way, but you can't exactly stroll into your local library looking like you're one misplaced book away from leveling the place. To top it off when it came to reasons to not wear full combat armor, the helmets—which I wore, complete with a retracted faceplate—reduced peripheral vision, which could easily mean I'd miss an important clue or an apex predator about to make me a snack.

As I pushed myself to my feet and worked out the stiffness in my joints, I noticed on the inside of both arms I had something scrawled across in black ink. On my right arm were seven long strings of digits and then the words "AO's World" written off to the side. On my left were six sets of digits with the words, "Helios IX," and then under that was a simple command: *Find Tolby.*

My chest tightened as the tempo of my heartbeat grew faster and faster. Had I lost him again? Or had I yet to find him? My head ached along the back and through my temples as I tried to piece my memories together. I could remember everything at Kumet, and even a bit afterward as I chased Tolby and that best-friend-stealing bitch of a clone across the galaxy and to a spaceport. No. It wasn't a spaceport. It was a Progenitor shipyard, or had been at least, right? Yeah...I had that part down.

But the shipyard wasn't a shipyard anymore. It'd been taken over by all manner of creatures and pretty much turned into a giant commercial mall or something. But I did find Tolby at some point, hadn't I? Or at least his trail? Did they get the webway there working, maybe, and I followed them to whatever planet this was?

I drummed my fingers on my breastplate, and when that didn't help fill in the blanks, I looked myself over thinking I might have left myself another clue or two. Apparently, I had the foresight to know my brain would be scrambled, so I was pretty hopeful I'd find something else.

A large plasma pistol hung off my left hip, and attached to my right were a couple of power packs for it, each one full. Tolby might have been one to run around carrying that much ammo, but I wasn't. I could only assume that meant where I was headed, it wasn't going to be a peaches-and-ice-cream kind of place. On my belt, I also found a little winged calculator-looking thing as well as a sweet RazoR ice axe.

"The thing you're looking at is the multi-phase subatomic matrix analyzer," came a tiny, muffled voice.

I jumped and screamed in fright before spinning around, trying to find who was talking to me.

"Whoa! Dakota!" it said again. "No need to panic. It's only me, Rummy. I'm inside the armor on your left wrist."

"Rummy?" I repeated. The name sounded familiar, which helped me get a grip. I wasn't sure how to take the guards to my forearms off, but I could angle them so I could get a peek inside at my wrist. There I saw a cute little bracelet, and memories of my time with Rummy came flashing back. "Oh! Rummy! Yeah...sorry, I forgot who you were for a minute."

"That's okay," he said. "Because you'll be happy to know that a full, uplifting life review is available for purchase and immediate delivery for the low cost of nineteen ninety-nine. Plus, if you act now, I'll throw in a deluxe spatula that is guaranteed to flip your pancakes, eggs, French toast, or Dexican pie with a simple flick of the wrist. Would you like to know more?"

"You're selling spatulas now? Now that's the weirdest pitch you've had yet."

"Yes...well, no," Rummy said, sounding disheartened. "To be honest, my brother got involved in a spatula pyramid scheme. I'm trying to help him move his excess inventory. But they are still a fantastic product. Would you like to know more?"

"How about you just give me the rundown on what I'm forgetting," I said, giving my arms a brisk rubdown to get some warmth back into them (which turned out to be pointless, thanks to my armor).

"You don't want the life review? It even comes with music and optional commentary, which if I may say, is hilarious when it comes to yours."

"No, but I'm going to guess by the fact that I'm in Kibnali armor and I've got a new plasma pistol strapped to my side, wherever I'm going is going to be rather dangerous," I said, shaking my head. "I'm also going to guess that if I don't know what's going on, you've got a high likely hood of being destroyed, too."

"Good point," he said. "However, I should point out that I'm still a program, and self-preservation isn't always at the top of my hierarchy of needs, especially when I'm behind on my sales quota for the month. And I have to say, while running around with you has been interesting, it's definitely impacted my numbers."

"And how much more do you think those numbers will be impacted if either or both of us are killed?"

Rummy grumbled something I didn't catch. "You drive a hard bargain, Miss Adams," he said. For the next ten minutes or so, he caught me up on all that had transpired and the fact that my recent memory loss was due to my interfacing with Jakpep once he was plugged into the engines and I made the jump to this planet. Actually, minor correction, his explanation on all that took ten minutes. We lost another half hour or so when he got to the part about me being a clone and I argued, cried, had a nervous breakdown, and then argued again before I finally came to semi-terms with it.

"Any questions?" he asked.

"Only if I've got my recap wrong: I sent myself to Helios IX to the time and place where I first met Tolby, to get him as a personal escort, because he can't be killed thanks to paradox issues since I'd never make it this far without him, and together we're going to find the Progenitor facility on this planet, warp to AO, sabotage his reactors, and warp out again before we're obliterated by the resulting explosion? Then, to keep the future from changing too much, you're going to wipe this portion of his memory before we send him back to this time and location."

"That's the plan everyone agreed to, yes."

I sucked in a nervous breath and exhaled sharply. It flew out in a white cloud and hung in the air, giving me something to focus on as I thought about it all. The thought of having such an intricate, apparently carefully laid out plan to follow with no recollection of how any of it came together left an unsettling feeling in my stomach.

"All right, well, I suppose we ought to get looking for the big guy," I said as I started to work the multi-phase subatomic matrix analyzer. At Rummy's suggestion (which turned out to be a reminder of things discussed prior to my memory loss), I used the Kibnali armor as my sample and then started searching for lookalike signatures in the area since not only would any armor Tolby be wearing have said signature but so would the ship he crash-landed in. Or at least, some of the gear inside still had Kibnali tech.

The side of my mouth curled into a snarl when I failed to get a signal, and I hoped it was simply because I was doing something wrong and not because my portal across the universe and millions of years was off a bit. I guess I should've been glad I'd at least made it to the planet.

That said, if I happened to be on the wrong side, that could complicate things, especially since as memory served (which again, was always doubtful) Helios IX wasn't tourist-friendly.

Killer animals. Killer plants. Killer diseases. Oh yeah, and a couple hundred scavengers swarming the place who were all out to kill anything and everyone who got in their way.

The last time I was here—or would be here, I guess—both Tolby and I barely got out alive. I am rather fond of that story, near-death aside, as when we met, we were practically BFFs at first sight. Well, maybe not *right* at first sight. He did try to kill me, but that was only due to a misunderstanding. Still, I made a mental note that when I found him, it would be a good idea not to be running full tilt in his direction with a weapon in hand.

I continued to make tweaks to the scanner as I worked my way down the hill. Snow crunched underfoot, which was normal, but I couldn't shake the metallic taste in my mouth. I knew it was lingering effects from brain mush, but that usually cleared up after a few seconds of portal hopping—definitely by a minute. But since I still had that awful taste in my mouth, I started to worry that said brain mush might be a permanent thing.

"Come on, stupid multi-phase thingy," I said, tapping its side a few times with the heel of my hand. "Do your magical stuff and find my soon-to-be BFF."

"I don't think that's going to work," Rummy chimed in. "Maybe if you—"

The scanner beeped excitedly, and a green arrow popped up on screen showing the direction of an eighty-eighty percent match on a lookalike signature, not even six kilometers away. "You were saying?" I said, grinning.

"I...uh...maybe we should add that to the troubleshooting section of the companion book?"

"Sounds good," I said. "I expect my share of royalties. Oh, and you'll want to add in a bit about having a lucky elephant, too, I promise."

"You'll have to talk to the publisher about royalties," Rummy said. "I don't handle that."

"Yeah, I figured that much," I replied. "Oh, speaking of royalties, did you know that I was working on my own book the first time I came here? *Dakota's Survival Guide for the Avid Treasure Hunter.* Or something like that. I never really settled on a name, I guess. But it was going to be chock-full of great info, tips, and rules to follow if you wanted to be an intergalactically famous xenoarchaeologist and treasure hunter like yours truly."

"I was under the impression you had yet to achieve fame and fortune," said Rummy. "I'm not sure what sort of platform you'd have available then to market your books. Might I suggest either *10,000 Ways to Be a Super Massive Success as an Indie Author* or *Burying the Competition: Tips from a Mob Boss*? Both have been utilized with great success, and in some cases, increasing earnings twenty-seven thousand percent (results not typical)."

"Well, I'm not famous, yet," I admitted. "But that's only a technicality at this point. I mean, once I get home—once *we* get home—it'll all be downhill from there. No one else has found the stuff I have, let alone traveled through time or across the galaxy."

"Maybe."

"Not maybe. Definitely! Follow my rules and stick to the plan, and you, too, can have awesome adventures others only dream of. Want to know what my first rule is? I'll give you three guesses."

"What do I get if I do?"

"I don't know," I said, shrugging. "I'll buy a starship full of spatulas off your brother when I'm rich. How's that sound?"

"Hope you like cooking lots of eggs," Rummy said. "Okay. Let me think...your first rule has to be cardio, right?"

"Ha! Not even close," I said, hands on my hips.

"Limber up?"

I pressed my lips together, trying to suppress a grin, and shook my head. "Nope."

"Don't be a hero?" he asked timidly. Before I could reply, he quickly changed his guess. "No, wait. I mean, be the hero. That has to be it."

"Sorry," I said, feeling a little bad for the guy. I could hear it in his voice throughout the entire exchange that he really wanted to move some spatula inventory. Maybe I could help him on that, too, regardless. Like set up a mega store for spatulas. Spatula City. I mean, I know it's stupid, and a little hilarious at the same time, to have aisle after aisle of different spatulas to buy, but since I was actually going to be ungodly rich (thanks to the sale of the resonance crystal that I assumed I'd get at least a portion of the money from) not to mention ungodly famous (you know, time traveling, space hopping clone with Progenitor tech installed and all), I could afford to have a few eccentric hobbies and investments. Hell, when you got right down to it, being famous pretty much required at least a half dozen oddities.

"It's get yourself a lucky elephant," I explained.

"Cardio seems better."

"Cardio is great and all, but that won't save you when all your carefully laid plans go belly up, which they will," I said. "Trust me on this. When I had my tiny plastic pachyderm, he was the best."

The conversation died, and I reached the forest a few minutes later. Getting through it was more arduous than I'd first expected on account of thick snow and rough terrain. More than once I nearly twisted an ankle finding an unexpected divot or stray stone. And though the moons above still provided decent lighting, I really wished I had more. As I'd mentioned before, Helios IX wasn't a friendly place.

This little factoid became even more obvious when I eased over a small rise and happened upon a pair of two-headed demonic canines, straight from a horror flick. They each stood hunched over a fallen something or other, faces full of gore as they stuffed themselves with a midnight snack. Even bent low, their shoulders came up to my ribs, and across their body they had long quills instead of cuddly fur.

I took in a sharp intake of air as a total of sixteen eyes fell upon me, four in each of the doggos' heads, and I immediately had flashbacks to my first time on this planet. Back then, or back in the future? You know what I mean. Anywho, last time I was here, I'd barely been on the planet at all when I ran across one of these Hannan terror beasts, and despite my excellent gunslinging abilities (i.e. nonexistent), I nearly died escaping it. The only reason I'm even alive was because Tolby saved me, but now there were two creatures and no Tolby.

"Easy there," I said, beating a slow retreat with my arms outstretched. "The last thing you want to do is chip a tooth on my armor. I promise."

"I would suggest running," said Rummy. "They don't look friendly."

"They're not. They're hungry."

"Still?"

"I've got the feeling they never stop being that way."

"In that case, I would like to second my own motion of running."

I guess they still didn't know what to make of me, because they didn't charge right away. That said, they didn't exactly leave me alone either. The larger of the two started toward me in a slow, methodical way, while the other began to move to my left, clearly intending to flank me.

With my right hand still up, I slowly drew my sidearm, and then wondered if it would do any good, especially in my off hand. I mean, in Tolby's paws, sure, but I wasn't the kitty commando. That said, I knew I was probably going to have to throw some telekinetic punches, and when my arm went numb and my hand became useless, I figured it would be a really bad idea to lose my grip on my gun.

The beast in front of me roared, charging forward with its mouths open. I darted right to put distance between myself and the other as

207

well, and socked the monster in the head with a phantom punch. I guess thanks to the frenzied, life-or-death situation, I didn't hold back on the punch one bit. The beast's left head exploded like it'd been hit by a train, and it crumpled to the ground, midstride.

My celebration lasted less than a second, which was the time it took for beastie number two to pounce. I managed to see it flying through the air, maws agape, before it struck, and thus also managed to flop my now mostly useless right arm in front of me for protection.

The terror beast's first set of jaws clamped down my right forearm, but despite the monumental increase in pressure, the armor held. Thank Inaja and her never-ending luck the Kibnali knew how to protect themselves, because without that armor, I'm certain my arm would've been torn off in a flash.

The second head bounced off my left elbow as the creature's body slammed into me. We tumbled to the ground and ended up with me on my back and the monster on top of me, still trying to chew its way through my armor.

Razor teeth flashed across my face, giving me plenty of foul slobber and putrid breath. I tried my best to keep the terror beast at bay using my feet, but the thing felt stronger than a rabid rhino. Not that I've seen any of them close up, mind you, but I did read about one poor guy who came across one. Went about as well as you'd expect.

I managed to kick the monster hard enough in the belly to get it to back off a split second, which freed my left arm that had been trapped between us. Then, when it drove forward again, trying to sink its other set of teeth into my neck, I shoved the pistol right down his stupid mouth.

"Snack on this," I growled, pulling the trigger.

A bright orange plasma bolt flew out of the back of its head, spraying charred bits of flesh and bone in all directions. Like the other terror beast, this one instantly went limp and fell on top of me.

"I can't believe you did that," Rummy said as I pulled my hand free of the beast's mouth. "You have no idea how disgusting that was. Sometimes I really wish I wasn't programmed for relatability. It'd be nice to not care about some things."

"Still, better than being eaten," I said, laughing as I squirmed out from underneath the dead monster. Once I got to my feet, however, my face twisted into a look of revulsion. Not only did my left arm look like I'd been rooting around in a carcass, but I had so much blood covering my chest and abdomen, a butcher three sheets to the wind probably looked cleaner than I did.

The soft crunch of snow grabbed my attention. I spun around in time to see something massive and covered in fur attack. Before I could think, say, or do anything, it jabbed me with a stun baton.

Electricity exploded from the head, racing through my body and sending me into convulsions. I dropped to the ground with a quiet thump. My vision darkened as wisps of smoke found my nose.

Consciousness slipped away moments later.

CHAPTER TWENTY-TWO
INTERROGATION

Around the time I was twelve, I took a keen interest in being an escape artist. It was one of those rare skills that people possessed that was cool no matter how you cut it. Not to mention, if you ever were hogtied, stuck in a burlap sack, wrapped with chains, and given a pair of cement shoes before being tossed off a bridge, it would be nice as you were sinking to the bottom that it was no big deal.

And so for about five months, I learned everything I could about how to escape from ropes, cuffs, jail cells, and so on. Most of my training revolved around how fast I could pick the lock to a vintage Mad Matt: Fury Canyon footlocker I got for a birthday present when I was seven. It was deftly kept secure by a total of three nefarious tumblers which would snap into place if you sneezed hard enough.

So you might say I didn't exactly become the master locksmith I'd hoped I'd be. Then toss in the fact that no one had used a lock and key for serious security in centuries, and you might say my lock picking skills were nonexistent, even if I had managed to score a fine set of rusted picks at a nearby pawnshop (dude traded them to me straight up for Darian Redwood's rookie Rocketball card that was barely in fair condition).

Did that stop me from trying to tease the Grim Reaper? If you said anything but "hahaha, yeah right," you haven't been paying attention to my story at all. Now, I didn't do anything like convince my little brother, Logan, to tie me up, strap a blindfold to my head, lock me in a safe, and eject me out the airlock to our family's corvette as we did a sightseeing tour near the famous Remani blackhole cluster, but that's only because we wouldn't take that trip for another two years.

No, instead, what I did was give him a set of cables, an old padlock I'd found in the junkyard by Dad's favorite R/C car racetrack, and I had him strap me to a metal chair after we made a pretty sweet Rube Goldberg machine that would knock me off the high dive to our pool in thirty seconds once it was started. You know, to add a little extra excitement to it all. I mean, anyone can get out of anything, eventually, I reasoned. If I were going to test my abilities and really grow as an escape artist, I needed a challenge.

Did I drown? Obviously not.

But did I escape? That's a big negative on that one, too.

The thirty seconds passed far faster than I'd expected, and right before the machine knocked me into the pool, all I'd managed to do was chafe my wrists and put a bruise on the inside of my left ankle. I sort of freaked out at that point and flopped around in the chair, and since I was on the high dive, there wasn't a lot of room to flop around in, and so I toppled off the side. My executor, the Rube Goldberg machine, ended up being my savior because in my panic, I got a foot tangled in a rubber hose so that when I fell, I didn't drop into the water, but ended up suspended in midair, about two meters above the surface.

I guess the reality of my predicament sank into Logan at that point, because despite my reassurances that everything was fine and this was all part of my master plan at getting free, he screamed bloody murder.

Which of course, summoned my parents and earned me a subsequent grounding, despite all my continued upside-down escape attempts.

Blah.

I bring this little story up because I hadn't thought much about that minor incident (and Mom and Dad's complete overreaction to it all), until I woke up, dangling upside down from the ceiling of a makeshift brig with my hands tied behind me. Thick, brown tubing wrapped around my ankles and held firmly to an anchor point in the ceiling, while florescent lighting from two corner lamps lit up the area. One of said lamps stayed continually on, humming as it did, but the other flickered with the occasional pop and spark, which didn't inspire a lot of confidence in me regarding the structural integrity of the place.

That thought was further amplified by what I could see about the rest of the place. My prison probably had been a storage place at one point, because I could see several tiedowns in the room, which was normal, but the olive-colored vines that had wormed their way out of the panels in the floor and ceiling? Not so much. In fact, I could make out a lot of flora, dirt, and even some rock down the hall that led to my little room. It was as if wherever I was, it had been built underground and was slowly succumbing to the planet's vegetation.

Did I mention I was naked as the day I was born? No? Well, I was, and since I was suspended from the ceiling, I'd hardly call my situation one that gave me a flattering look. Goosebumps covered my skin thanks to the crisp air, and the nailbeds in my fingertips had turned blue. At least my hair was out of my face.

Speaking of planets earlier, what planet *was* I on? I shut my eyes to try and focus my thoughts, but that didn't help clear their swirling, muddy nature. I remembered those two-headed dog things. I remembered chasing...chasing who? Holy snort, it hurt to think about anything beyond what was transpiring right then and there, which wasn't much.

I went back in time, or forward...was it? And that definitely scrambled my brain. I knew that. At some point, someone attacked me. Yeah, that was it. Knocked me silly with a stun baton right after I killed those terror beasts. I exhaled slowly, pleased I'd managed to piece that bit together. Maybe there was hope yet to figure things out, but I feared getting hit with a bajillion volts might have made my usual memory loss due to hopping through time more of a permanent Dakota feature.

I bit on my lower lip, trying to work out the rest. I spent maybe two minutes at the most when I simply gave up and decided I ought to work on getting free, getting my stuff, and getting the hell out of there before things got even worse. I mean, who knows what giant furry horned monster had made this place its home? If that were the case, I probably wasn't a prisoner. I was its next meal, hanging in its food pantry.

At least I hadn't been skinned alive. I've heard that's happened from time to time to those ambushed by aliens.

The first thing I did was to try a hanging crunch to get a better view of not only the bindings around my ankles but where the tubing was tied to in the ceiling. Though I ended up swinging a fair amount in the process, I did manage to get a good look at both before flopping back down. The bindings were even tighter than they felt, and the beam they'd been wrapped around up top was a good ten centimeters thick. There was no way I was going to either wiggle free or pop loose from the anchor point—which was probably a good thing, as falling a full meter and a half onto my head could put me out for good.

I really needed to get my hands free, but from what I could tell, the same type of tubing bound my wrists together as my ankles. That meant breaking free on strength alone was a no-go. Could I cut them somehow?

My eyes scanned the area. I didn't find a knife or scissors lying around, but I did see a small bit of metal paneling that was broken where some plant life had pushed in. The corner to it looked sharp. All I needed to do was get ahold of it and I'd be golden.

I shut my eyes and drew in a breath as I mentally prepared myself. Then, keeping my gaze fixated on my target, I used my Progenitor implants to punch, pull, and twist the plate as best I could, all the while trying to keep noise to a minimum and avoid draining all the energy stored in my arm's micro battery cells. I think I worked on it for a good five minutes, certainly no more than ten, when the panel, about the size of my hand, ripped free and shot across the air. It hit the far corner with a noisy clank.

"Good job, Dakota," I grumbled to myself. "Why don't you scream a little, too, and let everyone know what you're up to."

For the next few seconds I did nothing but strain my ears for any sounds of my approaching captor. All I heard were the quiet sounds of muffled machinery whirring along as well as some water dripping nearby. Thus, I went back to work. Three tries and a minor gash to the side of my right palm later, I managed to fling the panel through the air and catch it.

"Come on. Come on," I muttered, sawing away at the bindings with the piece of metal. My hands were slippery with sweat and blood, so working the impromptu knife with any sort of efficiency turned out to be difficult to say the least. Difficult, but not impossible.

The bindings broke free of my wrist and I nearly shouted in triumph as they fell away. I pulled myself up with my abs once more, wrapped my left arm around the tubing for extra support, and then started hacking away at it with my right. This time, cutting through was ten times easier. Less than a minute later, I dropped to the floor, smiling with pride.

Too bad Logan wasn't around to see me get out of that one. Maybe then he'd stop bringing up the pool story. Actually, check that. The nakedness would make things a little too awkward. And speaking of being trapped somewhere naked, god, how I hoped Jack wasn't lurking around. I hardly thought of him as a creep anymore, but it was fun to watch him pine over the fact that thus far, he'd been the only one sans clothes while stuck in a jail cell.

I perked at the thought of Jack and clenched my fist in triumph. Another memory back where it should be.

"All right, Dakota," I said, feeling ready to take on the world and get my life back. "You got this. You've got this."

I rolled my shoulders, rubbed my arms a bit for some warmth, too, and then eased out of the brig, checking the hall in both directions as I did. The corridor stretched pretty far on the left before making a ninety-degree bend right past a bulkhead, and to my right stood a closed hatch. A red light above it pulsed slowly, and the nearby console looked dead. Still, I checked it out anyway, but when I got nowhere with either the door or console in a few seconds, I decided to slink my way down the hall in the opposite direction.

With grace, speed, and stealth—yes, stealth; I know, shocker—I made it down the hall and around the corridor without making a sound. I even made it through the next room—remains of air and water processing, if I weren't mistaken—without incident as well and quiet as a mouse. By then, I was feeling good about not being caught and even entertained fantasies that my attacker had run off for a while, and I'd have plenty of time to not only get out but find my gear as well.

Because let's face it, I'm built for a lot of things, like capitalizing on any and all luck that comes my way, but surviving bitter cold? Not a chance. In fact, I hate the cold. Hate. Hate. Hate. Not only do I hate it, but I'm also well aware of the fact that humans are poorly suited for it. I probably wouldn't last the night outside without clothing.

I hooked a right at a T-junction on a gut-level inclination. It led me down another mostly ruined corridor and to one more hatch, which I quickly opened with a push of the console. The door zipped open with a whoosh. My eyes grew ten times their size at the sight of a massive feline sitting in a nearby booth with his feet kicked up on the table. His fierce eyes held no small amount of curiosity to them, and as he toyed with my helmet with one paw, he used the other to beckon me over with a single, large claw.

"Not bad, tailless," he said. "I'd like to know how you got that panel free. Can those implants of yours channel a magnetic field or something?"

"Yeah, more or less," I said, freezing in the doorway. "You were watching me? Why?"

"That's an answer you may never know. Now sit, please," he said. "There's no need for you to cower so far away. Besides, if you run, you'll only die tired—assuming I wanted to kill you."

I frowned. "Why are you treating me like this?" I asked. "If I did something to you, I'm sorry. I'm really a nice person. Ask anyone."

"There's no one around to ask or maybe I would."

My arms, now crossed over my chest, drummed across my ribs. In any other circumstance, I'd have felt a lot more threatened, but deep down, I had a feeling I should know him. Or he knew me? "Have we met?"

"We can talk when you sit," he said, this time a little more forcefully than before. "Or rather, I'll talk, and you'll answer questions. Then, depending on those answers, we'll see whether or not I want to keep you around or eat you."

My stomach tightened and so did my throat. I briefly considered making a run for it, maybe even throwing a little telekinetic punch or two to ensure my survival. In the end, I didn't. I simply nodded and inched forward because I couldn't shake the feeling that any sort of aggression toward him would turn out badly.

"What's your name?" he asked.

"Dakota," I replied, dropping into a chair and then hugging my legs close to my chest on account of the cold. "Dakota Adams. What's yours?"

The big kitty ignored my question and kept going. "Where did you get this armor?"

"I—I can't remember," I reluctantly admitted. My eyes drifted to the side, and I racked my brain for the answer. The armor was special, wasn't it? It had to be. Clearly it was special to him, too. Maybe if I knew who he was? I decided to ask my question again. "Are you honestly not going to tell me who you are?"

Mister Space Cat dropped his legs off the table, put the helmet to the side, and leaned over the table. "You are in no position to make any sort of request from me, Miss Adams," he said, making sure to enunciate every syllable slowly to impart the maximum amount of terror in my heart.

When my heart rate managed to dip under a few hundred beats per minute, and I subsequently managed to swallow the boulder in my throat, I spit out a reply. "Look, I'll tell you what you want to know," I said. "But I swear to god, I don't know what I did or why you're after me."

"You have no idea."

"Not a clue, I promise," I said. When he didn't ease back one iota, I shrugged and nodded toward my helmet. "You seem keen on my armor. Is that it?"

"Yes, you might say that has something to do with it," he replied. "Where did you get it?"

I shrugged again, even though I knew that was the wrong thing to do. I couldn't help it. My mind wouldn't come up with the answer. "I bought it somewhere," I said, knowing that was a lie. Or at least, I felt it was. The words tasted sour the moment they passed my tongue. But where else would I have gotten it? From what I could remember, it fit like a dream. "It's been a while," I tacked on. "So please don't ask me for specifics. I buy lots of things. I hardly keep track of it all."

Claws flicked out from his right paw as he dropped it on the table. His brow dropped, and he dug those mini daggers across the table's surface, making a horrid screeching noise as he did. "I won't ask again," he said. "Tell me where you got this armor or the last thing you'll see is your blood spray across this room."

I jumped back in fright. I'd barely cleared the chair when he was up as well. I don't know where it came from, but a carbine appeared in his paws. I tumbled backward and knocked the weapon aside with a telekinetic punch. The carbine fired as it flew from his grasp, and the shot tore a huge chunk out of the wall to my side.

Mister Space Kitty roared in defiance. I, in turn, scrambled back as fast as I could. Right as he went to pounce, I did the only thing I could think of. I used every ounce of energy I had in my arm to telekinetically punch his head off.

Let me be the first to say, I don't think I've ever summoned such a powerful blow in my life. I mean, when a half-ton angry, intergalactic tiger tries to rip your head off, you don't exactly hold back, you know? Right as I swung, however, this massive amount of pressure formed in my head, and the blow ended up going wide. Instead of shattering his skull, I blasted a quarter-meter wide hole in the ceiling. And as debris rained all around and smoke and flames poured from the hole, I felt blood gush from my nose. My eyes rolled back in my head, and I flopped to the floor.

Pushback from the Universe. I'd nearly caused a paradox. That was one feeling I'd never forget, no matter how much time travel turned my brain to soup.

Though I missed and now was prone on the ground, my attack probably was the only thing that saved my life. Mister Space Kitty hesitated instead of tearing me to shreds as he glanced over his shoulder. When he came back around, I was so weak and disoriented, I couldn't have cracked an egg to save my life. I think that's why he just picked me up and slammed me against the wall instead of separating my head from my shoulders. After all, he still had answers to get, and I wasn't a threat anymore.

"Your aim is abysmal, tailless," he said with a chuckle.

All I could do was weakly shake my head as much as his grip on my neck would allow.

His claws flashed in front of my face. "Last chance to talk, tailless," he said. "Tell me where you got that Kibnali armor, or I'm going to start removing your bones, one at a time, starting with your toes."

My eyes flickered at his species' name. Memories, all of them, flooded my mind, bursting free of whatever mental dam they'd been trapped behind. "Tolby," I gasped, half pleading, half smiling. "Oh god. It's you! I actually found you!"

Tolby eased his grip, tilted his head, but didn't let me go. "What did you say?"

"Tolby! I mean, that's what I call you," I explained. "Your real name is Tol'Beahn, right? House...House Yari was it? God, I'm so sorry for not paying attention more when you said that bit, but I've only heard it twice in all the time I've known you. You're also the second born to...damn...who was it? Undun? Rajap? That's right, isn't it?"

Tolby glanced nervously over his shoulders before looking back at me. "We've never met," he said. "How do you know this? Are you a spy of the Nodari?"

"No. We're best friends," I said. "Or will be at least."

"Will be?"

I nodded after sucking in a breath, and I couldn't help but worry how much of a nutball he was going to think I was. By the time Tolby and I had made it to the Museum of Natural Time, he and I had been together for quite some time, but we were hardly BFFs on first sight. Friends? Sure, especially after our wild adventure together on Helios IX (note to self: get that in book form, ASAP), but he was never the type of guy who'd believe in wild claims about jumping space and time. Worse, it's not like I had a lot to prove it with, physically speaking. I didn't have my portal device, and there certainly weren't any Progenitor webways nearby.

"This is going to be hard to believe, and I don't blame you if you think I'm lying, because I know you Kibnali are a shoot-first-and-ask-questions-usually-never lot, and my memory is a mess, but I'm from the future," I said. "I came here after...after you and I found a museum with a time machine."

"We found a museum with a time machine?" he repeated with exactly the amount of skepticism I'd anticipated: total.

I nodded. "Yeah. We also found other Kibnali there. You're not the only one left."

Tolby's grip vanished. He staggered back as I fell to the floor. "I can't believe it," he whispered. "But...no one here knows who I am, either. No one. I don't even know where I am."

"You're literally on the other side of the universe," I said after I picked myself up off the ground. "And the Last Act of Defiance? That happened like, millions of years ago, but like I said, it didn't kill all of you. I met Empress and her handmaidens. And back on my ship, there's another ten of you kitty commandos, too."

"Where is your ship?"

"A long time ago, in a galaxy far, far away," I said. When it was clear he wasn't following, I tacked on, "I told you. I'm a time traveler. I left them back in your home galaxy. The last planet of yours I visited was Kumet. Do you know that world?"

"In other words, you have no proof," Tolby said.

I turned my head so he had a better view of my cheek and the scars on it. "Empress gave me these honors," I said before showing off the other cheek as well. "I have more on my chest."

Tolby leaned close. His eyes squinted as he inspected the ritual scarring. He then dropped his head to see what was on my chest. I wasn't sure what the scars on my cheeks looked like, but thanks to the cold, the ones below stood out a little more as they'd turned a shade of light blue.

Slowly his face changed from outright denial to healthy skepticism and backed away a few steps. "Who are you?"

"I am Dakota Adams, *Ralakai* to the Empress Suiko, first-degree initiate of the Kibnali Guard, jumper of space and time," I said with as much formality as I could muster since I knew such things had their place in the Kibnali culture.

"What is your duty?"

"To serve the Empress," I said. "I am her fang and claw."

"And what is her will?"

"That the Kibnali should spread amongst the stars."

Tolby twitched his ears for a second before his eyes drifted off and stared blankly for a few beats. "Come," he said, waving me back to the table. "Tell me everything."

"Sure," I said. "But do you think I could at least have my clothes back? I'm a little chilly."

CHAPTER TWENTY-THREE
GARAGE SALE

Tolby took the news well.

Some of it, a little too well.

I tried to gloss over some of the details regarding Jainon and Yseri, specifically, their constant, wanton sexcapades, but he pressed hard for those details. Again, and again. And again.

Sheesh. At least I didn't have to do it freezing cold. He did give me my clothes and armor back.

During what little details I was able—and willing—to provide, his eyes glossed over, and his tail swished happily through the air. Thankfully, I managed to spend a minimum amount of time on that and got him the rest of our adventures together in about an hour: adventures ranging from our first meeting there on Helios IX to the Museum of Natural Time to our near-deaths on Adrestia, and of course, everything that took place on Kumet.

"I'm still trying to wrap my head around all of this," he said. "Never would I have dreamed any of it to be possible. To find others who survived the war. To see my species rise from the brink of extinction.

To have such a close relationship with a tailless such as yourself, no offense."

I smiled warmly at the big furball. Though he still wasn't my Tolby, he was getting there. "You could never offend me," I said. "Can I give you a hug?"

"Why wouldn't you be able to?" he asked. "Is your arm still numb?"

"No," I replied, laughing. "I mean, can I without you shooting my head off?"

"If you wish."

I bounded over the table and threw myself into him. He grunted as I hit but said nothing as I sank into his fur. I loved giving him hugs, obviously, even if he only sat there awkwardly, unsure what to do. To top things off, since he'd interrogated me not even an hour and a half ago, I was thrilled not to be on his bad side anymore. I guess I needed the physical confirmation of that, too.

"How long did you say we've known each other?" he asked.

"A few years, well—" I almost corrected that statement. Almost. He didn't know me. He knew Dakota. Part of me felt I should tell him, especially since I'd sort of omitted my clone nature when I recounted everything. I still hated who and what I was, and thinking about how many of my memories weren't mine, and the life I'd thought I'd lived wasn't mine as well, still cut me to the core. As such, it was a thousand times easier to let him think what he would. It would be nice to pretend for a few more hours, at least. Besides, Yseri wasn't keen on clones. Maybe Old Tolby, the Tolby before we'd first met, wasn't keen on them either.

"Well, what?"

I looked up at him from my official snuggled position. "Well, nothing," I said, putting on a happy smile. "I was just going to say, with all the time traveling, you could say millions of years, ya know? It's all relative."

I threw in a wink, which put him at ease.

"I see. Last question: If we need a…a webway, was it? If we need a webway to reach our foe, AO, to destroy him, do you have a plan on where to find one?"

"Yeah, I do," I said, pulling away. I sighed heavily, realizing that not only did he want to get down to business, we had to as well. "There's supposed to be one on this world, somewhere. We've just got to hope it wasn't wiped out when they were."

"This planet is big," he said. "And dangerous. Wandering around aimlessly isn't the brightest of ideas."

I grabbed the multi-phase subatomic matrix analyzer off the table and showed it to him. "This will pick it up, if we're close enough. I can have it search for tech similar to that in my arm and home in on the signal."

"How close?"

"Ten kilometers."

"This planet's a lot bigger than ten kilometers."

"Actually, it's on your arm," Rummy piped up. Aside from a brief intro with Tolby earlier when I got my gear back, he'd been quiet until now.

I looked both of them over but saw nothing. "It is? Where?"

"The coordinates to AO's world," he explained. "The first set are the latitude and longitude for the webway on this planet. The other six pairs are for the webway."

"They are? You sure?"

"Maestro found them off the archive cube back on the ship before you left," he said.

"Right, I knew that," I said, chuckling. "Or will at least. Guess the good ole noggin still has a few leaks in it."

Tolby's face twisted as he growled. "Hopefully that won't be problematic later on."

"We'll be fine, you'll see," I said, trying to stay positive. "So, how far away is this place? A few hours? Couple days? Can't be that bad of a hike, right?"

"I believe it was calculated to be forty-three thousand, seven hundred and fifty-five point nine-one-zero-eight kilometers, rounded of course," he replied.

My heart sank. My eyes rolled up as I groaned and collapsed on top of the table. "Oh god, please tell me Daphne missed that by a couple decimal places."

"She did originally," Rummy said. "She had it pegged at forty-three klicks, until Tolby double-checked the math."

"There's no way they'd send me here only to have to walk that far, would they?" I asked. "I mean, there's got to be something around we can use, right? Like the ship? Like it flies but it's just not space-worthy?"

Tolby chuckled and made a sweeping gesture of the room with his paw. "Does it look like that's the case?" he asked. "This ship hasn't been able to fly in nearly a decade."

I deflated even more than I already was with the news, but then the tiniest sparks of an idea hit me. There was a failed colony on Helios IX, one that had left behind a lot of equipment. Sure, it was outdated by a few hundred years, but that didn't mean it might not work—well, even.

"What about the colony here that was lost?" I asked. "There's got to be something there."

"The main settlement is a long way from here," he said. "But there's an outpost not terribly far away with an old garage I never managed to get open. Perhaps there's something there we can use."

"Hot damn," I said, slapping my palms on the table. "We're in business."

"I said, perhaps. It's no guarantee."

I laughed and hopped over to his side so I could squeeze his shoulder. "Tolby," I said, trying to sound serious. "My dear, dear, Tolby.

There's one thing you're going to eventually learn about me, so you might as well do it now."

"What's that?"

"If there's a chance, I'm going to take it."

Before we left, Tolby slathered my chest and the back of my shoulders in a teal goo. He said it was to help mask my smell, and since I didn't feel like attracting the attention of a pack of terror beasts, I let him stick it on me, despite the rancid odor.

The first couple of hours we spent hiking through a dense, snow-packed forest before sunrise. When the sun finally did crest the horizon, bringing with it golden rays of warmth and thank-god-I'm-not-in-the-dark-anymore, we were on our bellies, peeking over a ridge. Several hundred meters away and down a gentle slope and across a frozen pond I could see a few white-capped concrete structures as well as a half dozen construction vehicles of varying size. Even from this distance, I could see that they'd seen much better days. Crane arms sagged. A dump truck lay on its side, and a bulldozer-hydraulic-excavator hybrid had been torn in half—an impressive feat, not to mention unsettling feeling, given the thing was almost three stories tall.

"I count fourteen," Tolby said in a low tone. "They usually leave me alone one-on-one or even in small packs. But that many? They might try their luck."

"What are you on about?" I asked, squinting as if that would magically give me eagle eyes.

"Hannan terror beasts," he said, flicking a claw toward a section of the outpost.

"Where?" I asked, squinting even harder.

Tolby sighed. "Are all of you tailless creatures so helpless?"

"Ahem," I said, raising my arm.

"I'll take that as a yes," he said, shaking his head. "If you've had the foresight to augment your frailty in your body, perhaps you should've done the same with your eyesight. It's abysmal."

"No thanks," I said. "This girl will always be au naturel, time-traveling implants aside. Besides, I've got you. Always have. Always will, right?"

The corner of Tolby's mouth drew back, and his ears flicked with amusement. "That does seem to be the case," he said. "Though, I'm wondering what you bring to the relationship."

"You mean aside from getting you off this planet you're stuck on?" I said. "Adventure. Friendship. And plenty of root beer floats."

"Root beer floats?"

I chuckled to myself and shook my head. "Oh, right. You haven't had one yet. But you will, and trust me, you're going to love them."

"I'm going to hold you to that," he said. He then pulled off a giant set of binoculars and handed them to me. Well, they weren't giant for him, but since he was literally twice as tall as I was, my face was a little on the small side for them. "Most of them are twenty meters west of the farthest building, which happens to be the garage."

I spied the pack of creatures easily, thanks to the binocs. Sure enough, there were twelve there, with another two wandering nearby for a total of fourteen. "Can we wait them out?" I asked with a sigh. "Maybe they'll leave?"

"Not likely," Tolby said. "This is probably the start of a den."

"Are you sure?"

"I'm sure they're looking," he said. "It's that time of year. Whether or not they decide to live here for the next decade, I can't say. But it has everything they'd want. Water supply. Caves, or buildings in this case, to hide from their predators, and plenty of open space to run around in, and a forest to hunt."

"Did you say 'their predators'?"

Tolby's face went grim, and he snorted. "I did."

"Crikey, what the hell hunts those things?"

"Nothing either of us wants to meet."

My lips pressed together in a thin line of frustration. "There's sewers or an underground tram tunnel we can use to slip in though, right?"

Tolby shook his head. "Afraid not."

"Can we maybe draw them off and get inside the garage without them seeing us?" I asked.

"Possibly, but it's locked," he said. "We'd need a way in that didn't involve blowing up the door. Aside from potentially ruining what's inside if we tried that, the noise would undoubtedly draw them all back."

I held my PEN. Well, Original Dakota's PEN I guess. I'd found it tucked into a little holder on my belt as we'd been hiking here, and Rummy was kind enough to fill in the details. That was both clever and nice of her to let me borrow it. Hopefully, I wouldn't end up losing it. Okay, I'm rambling, I know. Important point: I had a PEN. "I've got this," I said. "I can hack the door, assuming it still has power."

"It does," Tolby said with an approving nod. "Okay, I'll draw them off. You get into the garage and get us a vehicle. Meet me back here or if things get bad, my ship. Do you know how to get there?"

I nodded. "Yup."

"Perfect," he said. "Soon as they're gone, move fast and quiet."

I nodded again, and Tolby slinked over the ridgeline and down the slope. Watching him prowl was a sight to behold. Never in a million years would I have guessed he could get so low without crawling on his belly. Hell, maybe he was, but you wouldn't know it by how much terrain he covered in so little time. Really made me appreciate having him on my side, you know?

Within a few minutes, he'd snuck his way to the very outer edge of the outpost. Through the binocs, I watched him shoulder his rifle, take aim at something hidden from my field of view, and fire off a trio of shots. Tolby then backpedaled a couple steps, fired again, and took off running.

The pack of terror beasts tore after him, howling as they did. They tore through the outpost with frightening speed, but despite their huge strides, they couldn't match Tolby's.

I waited a few seconds after they disappeared into the nearby forest before popping up and running down the slope. My feet sank into the snow a little more than I'd anticipated, and while that didn't make sprinting impossible, it did make it harder than I'd anticipated. It also meant that by the time I reached the garage, my heart hammered in my chest so hard I felt as if I'd just tried to place in the annual Steel Runner's 5K on Mars, which if you aren't aware, you better be running sub sixes to have a chance at.

Breathless, I reached the garage door and glanced to both sides to ensure no monsters were still hanging around. No terror beasts, thankfully, but I did see a lot of bones picked clean. That certainly didn't help my nerves.

I flipped out my PEN and went to work on the console. It did have power. It even responded to my commands, which was nice, since that meant I only needed to bypass the security instead of having to worry about repairing it all. Thankfully, getting around antique security with a PEN was a fairly straightforward and simple ordeal.

Using its micromapper, I quickly created a holographic schematic of the console I could reference, and then as I worked the console and issued basic commands, most of which were me guessing poorly at the five-digit code needed for access, I followed the power as it zipped through the circuitry. Given enough guesses and some trial-and-error prodding when it came to manipulating power nodes and microswitches, I could pop the lock.

Fairly straightforward process, and nothing terribly exciting, except for the part about being on the clock. Tolby could only keep those demon dogs away for so long. Eventually they'd get tired of chasing him and want to come home.

I was on my fifty-second try when I heard a rapid series of shots followed by a horrific roar that shook me to the core. I spun around, half-expecting to see the pack of terror beasts charging me and fighting over who got to tear into my body first.

What I saw was much, much worse.

Tolby had broken free of the tree line and sped toward me, covering the ground in great strides. Behind him followed a terror beast, trying its damnedest to keep up. That, of course, wasn't what stole my breath or caused me to drop my PEN. Seeing a fifteen-meter tall arachnid-rhino-dragon crash through the trees after them did.

It scuttled along on eight powerful legs, and when it got near the terror beast, it used the single horn on its reptilian snout to knock it away. The doggo momentarily sailed through the air before being snatched by a giant, whip-like tail when it was then thoroughly bashed into a nearby rock before being tossed into the monster's open mouth.

"Get that door open!" Tolby yelled.

His words snapped me into action. I fumbled with the PEN for a hot second trying to pick it up, but I quickly got back to work. I worked as fast as I dared, and then redoubled the effort when the next two tries at bypassing the locks proved futile.

"I thought you said you could get it open!" Tolby yelled as he slid to a stop next to me.

"I can!" I said, fighting tears of frustration and impending doom. "But you're the one who always did this when we needed it the most. I'm not the hacker of our little duo."

"There's not going to be a little duo much longer if we stay here," he said. "I think he's done with his snack."

I glanced over my shoulder in time to see the giant spider monster, who was still a few hundred meters away, flick a forked tongue over its mouth and then level its gaze on us. I spun back around, worked even faster, short circuits be damned, but still got nowhere, fast. The deafening thuds of the monster's fast approach didn't help either.

"Tailless! We've got to get out of here!"

With his panicked voice ringing in my ears, I decided to abandon conventional methods. I briefly considered using the spacetime flare thingy X-45 had made to carve a portal from where we were to inside the garage, but I didn't. I needed it for AO. Instead, I simply aimed the PEN at a series of micro power relays and sent a surge of energy through them.

Sparks flew from the console, a prelude to an electrical explosion that showered both of us with tiny embers.

"Damn it!" Tolby yelled.

He started to run, but I grabbed him by the arm at the sound of a distinct, muffled click. "The locks are disengaged," I said. "Can you get the door open?"

"I'll try," he said with a nod of determination. He then squatted and dug his claws under the door, and with one clean jerk, he sent it flying upward.

I jumped in the air, shaking two fists high overhead in triumph. "Yes! I told you we made the best team!"

"Let's save the tongue baths for when we're safe," he said, chuckling and running inside. "We still have that thing to get away from."

"You worry too much," I said, following.

A wide array of vehicles and no-longer-hovering transports filled the garage. Unlike the construction vehicles outside, all of these appeared intact, which did wonders to keep hope alive in my soul.

"Now this is what I'm talking about," I said, darting over to a six-wheeled Gemini Rover and flinging open the door. These babies might have been centuries away from their production line, but they were the undisputed kings of planetary exploration when it came to ground vehicles due to their reliability and ease of maintenance. The fusion reactors could take you a hundred thousand klicks before needing a tune-up, and even then, if you skipped it, you'd probably only see minimal loss when it came to horsepower. Not only did they rock it in the drivetrain department, but the cabins were extra plush and decked with options so you could not only traverse any landscape with ease, but you could do it in extreme comfort, too.

"Do you know how to drive one?" Tolby asked, racing over to the passenger side.

"Yeah, flick it on. Push the pedal. Point the wheels where you want to go," I replied as I fired up the reactor. "They're stupid simple."

"Flick it on. Throttle. Steer. Got it," he said before darting away.

"Hey! Where are you going?"

"Going to take care of our friend! Just don't leave without me!"

My brow furrowed as I didn't know what he had in mind, but that confusion only lasted a second. I saw him hop into another Rover, fire it up, and then rocket forward when he presumably floored the pedal.

"Oh snap!" I said, laughing and fumbling. I slammed my door shut and chased after him in my vehicle.

Due to the angle I'd been parked at, I fishtailed my Rover before lining it up with the exit. Tolby had already shot out the garage by then, and he was currently darting between arachno-rhino-dragon's legs. He jinked left to avoid getting stepped on before leveling out and racing away with the spider monster giving chase.

Tolby rounded a building, and as I saw the Rover clear the other side and head for open terrain, he leaped from the cabin, rolled, and raced back toward me. Giant spider monster, thankfully, had more interest in chasing the Rover than him. I guess it was more of a challenge? Who knows. Or maybe he was like a gargantuan puppy with tunnel vision chasing a tennis ball.

Anywho, picking Tolby up after that was a breeze, but I made a sliding stop for extra fun. Snow kicked up in the air, giving his fluffy coat a thorough powdering.

"Having fun?" he said, opening the passenger door and climbing in.

"Mm-hm," I replied. "You look good in white. Really brings out your eyes."

Tolby narrowed them both before grinning. Then he shook himself out, which ended up covering half the cabin and all of me in snow. "So do you."

"Thanks," I said, laughing. "Shall we go then?"

"Yes, please. I don't want that creature finding its way back while we're still here. I've had my fill of chases for the week."

I laughed again as I leaned over and patted his furry shoulder. "Oh, Tolby," I said. "What am I going to do with you?"

"What do you mean?"

"This is just the start of all the chases we'll have together. You're just going to have to learn to love them. They're part of the package."

"What package?"

"The Dakota Adams package, of course," I said. "The best, most coveted one in the entire universe."

"Can I take it back?" he asked playfully. "I think I still have the receipt."

I stuck out my tongue. "No, you don't, and no, you can't."

CHAPTER TWENTY-FOUR
ANOTHER FACILITY

Gemini Rovers. Gotta love 'em.

You've never experienced pure butt-warming bliss till you've plopped down on a leather Rover seat and turned on the seat heater. But Dakota, you say, aren't all seat heaters the same? Oh, my dear, sweet friend. I used to think that, too, back when I was young and naïve. Words can't adequately describe how amazing Rover seats are, and even if they could, I fear the depression you'd settle into if you knew how fantastic the seats were and how you'd never be able to experience them.

The leather cushions you in all the right places, heats you with the perfect combination of a blanket-from-the-dryer warm and the best hug from your best friend. It even has micro rollers built inside to prevent your legs from getting stiff on long journeys, while at the same time gently massaging your back.

Like I said, total bliss.

I plugged our destination into the nav computer and let the vehicle do the rest. Since the colonists who had tried to settle on Helios IX had been there for a while before a plague wiped them out, not only had the planet's entire terrain already been mapped out and loaded into the vehicle's computers, but we even found two pit stops. The first one we made about halfway and swapped the fuel rods and found a working GameKid™ with no less than fifty-five hundred classic games. Talk about a score!

While playing Joust Quest and clearing level twelve in record time, we happened upon our second stop, which was only three hours away from our destination. There we got to stretch our legs and climb the fire tower for a little sightseeing. The view afforded to us by the fifty-meter-high structure put a smile on my face, and while gazing across a lush field with a herd of thousands upon thousands of bison-like creatures hanging about, eating the grass and tending to their baby bisons, I almost forgot how much danger the near future held for us. Man, I really missed just traveling and seeing stuff without having to worry about how I was going to keep all my appendages intact. I needed to get back to that, especially with Tolby at my side.

Anywho, when we reached our final destination, I have to say, I was rather underwhelmed at the sight of it all. The site was located on a peninsula on the western edge of the continent. While the sound of angry waves crashing against a rocky shore put a little excitement in the air, and while the cawing of some sort of avian species above added a nice touch in terms of ambience, the place hardly screamed Progenitor webway.

I guess that's what happens when you get wiped from existence.

Aside from a lot of grass covering the semi-rounded area, the only thing that this little purchase of land had with it were several tall boulders jutting up from the ground, maybe ten meters tall. They didn't look as if they were a part of the webway whatsoever, and my first inclination was that they were some ancient relic like Stonehenge.

Hardly an exciting discovery when you're looking for a super-advanced facility complete with webway technology. Where was it all? Had the facility been wiped out with the bulk of the Progenitors' existence during the great backlash? I hoped not, but couldn't shake the feeling that maybe that was it.

"What now, tailless?" Tolby said, climbing out of our Rover and stretching his arms overhead. "There's not much here."

"I know you can't help it right now, but it would make me feel a ton better if you called me Dakota instead," I replied, exiting the vehicle as well.

"Apologies," he said with a short nod. "You've known me far longer than I've known you."

I flashed him a smile. "I know. But I still love ya."

At that point, I trotted out to the spires and looked around. This was the right place, wasn't it? I double-checked the writing on my arm to confirm. So where were the stupid controls for this place? Not to mention, the reactor?

"It's got to be here somewhere," I said, spinning in place and scanning the area. I frowned, huffed, frowned again, and even stomped my foot in a vain attempt to make a Progenitor facility appear out of thin air.

"Perhaps the coordinates are wrong?"

"No, this is right," I said. "I promise I wouldn't have been sent across time and space if we didn't know exactly where to go."

"Then where is it?"

I shrugged, but as soon as I did, I realized my error. I smacked my head and laughed at how dumb I was being. "It's underfoot."

"Subterranean?"

"Yeah," I said. "I found one like that not long ago. That's where I got X-45. Remember?"

Tolby shook his head. "You never really said where that facility was."

"My bad," I said. I shut my eyes for a moment, before opening one and tacking on, "Keep a watch, will you? What's inside might not be the most welcoming host, given everything we've been through."

"On it."

I sucked in a breath to refocus, and with my eyes closed, I reached out as best I could into the world with my implants, once again searching to make a connection with whatever Progenitor facility happened to be there. As with my attempt at Kumet, I found what I was looking for in moments.

A familiar pop sounded in my mind, and I quickly issued the mental command, *open door*. As what had transpired on Kumet, the ground rumbled in response. Tolby jumped back in fright, weapon up and sweeping the area. I probably shouldn't have giggled, but I did.

Five meters ahead of us, near the edge of a drop-off, the ground ripped apart and revealed a long ramp. Smiling, I led Tolby down said ramp until we reached yet another round bunker door that was set into a flat, beige wall.

"Impressive," Tolby said, giving the entrance a look. "How do we get in?"

"With the noggin," I said, tapping the side of my head. A quick mental command later, and I had the console next to the door lit up and ready to do my bidding. Reading what was onscreen, however, sent a chill through my core:

Please, Dakota. Don't do this.

"Don't do what?" Tolby asked.

I straightened and tilted my head with surprise. "You can read that?"

"Of course I can read that," he said with a huff. "You think I'm an illiterate kit?"

I shook my head as my gut tightened with unease. "No, but the screen has always been in the Progenitor language before. My implants always made an automatic mental translation."

"I can't speak to what happened before, but those words are written in Kibnali."

I bit my lower lip and wondered how much of a bad omen this was. Damn, what I wouldn't have given for Taz to show up right then and there for a belly rub. I could've really used the little guy's extra help. "This can't be good."

The hairs on Tolby's back bristled, and he brought his rifle to his shoulder. "Who do you think wrote that?"

"AO, I'm assuming," I said as I checked the area for any signs of my *ashidasashi*. There weren't any. "Not sure what it means though, other than we need to be cautious."

"Then I suggest you stand aside when you open the door."

I took a step to my right and gestured to the facility entrance. "After you."

Tolby aimed his rifle at the door and nodded, at which point I tapped the console a few times to get to the door controls and ordered it to open. Keeping in line with all the other Progenitor facilities I'd worked my way into, this one greeted us with a massive, pressurized hiss as the door sank into the wall a quarter meter before rolling off to the side. The screeching of metal grinding against metal also accompanied said hiss, and both Tolby and I set our jaws and cringed in response.

"Going in," Tolby said, easing through the door, weapon ready. I peeked around the corner as he swept the area with his plasma rifle, and when he saw nothing, he beckoned me in with his paw. "It's clear."

I stepped through the threshold and ended up gawking at what was inside. Whereas Lambda Labs and the facility back on Kumet had a bit of the abandoned look to it, this one was anything but. Crisp, white tile lined the floors while ample lighting hung from the ceiling above. Running down the center of this entrance hall were several sets of benches on either side of a long, decorative pool, complete with a cascading waterfall at the far end and a few schools of bright fish swimming about. Along the walls, spaced at regular intervals, stood bushy shrubs that had been manicured to perfection, as well as more benches, chairs, and small tables, which made the entire place feel more like the entrance to a grand hotel than anything else. The wide, curved desk made from marble and wood at the far end only solidified that feel.

We carefully made our way down the hall. My eyes constantly scanned every nook and cranny for whatever trap AO had left us, while my ears strained to pick up even the quietest of noises.

About three-quarters of the way, something burst out of the water behind us. Tolby and I spun around to see a spherical Progenitor droid launch itself toward me with a wicked-looking blade held beneath its round belly.

Both of us fired. The two shots I squeezed off from my pistol wiped out a nearby potted plant and put a deep gouge in the wall, while Tolby's singular plasma bolt struck the droid in the top of its eye. The robot dropped from the air, smashing into the ground and rolling a few meters before coming to a halt.

"Stupid droid," Tolby said with a snicker. "AO must be desperate to attack you with one of these, but let's make sure it's dead."

I doubted it was anything but. The droid's internal circuits popped, and the smell of burnt electronics filled the air. Tolby carefully approached, watched it for a few seconds, and then put all his weight into his foot as he stepped on it. What was left of its metallic shell crumped beneath him. "Let's keep moving," I said. "I'm not sure how many more there are."

A side door suddenly opened, and into the entrance hall whooshed another dozen of the bots. They whistled through the air as they came, and holy snort were they fast as they beelined toward me. Thank the lucky pachyderm Tolby was faster. He fired time and again, dropping them as he had the first and chuckling with each kill.

When the plasma fire stopped, a new sound filled the air: heavy stomping. The side door opposite where the little droids had come

239

through opened, and a pair of large, four-legged robots scuttled in. Their egg-shaped torsos looked similar to X-45's, as did the serpentine necks and heads, but size-wise, they were each twice as big and seemed twice as fast.

"You! Flesh-thing!" the one on the left said. "Mustn't kill-kill the species!"

"Die-die!" chimed in the other.

Not sure what else they were going to say, but whatever it was, the conversation halted as plasma bolts from both Tolby and me flew at them. To my dismay, our shots struck yellow forcefields that sprang up in an instant where they skipped off and destroyed more of the entrance room.

"Run!" I barked, turning on my heels and speeding off as fast as I could.

Tolby hesitated, but when more of the little flying bots came pouring into the room, he apparently decided a tactical withdrawal was the correct course of action.

We ran down the hall, taking pot shots at our pursuers the entire time. I actually nailed one of the little flying guys right after I vaulted over the desk and kept going. Tolby, of course, had much better success in taking them out.

At the far end of the hall, we reached a lift that was sandwiched between a pair of vending machines. Well, they looked like vending machines. I didn't have whatever card they took, and I wasn't exactly sure what popped out of the bottom. But they did have bright neon lighting and fancy artwork of delicious snacks.

I hammered the call button to the elevator. Thankfully, the doors slid open immediately, and I jumped inside with Tolby right behind. I nailed the button for the next floor and spun back around to see both of the larger robots barreling toward us with another dozen of the smaller bots flying after as us, too.

Tolby opened fire. His shots popped bot after bot, square in their central eye, but he couldn't penetrate the shielding of the larger ones. At least, however, every time they had to go on the defensive, they had to stop and root themselves in place. I guess it took all their power to their shields to do that.

The doors to the elevator closed, and the lift whisked us down to the next floor. The instant the doors slid open, we burst free into a hall that stretched in either direction. We hesitated for a second, unsure of which direction to go, but then the door at the end of the hall to our right slid open and another one of those damn X-45 robots came through.

"We've got to get the webway," I said, backing up and tugging on Tolby's arm. "Come on."

Tolby squeezed off a plasma round that once again bounced off a flickering shield before grunting. "Damn them," he said. "If only I could overload my shots with this thing."

We turned and ran. Through doors we went, took a couple turns at random, even made a fast button hook when the layout allowed. All the while, I closed every door between us and set it to lock, however much good that would do.

It felt like a lifetime of running, even if it had only been a few minutes' worth. When we finally got a reprieve, we ended up inside a narrow T-shaped room that smelled like formaldehyde. A slew of consoles beeped and chirped to our left, while their monitors cast soft, blue lighting across what would've been a dark, concrete floor.

With as much speed as we could muster without completely throwing caution to the wind, we zipped through the room. We got about halfway when Tolby, who was in front of me, glanced at what was on one of the screens and stopped.

"Am I seeing things?" he muttered, leaning close.

I stopped next to him, and my jaw dropped. Filling up two-thirds of the screen on the left was a wire-frame model of a Nodari scout. On the right, text gave a summary report on what I assumed were tests to the creature's abilities. Below that summary, however, was a fragmented message that caught us both off guard.

Tol'Beahn...of...House Yari...This is...You...as my...all costs...fang and claw...

CHAPTER TWENTY-FIVE
THROUGH THE WEBWAY

What in Hisoshim's name is this?" Tolby asked.

"I don't know," I said. "I wish I did, but..."

"But?"

"But we haven't the time to figure it out."

I tried to tug Tolby along, but he shrugged me off and tried to work the console. He managed to flip through a few different reports detailing Nodari effectiveness against the Kibnali, much like the ones Jainon and I had read back on Adrestia, but as for finding anything more on the mystery message, that came up as a bust.

"Tolby, we have to—"

I was cut off when the door we'd come through opened and in marched a bot, wielding a funky rifle made from two parts scrap and one part desperation. It snapped it up and fired. Tolby and I were already diving for cover, but we weren't quick enough. The shot skipped off his chest plate, while the second hit him in the side.

Tolby roared in defiance, and as I crouched behind a console, I saw him yank a small disc with six prongs from his skin before he crushed it in his pad. "Shock me, will you," he growled.

He jumped up from behind his cover and started to unload on the bot. Each shot he took struck the droid's shields, and for every one he fired, the bot shot back in return, hitting Tolby twice in the forehead.

As the two traded fire, I leaned around the console and drove a phantom punch into the back of the droid's head. The robot jerked to the side as sparks flew, and its shields failed. Tolby, predictably, capitalized on the moment and drilled a pair of plasma bolts through both its torso and head.

"By the gods, these hurt," he said, peeling off the discs and shaking his head. "I guess I should be grateful they're not bullets."

"Can we go now?" I asked, standing. "The rest probably know where we are now. Won't take them long to get here."

As if on cue, more robots and spherical droids entered the room, and we both ran as fast as we could in the opposite direction. I slid under a table, firing wildly backward as I did, before scrambling to my feet and darting through an exit on the far side of the room.

Off we went, down a hall and through a set of small labs filled with dozens of unfinished projects. When we entered the third such place, Tolby slid to a stop just inside the door and heaved a massive cabinet over on its side to block the door.

"That should hold them for a few," he said, admiring his work. He then grabbed its bigger brother and pushed it up against the makeshift barricade before then wedging a third between all of that and the wall. "And that should help, too."

I heard the door slide open a second later, which was followed by some high-pitched chirping. Then it all rattled from a heavy blow on the other side. To Tolby's credit, the barricade held, but it jarred so much, it probably wouldn't be long before it buckled and failed altogether.

"Come on," Tolby said. "Let's find this webway of yours."

"Hang on," I said, spying a console. "Maybe I can bring up a map."

"Just do it fast."

I nodded, raced over to the wall to where the console hung, and went to work. In the meantime, Tolby added what he could to the barricade. Pulling up a map took a few seconds, and finding the webway's location a few more, but I got it before we were at the mercy of a droid army.

"Got it! It's not far!" I shouted with joy.

Tolby stuffed the barrel of his rifle up and over the barricade where a hole had formed and snapped off a few shots. "Great. Lead the way."

Off we popped, racing through alien halls, praying the barricade would hold long enough for me to activate the webway so we could get out of there. I knew we were in danger, and where we were going would be even more dangerous, but I couldn't help but smile.

"What is it?" Tolby asked between labored breaths.

"I was just thinking how this is like the old days, you know?"

"No, I don't."

My smile brightened, and I shrugged unapologetically. "Oh right. Well, you will."

We took one final left hook down a wide ramp that dumped us into a circular room with a high-domed ceiling. My heart soared at the sight of webway spires surrounding a wide platform, and I practically burst into an ugly, happy cry when I saw the nearby control room that looked fully operational.

A large explosion came from behind, causing the room to shake and my heart to skip. Our barricade, no doubt, was no more.

"Hold them off!" I shouted as I took off for the control room.

"Gladly," Tolby said, retreating a few steps before taking a bead on the ramp with his rifle. "Let them come."

I found the control room to be very similar to the one back on Adrestia, which wasn't surprising but was a welcomed sight. I'd hate to think how much trouble we would've been in otherwise. The main bank of displays faced the webway's platform, while about a dozen screens ran perpendicular to it and hung from the ceiling. The moment I stepped across the threshold I heard the click of my mind interfacing with the computers.

"Oh yeah, we're in business," I said. "Now where's the part where I turn everything on?"

A small, blue rectangle popped up on the center screen. Inside were the words *power on* in white letters. I quickly gave it a push, and when a command to initiate start-up procedures popped up, I hit that button as well.

A deep thrumming filled the air. The lights inside the control room as well as those that surrounded the webway grew a little bit brighter, which probably was a good thing for Tolby as it gave him more light to shoot with.

And shoot he did.

Droids came flying in, most straight down the ramp, while others tried to take a more evasive approach. They didn't last long. Like all the other floating balls, they lasted a few seconds at the most before taking a shot center mass. They did, however, also have underslung miniature guns. With them, they fired disc after disc at Tolby, who had taken cover behind one of the webway's spires. Most of their shots went wide or slammed into the spire, but a few hit my bud. The little discs latched on to him like a mechanical parasite long enough to deliver their shocks before he could rip them off of his body.

"I swear, I'm going to find whoever invented these things and tear them limb from limb," Tolby snarled after plucking another disc from his forehead. "Hurry up and get us out of here. I'm getting a migraine."

"A few more seconds, I promise!" I said, directing my attention back to the screen. I bounced nervously on the balls of my feet for the start-up procedure to finish. The progress bar at the top seemed to grind to a halt, and to keep my sanity, I turned away and started popping shots at the ever-increasing swarm.

You know, a watched toaster never toasts kind of thing.

Droid parts and scrap thoroughly covered the floor by the time the start-up procedure finished. Tolby provided most of the new look, but I did manage a telekinetic punch that finished one off, too.

"Okay, okay," I said, sucking in a breath and navigating the menus. "Where do I put in these coordinates?"

A few flips of the onscreen menus later, I had my answer. Instantly, I went to work, carefully entering in the coordinates and double-checking each one before moving on to the next. Six pairs, twelve digits in total. All went in easily enough. All except for the last one, because of course it had to give me trouble.

Coordinate invalid. Re-enter.

I looked at my arm again and cursed up a storm when I realized I was missing a digit. The last number had been erased. By what, I had no idea, but it was mostly gone, and I guessed when I'd first put it in, I'd thought it was simply a smudge or scuff mark. What was it? A seven? A four? It was hard to tell.

"Any ideas, Rummy?" I asked, looking at my arm.

"No, sorry," he said. "I was doing bookkeeping when you guys wrote it down. You know, upcoming tax season and all."

I groaned. "That figures."

"Dakota!"

I snapped my head over my shoulder at Tolby's call. He was running toward me, full tilt, as a slew of droids took shots at him. "Get us out of here!"

I swore more than a drill instructor finding a wayward jelly donut in a recruit's footlocker and re-entered the code on my arm. When I got to the end, I tacked on a seven, because seven has always carried a decent amount of luck and four can just go straight to the fiery pits of hell as far as I'm concerned.

Something dug into the recesses of my mind, and I cringed. The world around me distorted and rippled, and suddenly I had a bird's eye view of everything that was taking place for a hot moment before it all turned black. Colors and abstract shapes filled my vision and streaked by my field of view, and before I could make sense of any of it, a gargantuan sphere, covered in Progenitor circuitry, appeared before me, hanging in a void.

This image lasted a few seconds as well before dissolving completely and allowing my normal vision to return. Blood ran down my nose, and I stumbled into the console. As I pushed myself off of it, I saw the screen displayed one simple line:

Coordinates locked in. Stand by.

And right after that line popped up, we got even further confirmation from a deep, electronic voice. "Spacetime folding in progress," it said. "Webway will be safe to use in thirty seconds. Twenty-nine... Twenty-eight... Twenty-seven..."

"Inaja be with us," Tolby said, forcing a smile after he was hit by yet another electrified disc. "Are there any last-minute things I should know?"

"Uh, yeah. Remind me what's going on again?" I asked with a sheepish grin.

Tolby's eyes grew tenfold. "What?"

"I...I don't know?" I said. "I mean, I guess if anything...don't let me die?"

Tolby groaned before snapping off a few shots out of the control room. "Cripes, Dakota, I thought your brain only went to mush using that portal device of yours."

"Dakota?" I echoed. "Oh, yeah. That's what some people call me. Pleased to meet you," I said, sticking out an open hand. "Want to go for a root beer float?"

"I would rather stay alive," Tolby said.

"As would I," Rummy tacked on. "I still have a lot of adventuring I'd like to do."

"We can still do all that and get a float," I said.

Lightning streaked across the webway platform with a deafening clap of thunder, and a bubble formed in the middle of the room, a bubble that bent spacetime around it. Inside that bubble, I could see a portion of a massive room filled with thick cables and sweeping, curved architecture.

"Spacetime fabric stabilized," stated our electronic announcer. "Pocket universe reached. Webway is now safe to use for ten seconds."

"Hisoshim guard us and Inaja grant us her luck," Tolby said, snatching my hand and dragging me along. "I hope you don't stay like this for long."

"Why?" I asked as he dragged me out of the control room, guns blazing. "Would I look better as a space kitty?"

Tolby's only answer was a grunt of frustration. As we ran for the portal, he dropped three droids with his rifle. I joined in the shooting fun because I always wanted to be a gunslinger. Or was that a mud slinger? Pop singer? Whatever. Doesn't matter.

I zipped off a handful of plasma bolts, too, and did a fantastic job redecorating the walls. Maybe I should get into the demolition business. I bet I'd be good at that.

A few meters from the portal, I caught a disc in the leg, and it sent a vicious jolt of electricity through my muscle. My thigh cramped, and I stumbled midstride, but thanks to Tolby's incredible strength and sheer force of will, we didn't slow. In fact, I even gained a little bit of speed when he slung me through the wormhole with one arm.

CHAPTER TWENTY-SIX
MEETING WITH EMPRESS

Now don't get me wrong, having the ability to surf spacetime is fantastic. You know what's even better, though? Having your best bud next to you when you've got goo brain.

"Tailless?" Tolby asked, leaning over me and patting my face. "I need you to snap out of it."

I cleared my eyes with my thumb and index finger, which helped me focus better on my surroundings. Organic lines comprised the room's architecture, while intricate circuitry covered every surface, including the floor. Tiny packets of energy zipped along the wires, numbering in the thousands, and a soft, blue light bathed it all. The smell of ozone hung in the frosty air, and the air itself felt lighter and fresher than any other I'd experienced.

A few portions on both the walls and ceiling, however, bore the signs of battle. Scorch marks. Melted electronics. Holes the size of soda bottles. Even a few cracked, out-of-commission screens could be seen. Who or what had had a shootout here, I hadn't a clue. Whatever battle had taken place, however, had spared the five-meter-wide screen that took up the majority of the opposite wall from us.

"Where are we?" I asked, pushing myself up with one arm while taking the assist he offered with my other.

"I don't know," he admitted. His pupils were large, and his voice held an unsettling tremor to it, one that I hadn't ever heard from him before. Fear. Confusion. Bordering on panic, even. "I'm not even sure what's going on."

"We just had our grand opening?" I asked.

"For?"

"Like I should know," I said with a shrug. "I'm guessing our newest store for Cuddle Monsters Inc. You know, lack of plushies on the shelves and all."

"There are no shelves."

"We should probably remedy that before we restock, you know?"

Tolby grimaced before shaking his head. "That doesn't sound right," he said. "But honestly, it feels like someone's digging an icepick through my skull, and I can barely remember what you said two sentences ago."

The big guy turned and surveyed the area. As he did, I spied a couple of those discs latched on to the back of his skull, the bright orange lights on their tops pulsating steadily. "Hey," I said. "There's something stuck on you."

Since he towered over me, I couldn't exactly reach one to pluck it off. I wouldn't have had the chance to, anyway. A door nearby slid open, and a scrapbot came racing through with a pair of giant, clawed hands outstretched. Tolby jumped to the side, quick as ever, and riddled it with holes.

Despite the damage done, momentum carried it forward, and it used what little it had left of its dying CPU to steer itself into me. The bot fell over, knocking me down and falling on top of me. At least it crumpled in such a way that I ended up only being pinned instead of being a pancake.

"Holy snort that hurt," I said, wheezing. "Get it off me before another comes."

"Hold still," Tolby said as he crouched and looked for a good place to get a hold so he could lift.

"Tol'Beahn, captain of the Royal Guard to the House Yari, if you can hear me, stop what you're doing immediately and listen. I can't talk for long."

Tolby spun at the sound of an all-too-familiar voice, and my eyes went wide with disbelief. When I strained lifting my head, everything took on a surreal nature.

Empress, *my* Empress, looked down at us from the giant screen. She sat on a platinum throne with golden inlays. Behind her stood a large mural filled with Kibnali art, while on both her flanks stood Jainon and Yseri, each dressed in ornate battle armor. Despite how real it all looked, my gut told me nothing good was about to come of this. I didn't know why, goo brain and all. Perhaps if I did, I could've stopped the exchange before everything went to hell. As such, I lay there, pinned, and tried to make sense of what was unfolding in front of my very eyes.

"Empress?" Tolby asked. He then shook his head and smiled brightly. "The gods do favor us. You survived!"

Empress nodded slowly. "I have, but the fate of our Empire hangs by a thread. Our survival now depends on you."

"I am your fang and claw," he said, bowing and placing his paw over his chest.

"That...*thing*," she said, pointing an accusing claw toward me, "is a spy. She has used you to infiltrate our last sanctum, our last defense against the horde her kind unleashed upon us."

"What?" I said, snapping out of my daze. "I'm not a spy, Tolby! We're best friends!"

Tolby, thankfully, looked confused at her statement. He shook his head, but grimaced as he did. "I don't understand," he said. "This human here has your honors and has offered me nothing but loyalty and friendship."

"Of course she has!" Empress bellowed, shooting up out of her chair. "They engineered the Nodari to kill us all! To serve their will and act as shock troops for a preemptive strike against our empire!"

"No, Tolby. I swear, that's not right," I pleaded. "I don't understand why she's saying any of this, but you're my best friend, and I love you with all of my heart."

"She's a spy, Tolby. Don't listen to her," Empress growled. "Now kill her."

I outstretched my hand, hoping it would be enough to at least get him to hear me out. Not sure if it was that simple act or something else, but portions of my memory came back, thankfully, portions that included what we'd discovered on Adrestia.

"Tolby, we didn't have anything to do with the Nodari," I said. "They were created millions of years after...after humans went extinct. The Progenitors sent them back in time. Not us. Not me. Empress is—"

"Is lying?" he growled.

I quickly shook my head, knowing I couldn't possibly say that to him. "She's mistaken," I said. "If...if I had my memory back, I could tell you maybe why she thinks that. Please, give me some time. I swear, Tolby, I'd never lie to you. I have her honors. Do you think she'd grant me those if I were a spy?"

Tolby looked to Empress, and she in turn narrowed her eyes and toyed with the hilt of a ceremonial sword which hung from her hip. "Those honors were forged," she said. "To my utmost disgust, they were forged well, but they are forgeries nonetheless."

Jainon stepped forward. "I am Jainon, High Priestess of the Kibnali Empire," she said. "Your hesitation, your confusion, is understandable, but Empress speaks the truth—and in the end, you have but one duty."

Maybe it was fright. Maybe it was luck. Maybe a combination of both. Who knows? But in that instant, everything snapped back. Everything. I knew who I was. I knew where we were. Most important, I knew what Real Me had told me about Empress's fate. And if she were dead, that left only one conclusion as to what was going on.

"Tolby! It's a trick," I shouted. "That's not Empress. It's AO."

"AO?" Tolby repeated as if the name sounded completely foreign to his ears. "Who?"

"The supercomputer built by the Progenitors!" I said. "He's the one who's orchestrated it all. He's the one we have to stop. We're in his core, Tolby! We've got to destroy him if we have any chance at surviving!"

"Captain Tol'Beahn, do not fall for her deceptions," Empress said. "She—"

"Empress is dead!" I yelled, interrupting. "None of this is real!"

Tolby balked. Though I was glad he didn't shoot me on the spot, his tail was stiff and his fur bristled. My life teetered on the edge, I knew, and it would all boil down to who could convince him of what. God, if only he knew how close we were. Tears formed in my eyes and ran down my cheeks. "Tolby," I said, my voice cracking and barely making a sound. "Look at me. Look at me like you did when we first met. You know I'm not a killer. You know who I am, even if technically we haven't been partners yet."

"Tol'Beahn, your duty is to the Empire," Empress said evenly. "Ask yourself this: Which is more believable? A tale wrapped in time traveling where your real enemy are these 'Progenitors' who are a species you've never heard of? A race that hates us more than any other but that we have no record of? Or is it more believable that her kind attacked us the moment we discovered each other and that they proved to be a lethal foe? Would you listen to the word of an alien over my own? The facility you're in is one I had made in secret, our last hope of survival. With it, we will rise from the ashes anew, stronger than ever before. But if she destroys it, she kills us all. You must stop her, Captain.

Everything she's said, everything she's done, has been a ruse to get you in here and betray us all."

Tolby winced and crumpled into a half-crouch before growling and shaking it off. "By the gods," he muttered. "I can't think."

"She's infected you, Tol'Beahn!"

"Tolby, I'd never hurt you!" I cried.

The screen flickered, and instead of a view of Empress and her throne room, what was displayed was an off-angle view of some random person standing over the corpse of a Kibnali who lay on a steel table while several Nodari scouts stood idle in the background.

"See it with your own eyes, Captain!" Empress said. "I lost three of my best spies to get this intel smuggled out of the humans' research facilities! They've been capturing us! Testing on us! Developing the perfect organism to kill us all! What more proof do you need?"

"That's not Empress!" I said. "Don't listen to her! Rummy, tell him!"

Rummy didn't say a word. I didn't understand why that was, but I was too fixated on Tolby to give it much thought. The big guy remained silent for a few seconds as he stared at what was on the monitor. Eventually, his eyes drifted away from the screen and to me, at which point he finally said, "If she's a spy, then why does she need me?"

As glad as I was to hear Tolby's skepticism, Empress's response not only came swiftly, it also ended up being a perfect reply. "She needs you to bypass security at the reactor," Empress said. "She's already disabled what defenses we had in place. Kill her now before she does any more damage."

Tolby's claws flexed, and he fidgeted with his gun. "You have my utmost apologies Empress if I offend you by what I'm about to say," he said. "But if I'm to act on your word, I need to know you are who you say you are."

To my shock and subsequent horror, Empress eased both her tone and posture. "I commend you on your due diligence, Captain," she said.

"You and I both know each house is given a set of signs and counter signs that are entrusted only to those most loyal to the Empire—if I'm not mistaken, as Captain of the Guard, you are aware of these."

Tolby sucked in a breath and nodded. "I am."

"Then I suggest you use them."

Tolby nodded and pressed his lips together before rolling his shoulders back. He stared at me with an icy calm, but I didn't miss his claw easing its way to the trigger on his rifle. "The ninth black colony needs a detachment," he said. "When can they get one? Twelve or two?"

I froze, wide-eyed, scared out of my mind. I hadn't a clue to the answer, but more importantly, I couldn't believe my own best friend was treating me like the enemy. I knew I had to reply, but I also knew that whatever the countersign was, it sure as hell wasn't two or twelve. I sucked in a breath and prayed that between my former lucky elephant and wherever Taz might be, I'd guess the right response. "Ten."

Tolby didn't react one way or the other. Instead, he turned to Empress, who promptly said, "By the will of Hisoshim, they are gone," she said. "Fourteen guard remain, and twenty have fallen." When Tolby nodded approvingly, she then added, "Since that is settled, Captain Tol'Beahn of the House Yari, who are you?"

"I am your fang and claw," he said, bowing deep.

"Good...good," she said. "Now kill her."

CHAPTER TWENTY-SEVEN
SHOWDOWN

Tolby? Tolby!"

The Kibnali turned around, and where my best bud had been only seconds ago, now stood a complete stranger. His cold eyes looked at me without any hint of emotion, let alone remorse, as he raised his plasma rifle.

I socked that weapon right out of his hands, hitting it with a sizeable phantom punch. My next hit cracked him across the nose. It wasn't enough to shatter his skull, but I did put enough behind it I could hear the crunch and see blood spray.

"You've got claws. I'll grant you that," Tolby said, wiping his nose.

"I'm so, so sorry, Tolby," I said, trying to worm my way free of the robot who still had me trapped. "Please, don't make me hurt you again."

Tolby leaped toward me without a word, his razor claws drawn back and ready to tear me to ribbons. I knew the attack was coming. It would've been foolish to think otherwise. Thus, I already had my own reply set in my mind. I used everything I had, telekinetically, to shove the robot off my body and send it careening into the big guy.

Predictably, my right arm froze up and went numb, but at least it got the job done. The robot corpse was too large and flew too fast for Tolby to get out of the way. It struck him square in the chest, and since it weighed a hell of a lot more than Tolby did, it knocked him over without trouble.

"I'll make this right," I said, scrambling to my feet while he struggled to get out from under the heavy scrapbot. "I swear, Tolby. You'll see I'm not your enemy."

"Run, coward," Tolby sneered. "You'll only die tired."

I spun on my heels and darted out of the room, but not before scooping up my fallen gun. I'd die before I'd use it on Tolby, but that didn't mean keeping it handy for whatever else AO had around there wasn't a good idea.

Once I was out of the hall, I used my armor's tactical battle computer to bring up the schematics of AO's world. I had no idea where I was in relation to the control room, but according to both Tolby and Jainon, if I ran around enough, the auto mapper would be able to pinpoint my location.

Easier said than done, seeing how not only would AO be trying to kill me, but Tolby as well.

I sprinted down desolate, battle-worn halls and rooms packed with enormous devices not unlike my archive cube, only a thousand times bigger. Most hummed along as I raced by and were warm to the touch. A few, however, had lost all signs of life, their ice-cold surfaces dark and in some cases, broken, exposing melted circuitry inside.

"Any ideas, Rummy?" I asked. "I'm all ears."

He still remained silent, so I dared a peek inside the armor on my forearm to see what was going on. Rummy, or rather the bracelet I wore that held Rummy, had been split almost completely in two. I muttered a few curses as I tore my eyes away from his mutilated body. As annoying as he'd been throughout our adventures when it came to constant sales pitches, I did like the guy. I could only hope whatever damage had been done was repairable.

My lungs continued to gulp air as I redoubled my effort to race through the halls. From panting heavily, my heart thundering along, and the faint buzzing in the air, I couldn't hear a thing. Had I lost Tolby? I doubted it. He was probably only one step behind, or worse, one step ahead, getting into a perfect place to make an ambush.

I rounded a corner and ended up stumbling for balance when the floor unexpectedly dropped a quarter meter. Though the ceiling had lighting, most of it was cut off by the constant thick cables that seemed to run everywhere.

"Come on. Come on," I said, daring to slow long enough to fiddle with the auto mapper. "Shouldn't you have found where I'm at yet?"

The auto mapper didn't reply, so I kept going, taking passageway after passageway, branch after branch. More than once I stumbled on the remains of someone long gone. The bones looked like any other bones, not that I stopped to study them, but the clothes, and in some cases the armor, looked all too familiar.

I tried not to think about that.

I came to an abrupt halt when I zipped up a ramp and stepped foot on a catwalk that ran around the perimeter of a giant, vertical shaft. From the bottom of said shaft came a hot and howling wind, and in its center, accessible via the catwalk, too, was a platform which held lots of machinery.

Realizing my right arm was still useless, I extended my left arm over the railing so it could be exposed to as much of the hot air as possible. I then tried to draw energy off of it, which thankfully, both worked and didn't take long before I could not only feel my fingers again but could use the hand as well.

"Oh thank god," I said with a sigh of relief.

A rapid series of beeps sounded in my helmet a moment later. Elated, I punched up the auto mapper. I nearly cried when I saw it had pinpointed my location, and even better, I wasn't that far from the control room. Maybe I could get there and end this before Tolby ended me.

Movement caught the corner of my eye, and I spun around to see Tolby aiming his rifle at me. Again, I sent a phantom punch at the weapon, knocking it free from his grasp and sending it careening down the shaft. Despite my lucky hit, Tolby still got a shot off. The plasma bolt skipped off my hip, vaporizing one of the multi-dimensional burst relays that X-45 had built for me. It wasn't the one that would help me get into the control room. It was the one that I was supposed to use to get me home.

In all honesty, I'm still not sure which one would've been worse to lose, but at that time, all I knew was I was in deep crap, one way or the other.

That said, however, I had more pressing matters to attend to than how to get home or how to infiltrate the control room. I had a three-meter-tall, angry space kitty looking to rip my face off.

"Tolby! I'm not your enemy!" I shouted, backpedaling with my hand raised in defense.

Not surprisingly, he felt otherwise and ignored my attempts to keep him at bay.

Tolby charged, and before my mind could even register what was going on, he was sailing through the air, about to smash me into the wall, which he did.

With one paw, he drove my head back until it connected with a pipe. My helmet was the only thing that kept my skull from shattering, but that was only a temporary thing. While I was still dazed, Tolby drilled my head again.

While the first hit felt like someone had hit me with a sledgehammer, the second felt more like being clobbered by a huge pillow—and not because he was being gentle, but because my poor little brain was getting pulverized.

I held up my left hand in a feeble attempt to push him away, but he knocked it aside with a swipe of his claws—claws which found gaps in my armor and tore deep into my arm. Though having blood spurt from your arm in mass quantities is usually considered a bad thing, the fact that he'd stopped bashing my head in and the fact that with this new injury came a flood of endorphins and adrenaline, I was able to stave off death, even if it was purely out of reflex.

I hit Tolby in the chest, dead center, with a telekinetic blast. The blow was more than enough to knock him backward and over the rail to the catwalk.

For a second or two, everything about the situation and the world around me felt surreal. Even the blood coating my left arm seemed like it was nothing more than paint, when it should've been scaring me to death.

Once reality snapped back in, however, my concern wasn't for myself, but for my best bud. I threw myself at the railing and shouted. "Tolby!"

At first, all I saw was darkness, but then my eyes spied him on another catwalk a couple stories below, and I exhaled sharply with relief.

"You won't get away from me again," he said, pointing a claw at my head. "I promise."

I nodded slowly as my throat constricted. He was right. As much as I wanted to pretend otherwise, he'd get me next time. It was probably only blind luck that I saw him when I did.

For the next few moments, we stared at each other, and then he slipped off into the shadows. Before he was completely gone, I sent a whisper after him. "I love you."

I probably stood there another beat or two before I snapped out of my miniature pity party and checked the map. It was a few hundred meters to the control room, or rather, where I'd need to portal in to the control room.

I set my jaw and took off for one last run. I'd barely made three strides when my heads-up display flickered, and AO's holographic orb splashed across the faceplate.

"Dakota Adams," he said in my helmet. "Cease your hostilities. I do not wish to kill you."

At the sight of him, I came to an abrupt halt and nearly fell flat on my face in the process. "AO?" I said. "How are you in my helmet?"

"Kibnali transmission protocols are well-known to me and easy to duplicate," he said. "Now that you have adequate explanation, you should use your brain to process the futility of your actions and compute the nonexistent odds of your success. If you are unable to do either, I am happy to provide you with the data."

"I've got your bad odds right here," I said, flipping him (and I guess myself), the bird before running once more. "Now you sit right there and watch me take you down."

"Your continued denial as to the nature of the Kibnali is unfortunate," he said. "You've seen what they do. You've seen the species they've enslaved. The species they've wiped out. Are you willing to condemn all of humanity, too, just so you can save them?"

"I'm not listening to you," I said.

"Stress in your voice indicates otherwise," AO said. "My creators were peaceful. My creators reached out to them in good faith, wanting nothing more than to have an exchange of ideas and technology. The Kibnali, as you've seen, had other plans."

"I told you, they've changed."

"Erroneous conclusion that I've tried to demonstrate with your friend Tolby," he said. "Even now, he's trying to kill you, and you've done nothing to him."

"Because you lied!"

"The Kibnali are inherently distrustful of all others," he said. "I merely demonstrated this fact. Even if the two of you lived for a hundred years together, that would not change the fact that he, along with the other Kibnali, would never trust anyone outside themselves. You've seen this firsthand with Yseri."

I shook my head as I rounded a corner. He was wrong. I knew he was. He had to be. "No—"

"I am trying to save your life, Dakota, before you force my hand. Why do you think my drones have used non-lethal weapons against you?"

"Don't know. Don't care," I said. "All I really know is you're trying to save your own hide."

"I do not have a hide," AO replied evenly. "But yes, I am working to preserve my existence, but I'm also attempting to not only preserve yours, but your entire species as well. If allowed, the Kibnali will rebuild, and once that is done, they will wage an even bloodier campaign across the stars until the entire universe is crushed under their heels."

Try as I might, I couldn't shake his words. They didn't sound like ones spoken of desperation, or those coming from one who was ignorant on a matter. No, the words he spoke had a calm authority to them. He knew...

I slowed my pace. He knew...

And why wouldn't he? AO, a multi-dimensional supercomputer built by the most advanced species ever to exist, truly had seen it all.

"Your hesitation indicates new thoughts," AO said. "Though I have reservations, I am hopeful we can resolve our differences without further need of conflict."

My run came to a halt at a T-junction. Where I needed to be lay off to the right, some fifty meters or so.

"You can't win, Dakota," he added. "Forty-one iterations have struggled against me. Some have made it this far. Most did not. You, Dakota—the unexpected clone—will be the last. Time eddies are settling. There will be no further cycles."

"You're saying that no one else will be coming after me?"

"That is correct," AO said. "I can still repair your body and transport you back home using a nearby unidirectional webway. I can give you the life you long for, with your family, with Tolby, even."

"Your original offer…"

"Correct," he said. "I am still willing to give that to you, including new memories and clear conscience if you so desire."

"And let you kill his family…"

"Also correct," he said. A pause settled between us, one I hadn't expected, but when he came back to the conversation, I wasn't prepared for what came next. "You are morally correct to weigh the consequences of each action," he said. "I would also like to point out that if you go home, I'll guide you to lost Progenitor technology that will take your medical and agricultural levels to unfathomable heights. The lives you save introducing humanity to these advancements will be in the trillions of trillions."

"Until someone weaponizes it," I muttered off the cuff. Now that I think about it, I think that little bit of flash insight was the only thing that didn't make me take the offer right then and there, or at least, seriously consider it.

"Are you agreeable to this?" AO asked. "If so, start walking to the left until I direct you otherwise. If not, I will be forced to direct Tolby along with all droids to your location where there is but one outcome."

"One?"

"Your death," he explained. "You cannot kill him due to the universe abhorring a paradox. You cannot keep him at bay for long anymore, if at all. As he will not listen to you, there is but one outcome, especially when you factor in the extra service bots converging on your location as we speak."

I clasped my hands in front of my chest before fidgeting with my fingers. I wanted to go home. I wanted to see Mom and Dad, and Logan, even if they weren't mine. I wanted to down a colossal root beer float with extra cherry and go to sleep in my own bed in my own apartment.

I wanted to hug my best friend again and lay up against him under a starry sky as we talked about all the adventures we'd go on together and priceless artifacts we'd find.

I wanted to be able to do all that, but at the same time, I wanted to be able to look myself in the mirror. But I could...I could if AO wiped my memories and gave me new ones. I'd never know any of this happened. But...

But it wouldn't be real.

And that's what I wanted more than anything. I wanted to be real.

Not a fake.

Not an artificial construct.

Real.

"Even with the ability to create an extra portal, you'll die here," AO said.

His words snapped me back into the moment. "Come again?"

"I am aware both you and Dakota 42 can use the prime mover," he said. "It will not make a difference."

My mouth opened. I almost argued. Almost. If I had, maybe he would've talked me out of what I wanted more than anything:

I wanted to be real.

CHAPTER TWENTY-EIGHT
DEATH

I pivoted right and shot down the hall, intent on destroying this place.

"A sad but expected decision," AO said. "Your family will never be the same, and your brother will never forgive himself for getting you wrapped up with Pizlow and thereby finding the museum."

"I'm not listening to you," I said. "You have to be stopped. That's all there is to it."

The corridor bent sharply to the left and ended at a sealed blast door. According to the map, some thirty meters beyond it and through two more security doors lay the control room I needed.

"All right, Real Me, don't let me down," I said, pulling off the multi-dimensional burst relay from my belt. The thing, built by X-45, looked like an old soda can with three antennae sticking out the side. I had no idea how it worked, only the possibly foolish hope that it would.

I aimed the top at the blast door while keeping the rest parallel with the floor and pulled the safety ring at the top. The moment it slipped free, the device hummed and vibrated in my hand.

"This is your last chance to surrender," AO said.

"Duly noted," I replied.

As I waited anxiously for a wormhole to pop up, I started bouncing on the balls of my feet. I tried not to think about how much time was being wasted as I stood there, but I couldn't help but count the seconds tick away. When I got to the double digits, I distracted myself by looking back the way I'd come.

Damn. I really shouldn't have done that. Four scrapbots rounded the far corner and lumbered toward me. Large, powerful hydraulic legs kept them aloft while arms that ended in torches, industrial claws, and pneumatic hammers promised a swift death.

"Come on, Dakota!" I said, feeling my heart jump in my throat. "I need to get out of here!"

Despite my pleas, the wormhole didn't come. So I did the only sensible thing I could, I pointed my pistol at the approaching bots and start shooting. Plasma bolts sizzled down the hall, carving chunks out of everything they hit. Most went wide or struck the ceiling or floor, which didn't help my confidence or outlook on the situation. And with each shot I took, one of three questions ran through my mind:

Had I done something wrong?

Was this plan even going to work?

Or did making a portal in this world from another universe take far more time than I had?

To keep from going mad, I concentrated on my aim rather than those questions and squeezed off another shot. This time, Tolby himself would've been hard-pressed to have done better. The plasma bolt struck the lead bot square in the face, dropping him instantly. And since the corridor was relatively narrow compared to its bulk, after it fell, the others had a hard time getting over it.

Too bad I couldn't have capitalized on that. But instead of dropping bots two, three, and four, I shot up the walls some more.

A flash of light drew my attention, and I twisted around to see a portal spring up with perfectly round edges and a crystal-clear view of a room filled with consoles. Without a moment's hesitation, I dashed through.

Maybe I shouldn't have careened into the room so recklessly, since I ended up smashing into the back of a white chair. In my defense, however, I didn't want the portal to close—which it did the moment I was through—and I also hadn't expected the room to be so small. Though I didn't take any measurements, I was pretty sure I could've fit the whole thing in my bedroom back on Mars with room to spare, and that bedroom was bursting at the seams with just me and my mattress in it.

In a flash, I jumped into the chair and reached out with my implants to make the mental connection to whatever control station I was at. I found that connection immediately. Everything around me sprang to life. Lights danced across consoles, monitors displayed start-up procedures, and even the seat cushion warmed slightly, which amidst the chaos, I had to say was a nice touch the Progenitors put in.

Menus began to pop up all over, and I immediately went in search for something that said "Kill Super Computer." I didn't see that, but I did see something almost as good. Well, maybe not almost, but it still lit the fires of hope in my soul. That little something was the command "Lockdown Room."

The moment I hit that key, I heard heavy metal locks slide into place, presumably locking not only the one security door behind me, but the others as well. They'd barely gotten set when I heard something massive beating on the door with rhythmic blows.

"Ooo, I hope you guys knew how to build vaults," I said to myself.

"Perhaps you should hit the fifth button down on the screen to your nine o'clock high," AO suggested.

"Yeah, like I'm going to listen to you," I said. Despite my words, when I found the key he was referencing, I couldn't help but push it.

The monitor next to it flickered and gave a view of the hall outside where a scrapbot hammered at the door a few more times before backing away to let another with a cutting torch take its place and go to work.

"They'll be here in five minutes," AO said. "As one last offer, I'm willing to pass on any final words you have for you family. Perhaps this will help bring them closure when you disappear from their lives and never return."

I shook my head as a reply, and instead kept working, kept searching for something, anything, that seemed to do with the power regulation. There had to be something here. There had to be.

A few clicks of some buttons later, I found a way to bring up a camera view of the main power core. It looked a lot like the one back at the Museum of Natural Time: a circular room that had a massive, cylindrical body standing on end at the very center with dozens of equally spaced portals around the center from which gouts of plasma flowed. It looked a lot like the reactor Tolby and I ruined, that is, except about fifty times bigger.

That was promising. Now if only I could destabilize those portals or shut down the containment fields that kept the plasma in check.

"Four minutes."

I nodded this time but continued my relentless search through a myriad of controls that seemed to do nothing and menu selections that led nowhere.

"Three minutes."

"Holy snort," I said, beaming and leaning back in the chair, not at what he'd said, but at what I'd found: an array of a dozen buttons, each inscribed with a twelve-digit serial number with the words "Containment Field" written above and "Shut down?" written below.

"Checkmate, buddy," I sneered, but when I reached out and pushed the button to turn it all off, nothing happened.

"Your inability to follow directions is intriguing," AO said. "I would have been interested in studying you further to see how you managed to stay alive this long if you hadn't forced me to terminate your existence."

I cursed and snarled, both at his jab and the fact that, somehow, I'd managed to miss the most important part to all of this. Underneath all the buttons to switch off the containment fields was a line that read:

Enter the failsafe code below for verification:

"Failsafe code?" I said, eyes going wide and mouth drying. "What damn failsafe code?"

I desperately looked all over my armor, hoping to find another set of scribbles, before scouring the control room, too, for any sign of them. After a dozen, panic-stricken seconds, I realized it wasn't asking for them as a security measure, because it was telling me right where they were.

They were below, at the bottom of the screen.

My eyes darted down. I found the line, but I couldn't read the code, try as I might. The numbers and letters kept blurring and shifting around. Worse, the more I tried to read them, the more a newly formed headache grew, threatening to incapacitate me at any moment.

After a few more excruciatingly painful seconds of trying, I flopped back in the seat, panting and drenched in sweat. The pressure in my head lessened, even more so when I turned away from the monitor.

"A paradox," I muttered.

I couldn't destroy AO with Tolby still here. The Universe wouldn't let me. I had to get Tolby out. Somehow.

"Ninety seconds," AO announced. "It's too bad it took until now for you to see the futility of it all."

"No, it's not futile," I said, straightening at an unexpected revelation. I'm not sure what AO said at that point, but I knew he was talking, because I was fully concentrating on searching the map for what I knew was there. I found it in less than five seconds: the location to the unidirectional webway. Not only did I find that, in those few moments, I also realized how I might be able to get Tolby through it.

Sparks shot out of the top of the security door and then started moving around its edge as the torch-wielding bot began to cut.

"Damn," I said, realizing I had to work fast. I picked up the communicator off my belt and prayed Tolby's lust for blood wouldn't trump the big softie I knew he was deep down. "Tolby?" I said. "Can you hear me, bud?"

"I hear you," he said. "And I'm about to see you, too."

"I know. That's why I'm calling."

"Wanting to beg for mercy?"

"No," I said. "Before you come in here, I want you to know something: We really are, or will be, best friends. I've pulled you out of a tight scratch or two, but if I'm being honest, you saved me far more times than I deserved, given how much I've put you through—or will put you through. I guess my charming personality won you over."

"I'm not interested in your lies."

I shut my eyes and drew a deep breath to focus and center myself. I had to deliver this calmly.

"Tolby, I know something about you no one else does, not even Empress," I said. "Not long ago, you told me you always felt you were a fake. You told me this because I was having a nervous breakdown because I found out I was a fake, too. Or at least, I felt like I was, depending on how you look at it. Anyway, you never liked how the Kibnali were, how they always shot first and asked questions never, but that's who they were. That's how you were supposed to be. And worse, you couldn't tell anyone, especially as Captain of the Guard, because that would be blasphemy of the highest order—to say that the Kibnali shouldn't be conquering, enslaving, and annihilating, even if it was in the name of the Empress. If anyone knew the real you, you'd have been executed long ago."

I paused, even though I had a few more things to say, hoping he'd reply and give me some sort of indication he was listening to me. Thus, I kept going. "You know what else? You never wanted to fight since I knew you. I mean, you sort of had to with the Nodari, but even when this crazy adventure started, and I was being run down by sentry bots, you know what your first words to me were? 'Have you tried talking to it? Maybe it's misunderstood.' You didn't tell me to shoot it, blast it, or whatever. You wanted me not to resort to violence, even though that damn thing was hell-bent on trying to rip me apart."

Again, I paused, thinking he might want to reply. I didn't get one. All I got was the realization that the bot was about ten seconds from cutting through the door. "Anyway, Tolby, I might not know all the codes, but if I weren't telling the truth about time traveling, if I weren't your best friend in the future, you'd never have told me that. And I just thought maybe...just maybe...that might change your mind. I'm putting my pistol down, and I'm not going to fight you. I never wanted to, and I never will from this point on."

The door fell forward, causing me to jump back in fright. On the other side stood the bot along with two others and Tolby as well. It probably only lasted a breath or two, but it felt like eternity before any of us moved, Tolby being the first.

The big furball drove forward and rammed me with his shoulder. I flew back, striking a console. The next thing I knew, he had my pistol in his hands and fired exactly three times. When he was done, the three bots dropped like a sack of potatoes, smoke rising from newly formed ventilation holes in their heads.

"I...I thought I was dead," I said, staring at the fallen robots.

"If you don't get us out of here soon, we still might be," Tolby replied, handing me my pistol.

I cried, and despite that we had no time to waste, I threw my arms around him and squeezed. "I love you."

"I love you, too—or will, if that sounds weird right now," he said.

"No. That will never, ever, ever sound weird coming from you."

"Good. Now can you get us out of here?"

"Yeah," I said, laughing and wiping my nose. "Watch the door. I'll only need a few seconds, I think."

I was back in the chair, and to my utmost elation, not only could I read the failsafe code, but my headache completely disappeared.

"No! Stop!" AO yelled, his voice panicked for the first time ever. "You don't know what you're doing!"

"I know exactly what I'm doing," I growled.

"You're going to kill—" He never got to finish since I cut the volume.

"In more uplifting news, get ready to run," I said, flashing a grin to Tolby as my fingers danced across the touch screen. One by one, I flipped off the containment fields, and each time I did, I'd check the reactor monitor to see jets of plasma escaping their forcefields and carving large swaths of destruction out of everything.

Alarms blared, and a new voice cut through the air, or rather, one I hadn't heard in a long time. Curator's. I'll never forget how calm and soothing it always sounded. "Attention. Emergency containment procedures are now in effect," he said. "Core planetary processor will be vaporized in t-minus seven minutes."

"Seven minutes!" I shrieked. "Last time we had nearly thirty!"

"Then we better hurry," Tolby said, tugging my arm.

"Unidirectional webway egress system will be offline in three minutes," Curator went on.

"And now we leave," Tolby said, dragging me out the door.

I found my feet, and together, Tolby and I ran through the halls, following the map to the webway. After taking our second corner, everything around us shook, and a wild jet of plasma, nearly two meters wide, tore through the floor before ripping through the ceiling, sending molten metal and sparks everywhere. A second jet erupted from the wall, and Tolby and I barely had time to flatten ourselves on the ground before it shot by our heads.

"Go! Go! Go!" Tolby yelled once it went by.

I didn't need the encouragement. I sprinted for all I was worth. We bolted into a large room where two more bots came lumbering at us. The first was crushed when more plasma carved out the ceiling and something big and heavy smashed on top of it, while Tolby promptly dropped the other with a shot to the head.

"That's why I pay you the big bucks," I said, chuckling.

"I didn't realize root beer floats were considered the big bucks," Tolby replied.

"They could be," I said with a sheepish grin as we ran on.

Less than two minutes later, we found the webway. It looked like all the others we'd seen, raised platform with spires, only on a much smaller scale. I found the controls easily enough. Fired it up without trouble as well using the only coordinates I had: Helios IX, a day after we left.

"Is this going to warp your brain again?" Tolby asked.

"If I'm lucky," I said.

"And if you're not?"

"I get the feeling it might turn me into a permanent vegetable."

"We can fix vegetable," he said. "Dead? Not so much."

"Yeah, well, there's something else you really ought to know about me."

"What's that?"

"If I die, I want a Viking funeral."

Tolby stared at me blankly. "I have no idea what that is."

"I guess you better not let me die, then, huh?"

The conversation halted as my mind, now fully hooked into the webway, issued the final commands to open a portal. I grimaced as my vision wobbled and pinched before turning into a swirl of colors and elaborate equations that seemed never ending. I dropped to one knee right as my vision returned. I think I was bleeding out of my nose again, but it was hard to tell since my left arm still stained everything red.

Tolby was at my side, trying to get me up. "Dakota! Are you okay?"

I tried to stand, but my body refused to move. All I could do was shake my head in response.

"Then I'll carry you," he said, slinging me over his shoulders. "It'll be good practice for later, right?"

I shrugged. I had no idea. Hell, I didn't really understand why I was getting a piggyback ride from a super kitty, or why fire and debris was raining all around us. I had the vague idea it was part of a school play I was in, though.

I probably should've studied my lines more in that case.

Damn.

Oh well, maybe I'd remember what I was supposed to say in the next scene—where whatever happened after we jumped through that cool-looking sphere with all the lightning shooting out.

CHAPTER TWENTY-NINE
FIN

Huh, she's coming out of it," Daphne said. "I've really got to stop doing that."

I blinked, and the world around me slowly came back into focus. I was lying on my back, staring at the cold ceiling of the medbay onboard Original Me's ship. My left arm had some sort of carbon-fiber splint while my right was hooked into an IV. Old Tolby stood next to me, face full of worry, while New Tolby stood at the foot of my bed, his face full of worry, too. And while seeing two Tolbys was one of the weirdest things I'd ever seen, Daphne's comment was what I went after first.

"You've really got to stop doing what?" I asked, trying to sit up and immediately wishing I hadn't as pain exploded through my head.

"Losing money betting on your survival," Daphne said.

"You bet I'd die?"

"Yes, and thanks for costing me another twenty credits," she said, sounding put off. "Oh, and then another twenty on top of that for not staying a vegetable. I can't believe you're like that. I thought we were friends."

"Me? I can't believe you're like that!"

"Why? Don't you want your loved ones taken care of after you're gone?" she asked. "People bet on dying all the time. That's quite literally the entire business model for life insurance."

"Don't worry," New Tolby said. "You're not the first person she's done this with."

"She's not?"

Original Me, who was leaning against the wall nearby, pushed off it with her shoulder and grinned. "Nope. She bet against me twice, too, when we were escaping Kumet."

"You know what? I'm not feeling very appreciated at the moment for my attempts to turn tragedy into a financial windfall," Daphne said. "Just so everyone knows, when I hit it big on the Death Jackpot, I'm not sharing with any of you."

I didn't feel like arguing and knew it wouldn't matter anyway. Daphne's quirks would forever be, and no one would ever be able to change that. As such, I had to ask the obvious question. "What happened?"

"Do you want the long version or the short?" New Tolby asked.

Old Tolby snickered. "From what I understand, the stars will have all long burned out by the time you finish the long version," he said. "Give her the short."

"Or maybe the short, short, *short* version," Original Me added.

"Right," New Tolby said. "The ultra-short version is this: A few minutes after you left the ship and stepped through a portal to Helios IX, the fighters AO sent caught up with us. Thankfully, with you operating in a different timeline, you destroyed him before they chewed through our defenses, and Daphne ordered them to stand down. But you never returned, which meant you either died or managed to escape back to the only planet you could: Helios IX. Almost everyone bet on the latter. You can guess who bet on the former."

"And that's a double amount of nothing you're getting from my winnings, buddy," Daphne said.

277

"But how did you get to the planet to find us?" I asked.

"That's the long, long story," Original Me said. "Might make for a good book one day. We'll see."

"Then what's the ultra-short version?"

"Got the webway working back at the station," she said. "With it, popped everyone forward in time and across the universe to the good old Milky Way. Then it was a simple flight to the planet where we waited for you to pop up in, which of course you did, albeit a hell of a lot bloodier than we were expecting, hence the immediate trip to medbay."

"Not sure I'd call having to deal with a herd of carnivorous, spacefaring uni-pigs simple," New Tolby added.

"Compared to that relay race, it was," Original Me countered. She then turned her attention back to me. "Anyway, what tore you up? You still look like hell."

Old Tolby tensed as regret washed over his face. He started to say something, but I quickly cut him off. "AO's not-so-friendly minions," I sort-of lied. "Thankfully, my best bud was there to save the day."

Old Tolby relaxed. "You give me too much credit," he said. "I'm not the one who killed AO."

"I guess that's why we're such a great team," I said, smiling and patting his arm. I then turned to Original Me. "Where's everyone else?"

"X-45, our new chief engineer, is still working on ship repairs along with Jack," she said. "He practically shorted out his entire electrical cortex when he had enough time to inspect the damage caused by those fighters."

I grimaced, but that didn't last thanks to New Tolby's deep laugh. "It was pretty funny," he said. "Kept saying 'No-no! This is all wrong-wrong!' before launching into a tirade of made-up expletives."

"Any chance he can fix Rummy?" I asked, noting my bracelet wasn't on my wrist and hoping they hadn't tossed it in the garbage. "I really took a liking to the guy."

"Yeah," Original Me said. "X-45 said he could fix him up quick-quick once he was done-done making sure we didn't die-die."

"Well that's good," I replied. "I'd rather not die-die, if that can be helped. What about Jainon and Yseri?"

"Yseri is looking at star charts, trying to pick where they want to start a colony," Original Me said. "Jainon is meditating."

"Really?" I asked.

"Why wouldn't they be?"

"I guess after all I heard about them, I assumed once the action died down, they'd be wanting some quiet time with Tolby again—especially now that there're two of him around."

Original Me snorted and rolled her eyes. "Oh, they did that all right," she said. "And they were anything but quiet."

New Tolby shot Original Me a playful glare. "I'll be sure to comment on what noises you make when you and Jack mate."

"Never going to happen."

"Would you care to make a wager on that?" Tolby asked, grinning.

Before I could reply, Daphne jumped in the mix. "Oh! Oh! I would!" she said. "I'll even give you five to one odds saying she won't."

Original Me and I exchanged worried looks at Daphne's ability to predict the future, and both Tolbys burst into deep laughter.

"You, quit it," I said, pointing to New Tolby before scowling at Old Tolby. "And aren't you supposed to be back at your ship, sans memory yet?"

Old Tolby feigned a deep hurt and put a paw over his chest. "Ready to be rid of me so quickly?"

"After that remark, you're damn skippy," I said. "You should know I'm not ready to waddle around, feeling like a hippo."

"I should?"

"Well, you will. So that's just as good," I said, sticking out my tongue.

"If you say, Dakota. If you say."

A few hours later, Tolby and I were back inside his plant-infested ship, back where he slept, while everyone else waited for us patiently outside to say our sort-of goodbyes.

"Do you think this is safe?" Tolby said as he toyed with the circlet X-45 had made with both Daphne's and Rummy's instruction.

Once he activated it, the device would send him into a deep sleep before wiping all his memories over the last however many hours it'd been since I met him. Even though I could understand why he'd be apprehensive about having something screw with his brain like that, I didn't want him to worry. "Yeah, of course it is," I said as upbeat as I could. "We're going to go through a lot together in the not-so-distant future, and you always seemed right in the head during all that."

"But this is the first time you came along, remember?" Tolby pointed out.

"Yeah, well, how do we know all those other Dakotas didn't find you before, too?" I asked. When he didn't have an answer, I crossed my arms over my chest and gave a triumphant nod. "See? Exactly. Besides, the universe abhors a paradox, remember? I haven't felt any pushback with you our entire time—AO aside—so things have to all workout, right?"

Tolby nodded and dropped onto his bunk, still eyeing and playing with the device. "I hope everything works out," he finally said. He then chuckled. "And it's weird to think I'm going to wake up in a few hours and not recall any of this."

"I know," I said. "But don't worry. You'll be fine, what with all the important things you're destined to do."

"Like saving you?" he said, the corners of his mouth drawing back.

"Yup," I replied. "And don't forget about finally getting some root beer. Gah! I wish I could be there again when you try it for the first time. You nearly broke the soda fountain trying to refill your glass."

Tolby snickered. "I look forward to it, then. But I didn't mean I hoped things worked out with me. I meant, I hope they work out for you."

"Oh," I said. "They will. You'll see."

"Will I?"

"Part of the crew now," I said. "So yeah, you'll see. Unless you run off with your Kibnali princesses and leave me again."

"Handmaidens, and never."

"Promise?"

"Promise," he said before wrapping me up in a hug. When we pulled away, his eyes found mine, and the tone in his voice turned as serious as I'd ever heard it before. "And thank you for reminding me of who I am. I can never express my gratitude enough for that."

I smiled. "Anytime, bud. But not eating me is all the thanks I need. You know?"

Tolby laughed. "I doubt you'd taste good anyway," he said. "I prefer meat that's not scrawny."

"Gee, thanks."

Tolby flipped the circlet around in his paw. I thought he was about to put it on his head and start it up, but apparently, he had one last question for me. "Have you settled on a new name yet?"

"No," I said. "Not sure what else I'd like to be called the rest of my life."

"Still want a new one, though?"

"Yeah," I said after some thought. "She's Dakota. I'm...I'm not sure what I am."

"Might I have the honor then of naming you?"

I straightened, caught off guard by the request. "Of course you may," I managed to stammer. "As if I'd ever say no."

Tolby nodded as he donned the circlet. "Karri, then, is what you're to be called from this moment on," he said.

"Karri..." The name rolled off my tongue so smoothly, I could scarcely believe I hadn't thought of it on my own. "What's it mean?"

"No idea," Tolby replied. "I just like the sound of it."

We shared a laugh and a few more bits of banter back and forth before Tolby decided there was no point in stalling the inevitable any longer. He pushed the little blue button on the side of the circlet and lay down in his bunk. A faint hum emanated from the band, and a small status screen on the side displayed a myriad of fast-scrolling information.

"Take care, Tolby," I said as his eyes grew heavy and then closed within moments. I leaned over and kissed his forehead before adding, "I'll see you soon."

His eyes fluttered open for a brief second. "I look forward to it, Karri."

Then he was gone, whisked away to whatever world his dreams had in store for him. I left his room to rejoin the others, and for the first time in my real life, I was eager to see what the future would bring.

I knew.

Family. Friends. Lots of root beer. Oh, and that one adventure I wanted to take that would change it all...

Would you like to know more?

(End of Book IV)

ACKNOWLEDGMENTS

As always, I have the usual crew to thank: My wife for putting up with a lot of bad writing over the years, my wonderful editor Crystal for turning slop into something decent, and my kids for giving me endless ideas on what's fun and adventurous.

I'm also forever grateful to Katherine Littrell who breathed wonderful life into the characters and gave Dakota the voice she needs for the audio narration of the series.

Of course, none of this would be possible without all my brilliant readers, new and old; so here's to hoping you enjoyed this book and are chomping at the bit for more.

ABOUT THE AUTHOR

When not writing, Galen Surlak-Ramsey has been known to throw himself out of an airplane, teach others how to throw themselves out of an airplane, take pictures of the deep space, and wrangle his four children somewhere in Southwest Florida.

He also manages to pay the bills as a chaplain for a local hospice.

Be sure to drop by his website https://galensurlak.com/and sign up for his newsletter for free goodies, contests, and plenty of other fun stuff.

ABOUT THE PUBLISHER

Tiny Fox Press LLC
5020 Kingsley Road
North Port, FL 34287

http://www.tinyfoxpress.com

Lightning Source UK Ltd.
Milton Keynes UK
UKHW011934310820
369124UK00002B/28/J